Reviews

"This gripping collection of detective stories is an excellent blend of contemporary and traditional crime drama. Each story is tightly plotted, exciting, and each with a satisfying twist at the end. There is a variety to the stories, ranging from dark secrets being exposed to genuinely tragic family secrets coming to light.

"But the real success of these stories are the two main characters and their relationship. Rathe is a fascinating and original character, a troubled man trying to make sense of his life in the wake of a tragedy which still haunts him. Contrasted with Rathe's private quest for redemption is Inspector Cook, a man with his own troubles, trying to come to terms with the violence he sees in his everyday life in the best way he can.

"The contrast between the two of them is set off against their mutual desire to find the truth and it forms the basis of an uneasy alliance. It is their uncertain partnership which sets these stories aside. It is not the usual detective duo combination and this amiable hostility between them is a welcome change. Rathe and Cook are wary of each other but what these stories show so well is the slow building of trust and respect between them as they investigate the crimes at the centre of these four excellent stories. A sequel can't come soon enough."

Shirley Rothel

"I thoroughly enjoyed this book and marvelled at both its pace and great character in Anthony Rathe with its intriguing twists and turns in four great imaginative tales."

Emyr Williams

"Anthony Rathe is a disillusioned former lawyer having left the bar because an innocent young man called Marsden, whom he prosecuted, committed suicide in gaol. As a result, haunted by guilt and shame, Rathe finds himself investigating crimes of passion where injustice is evident. 'The Marsden disgrace', as Rathe views the matter, is a connecting thread through the four stories in this excellent collection as he attempts to atone for his perceived sin.

"Anthony Rathe is a fascinating character who works in a solitary fashion down the narrow line between the police and the legal system. He is a wonderfully incongruous mix of the stoical and passionate. Here we have a character who is intriguing and pleasingly different from the run of the mill sleuths who people modern crime fiction. Indeed his heritage is in the tradition of the unusual golden age detective who is neither a tired policeman nor the risibly eccentric private detective. He is a very welcome addition to the raft of modern crime solvers.

"In this collection we have a quartet of stories in which Rathe solves a series of murders. I think of these as cabinet detective tales in that the mysteries are tightly plotted and cunning, while involving only a small cast of players, which works well with Booth's rich and intense storytelling style. He is particularly good with atmosphere and Rathe's internal monologues. The characters are expertly drawn and psychologically accurate. While at times we are in Agatha Christie whodunnit territory with the plots which challenge the reader to spot the culprit before the denouement, the literary quality of the writing adds an elegant and realistic patina to the narratives.

"One of the added pleasures of these stories is the growing uneasy relationship Rathe has with the police detective Inspector Terry Cook, a belligerent but very human copper who tolerates rather than accepts Rathe's interference in his cases. Indeed on occasion he sometimes seeks his help, albeit begrudgingly. The two men rub each other up the wrong way most of the time, but Booth subtly reveals that there is a respect growing between them. It's an engaging double act.

"Anthony Rathe is a new star on the crime fiction stage and this reviewer wants more, please."

David Stuart Davies

"Four stories focus on the quest for truth and justice, no matter how inconvenient. To build up trust and tension Rathe's private investigations are contrasted to Inspector Cook. The stories read like a classic crime story on TV, concise, and conversations to look into the investigator's line of thought to solve the whodunnit puzzle."

Henk-Jan van der Klis

"This was not my usual read but I enjoyed it. I liked the character Rathe very much. This felt more like a gentlemanly approach to crime detection. The fact that Rathe was trying almost to redeem himself from his previous behaviour made him even more appealing. Each case was self contained and fairly succinct. I enjoyed the change in pace from more grisly stories."

Sue Ross

"This had a perfect balance of deduction and soul searching to make the main character compelling. The mysteries were well written with refreshing style."

Bridgit Davis

Comhairle Contae
Átha Cliath Theas
South Dublin County Council

LIBRARY SERVICES ONLINE at www.southdublinlibraries.ie

Items should be returned on or before the last date below. Fines, as
displayed in the Library, will be charged on overdue items. You may renew
your items in person, online at www.southdublinlibraries, or by phone.

Cover design based on an image © iStock.com/Viktor_Gladkov, by Larch Gallagher

British Library Cataloguing in Publication Data. A catalogue record for this book is available from the British Library.

ISBN: 978-1-907230-68-4

Printed in the United Kingdom by Grosvenor Group (Print Services) Ltd

1.0

@SparklingBooks

Matthew Booth is the author of *Sherlock Holmes and the Giant's Hand* and one of the authors contributing to *Further Exploits of Sherlock Holmes*. He is an author in the MX Publishing Undershaw Preservation project, having contributed to their anthologies of new Sherlock Holmes stories.

Matthew was a scriptwriter for the American radio network, *Imagination Theatre*, syndicated by Jim French Productions, contributing particularly to their series: *The Further Adventures of Sherlock Holmes*.

To Mum and Dad

and to Jodi

with thanks for all the love, fun and support

The stories:

Burial for the Dead

Burial for the Dead

"Why do you come here, Mr Rathe?" she asked. "What do you want to find?"

He gave no immediate reply. They were the same questions which he had asked himself, time and again, but he had never been able to provide a satisfactory answer so there was no reason why he should find it possible now. Instead, he kept his eyes on the grave in front of him, the gold lettering providing a sharp contrast to the black sheen of the stone. The name which lingered in the darkest corners of Rathe's conscience stared back at him, the two dates with the cruelly brief time span between them shouting his guilt in his face. The woman edged closer to him, but Rathe did not turn to look at her even then. His attention was gripped only by the details on that black marker of death. But, after a few moments of no noise except the rising wind of the autumnal morning, Rathe dared at last to answer the questions.

"Forgiveness," he said. "I want to find forgiveness."

Kathy Marsden placed a hand on his arm. "You didn't kill my son, Mr Rathe."

"We both know that isn't true."

"He did it to himself," she insisted. "Nobody else did anything."

Rathe turned his face to hers and she stared into his dark, austere eyes. His expression was paralysed with a bitter sadness, the same expression she had seen each time she had found him standing in front of her son's place of rest. He seemed about to speak, but initially no words came. She did not need him to speak; she knew well enough from their previous discussions what it was he would want to say.

"You don't believe that," he said at last. As she had expected.

"It's not a question of belief. It's the truth. You didn't kill Kevin, no matter how much you convince yourself otherwise."

"He was innocent." Inside his pockets, Rathe's fingers turned in on themselves, bunching into fists. "I can see that now. I just couldn't see it then."

"You didn't convict him of any crime, Mr Rathe. The jury did that."

"Based on what they heard in my arguments against him."

Kathy Marsden did not argue the point. She saw no reason to dispute what he had said, not given that it was true. Instead, in a soft voice, she made a different point. "What happened at the trial, and afterwards, who said and did what... none of it means you have to come here every day. You should stay away."

"I can't. I don't know what else to do to make amends for what happened to your son, Mrs Marsden."

"Isn't walking away from your life and career, this punishment of yourself, enough?"

"It doesn't seem to be."

She sighed heavily, a tired and frustrated expulsion of air. Rathe did not react to it. From somewhere behind them, the church clock struck the hour. Rathe wondered how long he had been standing at Kevin Marsden's grave, living through the events of the recent past. No idea.

"You talk about finding forgiveness," Kathy said. "Whose forgiveness do you want? Mine, or your own?"

Briefly, he smiled but it was not enough to erase the traces of melancholy from his face. "Perhaps both."

She nodded, as though she had been expecting the answer. "You haven't ever needed my forgiveness. But, if you feel you need it, you have it. You should move on from the past, Mr Rathe, and the first step to doing that is to forgive yourself."

He shook his head. "I don't think I can do that."

Kathy Marsden leaned closer to him as the first spots of rain began to fall. "Then how will you ever find any peace, Mr Rathe… ?"

* * *

The vicar paused at the church door. The night sky was the deepest black, barely a star in sight, and the only light available to him was the meagre beam of the small torch which he held in his shaking hands. He could see that the door to the church was ajar, the wind gently whispering in the opening, as though willing the vicar to enter, enticing him into the darkness of the house of God. He muttered a brief prayer under his breath and, in a moment of indecisive anxiety, he looked back towards the sanctuary of the warm, cosy vicarage behind him.

He had been sitting in the living room, idly reading a Dickens novel, when he had become conscious of a strange light in the church. Not strange in the sense of it being alien, but rather that it was a light which should not have been lit at all. The Reverend Thomas Healey himself had locked and bolted the church earlier that evening and, as he was accustomed to do, he had ensured that all candles and electric lights had been extinguished and that the door to the church had been locked and bolted. Healey was not a man to be remiss about such things; if anything, he erred on the side of over-caution where the question of security was concerned. He had been surprised, not to say alarmed, therefore, to find that the stained glass artwork of the arched windows was now glowing with flickering candlelight. He had wrapped a scarf around his neck, grabbed his torch, and made his way rapidly along the small gravel path which connected the vicarage to the church itself.

Now, standing at the open door, he was unsure that his course of action was altogether wise. If someone had broken into the church, the intruder might still be inside. Whatever business he had there could not be legitimate, it seemed to Healey, since otherwise whoever it was would have waited for the morning and approached the elderly vicar personally. Healey could not dismiss his apprehension but, by the same token, he felt unable not to investigate this intrusion into the Church of St Augustine.

He pushed the heavy oak entrance as slowly as he dared, his breath held tight in his lungs, and he peered round the door, barely prepared for what he might find inside. The beam of the torch illuminated the concrete floor and the backs of the pews which were immediately in front of him. There was the smell of cold stone and the deathly silence of a building at rest. From behind him, the wind rushed through the widening gap of the entrance and the flames of the candles danced themselves into extinction. The sharp scent of smoke and wax drifted towards him and Healey creased his nose at the sensation. His only light now was the conical beam of the torch, lighting no more than two or three feet in front of him. His shoes clicked on the stones beneath his feet, the resulting echo seeming to fill the vastness of the old building, so deep was the silence into which he walked. The light from the torch moved across the pews and the walls and, once, Healey shone it behind him as if to dispel the irrational fear that somebody was following him. But there was nobody there. The old man was alone.

As he moved the light in front of him once more, however, he found that he had been wrong in his assumption. He was not alone in that church. There were two other men in there with him. At the sight of them, Healey caught his breath and he raised a hand to his mouth in shock. In front of him, there was a man lying face down on the altar steps, his arms outstretched towards the effigy of the tormented Christ which towered over the altar itself. The divine head hung on the battered breast, an expression of humble suffering etched onto the noble features, looking down at the horror which was sprawled out below those nailed, bloodied feet, as though recognising a sin which could never be absolved.

The dead man on the altar steps was dressed in an expensive suit, dark blue if that mattered to anybody, and his well-polished shoes exposed their soles to Healey. The vicar paid no attention to them. Instead, his eyes were fixed on the repulsive trauma which had been inflicted to the back of the man's head. The deep crimson of his life had ebbed out onto the scarlet of the carpet which adorned the steps of the altar and, lying across his back, there was the instrument of death. One of the heavy, gilt candlesticks which normally stood on either side of the altar, the base of it stained with the same red smear of death. Its brother stood in its rightful place, innocent of any connection with the horror which had played out before it.

For a moment, Healey could see only blood. It seemed to him to be everywhere: seeping still out of the man's head; staining the carpet of the altar; glistening on the golden base of the candelabra; pounding in his own ears as his heart raced in disgust at the scene which had played out before him. For a moment, he was incapable of registering anything other than the sight and smell of blood. But then, as if from some place far away, he heard the whimper of a voice. An adult voice, but oddly childish in its terrified pitch. Healey broke free from his blood-spattered spell and looked at the other man in the church. Not the horrible thing which had once been a man, but the undeniably human form which was standing over the corpse. He was staring at the vicar with the wild eyes of a madman, his face twisted in some emotion which might have been fear, panic, or guilt. Perhaps it was a mixture of them all. His hands were outstretched to Healey and at once the vicar was again conscious of the presence of blood. This time, it was smeared over those outstretched palms, as though begging the holy man to cleanse them. As the stranger took a step towards him, Healey made an instinctive move backwards. The man seemed bewildered by the vicar's movement, frowning in confusion into the light of the torch's beam. Then, as though his senses told him what was in the vicar's mind, the man began to shake his head. A finger snaked out and pointed towards the body beside him.

"I didn't do this," he stammered. "I swear to God, I... "

But Healey heard no more. He had no thought for anything other than his civil and moral duty and the need for a police presence in the house of the Lord.

How many hours passed between fleeing from the church and the arrival of the police was impossible for him to determine. But, now the churchyard was illuminated by the bright blue lights and the glare of the floodlights surrounding the entrance to the church, those same lights which he had seen before only in television dramas. The scientific officers in their protective suits wandered around the place like ghouls, adding more light to the area with their flashing cameras. The churchyard was alive with activity but it seemed to Healey that none of their movements were appropriate in what should have been the respectful silence of the cemetery. The whole thing sickened him, leaving a bitter taste of violence and death in the back of his throat.

Healey was grateful for the cup of tea which he had been given, but he barely tasted it as he drank. His mind was still seized by the scene which he had interrupted earlier that night. The night was everlasting and, similarly, Healey wondered whether his church would ever purify itself of the sin which had been inflicted on it. He had been given a blanket which now hung loosely over his shoulders, barely serving the purpose for which it was designed. Healey had a chill about his person which seemed to penetrate through his bones into his very essence. Was it ever possible to recover from the effects of violent death, he wondered, and no matter how deeply he sought within himself for an answer, Healey could not find one. He doubted God had an answer either; if He had, would He not have provided it by now? Heaven alone knew, in the space of time which had elapsed, Healey had asked often enough for God's guidance. But the silence had continued. Healey drained the tea, as though in an effort to drown out the fear and the doubt which threatened to consume him.

The man sitting beside him looked as though he was ready to go home. His face was pale with exhaustion and his eyes were heavy with responsibility. His suit bore the shine of age and the tie which was hung around his neck was as limp and fatigued as the man himself seemed to be. His hair was grey, in need of a trim, and there was a day's growth of patchy stubble about the chin. His slumped shoulders suggested the heavy burden of long hours and minimal sleep. Despite all that, his blue eyes were shrewd and alert, fixing themselves now on Healey with a determined glare.

"You knew one of the men you discovered in the church, is that right?" he asked now. His voice was harsh, practical, the hoarse whisper of a man not to be crossed.

"Not very well, but I knew the… " Healey struggled to find the words. "The man who died. I knew him, yes, inspector."

Detective Inspector Terry Cook stood up, stretching his spine as he did so. Any more sitting about and the temptation to lie down would be too much. "Tell me exactly what you did know about him."

"There's not much to tell. His name was Richard Temple. I had met him only a few weeks ago."

"Where?"

"Here, at the church. I found him sitting on one of the

pews, in silence, alone with his thoughts."

"Just wandered in off the street, did he?"

Healey could not fail to detect the tone of voice. "Some people do, inspector. Some people need peace once in a while and there is no greater peace than within the sanctuary of God."

Cook's expression remained impassive. "I'll take your word for it, Father. I don't see much of any sort of peace by and large."

"I'm not a priest," said Healey. He looked up at the bemused Cook. "You said father. That applies only to Catholic priests. I'm not a Catholic."

Cook made no reply. The niceties of religious etiquette didn't seem to him to matter very much when brutal murder was the business in hand. "Did Mr Temple say why he needed this special bit of peace?"

"No," replied Healey, his head lowering once more. "And I never asked."

"I'm guessing you didn't let him in last night. So, he must have had a key, right?"

"Yes."

"How come?"

"I gave it to him."

"Why?" pressed Cook.

"Because he asked for it."

"You're going to have to give me more than that, Father. Didn't it strike you as a bit odd, him asking for a key? You don't just give random people keys to the church like those wafer things you dish out, do you?"

"I'm not a Catholic," repeated Healey. "I don't perform mass. And, no, I don't give out keys to anybody."

"So why did you give one to Richard Temple?"

Healey's eyes widened and his mouth hung open impotently. It was a question for which he could offer no answer. "I don't know. Not really. It's hard to explain."

"Try," demanded Cook.

Healey shook his head, giving a slight shrug of his shoulders. "It seemed somehow important for him to have a key."

"Important to you or him?"

"Both. But to him especially. And, if he needed help and I could offer it by giving him a key, that made it important to me too. So, important to both of us."

"When did you give it to him?"

"A couple of days ago."

"Was it a spare, or did you have it cut just for him?"

"It was a duplicate."

Cook fell silent for a moment and he began to kick the gravel of the pathway with the toe of his shoe. "What about the other man, the one you found with the body? Know him?"

A brief shake of the head. "I've never set eyes on him before."

"His name's Nicholas Barclay. Ever heard of him?"

"Never."

"Sure about that, sir?"

"Of course. I don't know him."

"You've no idea why the two of them might be in your church?"

The shake of the head again. "None. How do you know who he is, this other man? Surely he fled as soon as I left the church."

Cook nodded and a smile might have flickered across his thin lips. "He ran off, all right. But a bloke legging it down the road covered in blood attracts attention. He was picked up less than half a mile from here."

"I see," murmured Healey.

"He's sitting in that patrol car over there. I had him

11

brought back here, so you could identify him as the man you saw in the church. Get me?"

"Yes, I understand that. And it is. Him, I mean. He's the man I saw."

"But you can't give me any reason why Barclay would be with Temple in your church and why one of them might be lying dead, with the other one standing over the body?"

Healey's voice rose, with frustration, fear, and sadness. "How many more times must I make that clear to you?"

Cook squatted down on his haunches, peering into the vicar's face. "This is important, sir, and I want you to give me the truth. Did you see Nicholas Barclay kill Richard Temple?"

"No, I did not."

"Positive?"

"Absolutely. Mr Temple was already dead when I came into the church. This man, Barclay, was standing by the body, his hand covered in… blood."

"You didn't see Barclay strike Temple with the candlestick?"

Healey sighed and shook his head, suddenly feeling exhausted. "I did not. And I thank God that I did not."

Cook rose to his full height. "I hope He listens to you, sir. He doesn't listen to me much."

"Perhaps it is you who is not listening, inspector."

There was very little to be said in reply to that. Cook shrugged and walked away from the vicar, keeping his hands deep in his pockets. He gave a brief yawn and the thought of food crept into his brain. Conspiratorially, his stomach gave a faint rumble. Cook ignored them both. He refused to be bullied by his own body. He looked over to where Nicholas Barclay was sitting in the back of the patrol car. Thin, nervous, with dark hair gone wild with the trauma of the night. The expression was vacant, the eyes wide but

12

lifeless. Shock. Or guilt. Cook had seen enough of both, but sometimes it was difficult to tell them apart. His stomach complained again and with an optimism quite unlike his nature, Cook thought it might not be long before he could satisfy his basic need for sustenance. He had no doubt in his mind that Barclay had murdered Temple. The vicar himself was proof enough of that. To Cook, the simplest answer was often the right one, and it was difficult to argue with the facts. All he needed to know was why. He looked back at Barclay, those thin features flickering blue in the glare of the official lights. A weak looking man, frightened by what he had done, allowing all sorts of dark scenarios to play out in his head, no doubt. Cook knew the type. It wouldn't take long to bully him into explaining why he had been driven to murder. Not long at all.

And then, Cook could enjoy a good English breakfast and a few hours in bed. He felt he deserved it.

* * *

Rathe handed the woman another tissue. The tears had begun to subside but the last few moments had been uncomfortable to endure. For both of them, he suspected, but for himself particularly. He had felt the human instinct to comfort the distressed woman, but it had been overtaken at once by the similarly human failing of the deep sense of inadequacy. Nothing he thought to say seemed to offer any practical comfort; his words seemed to be nothing more than empty platitudes, no matter how earnestly he may have intended them to be. So he had simply let her cry until her eyes could shed no more, content for silence and time to offer that support which he felt unable to give.

Caroline Barclay had always struck Rathe as a handsome woman, certainly capable of attracting a man with more presence about him than Nicholas. Rathe had never under-stood the bond between them. Caroline was vibrant, gregarious, always ready with an opinion which would be delivered with a smile; Nicholas was almost insignificant beside her. A man who hadn't found his place in the world, who was unsure both of his abilities and his responsibilities, never wishing to provoke an argument, even if it meant he would condemn himself to submission when he knew he was in the right. So eager to keep the peace that he never made any mark. And it was not that Caroline should find him so sexually attractive that all his other faults could be forgotten. Lank rather than slim, weak rather than sensitive, his face timid and his demeanour apprehensive. He was kind, no doubt, and Rathe couldn't think for a moment that he did not love his wife, or vice versa, but it had always seemed to him to be a mismatched coupling.

In contrast to Nicholas's ordinariness, Caroline seemed almost incredible. Rathe could never bring himself to say that she was beautiful, because her features lacked the delicacy which he felt should always be present when assessing true beauty. But it was impossible to deny that the high cheek-bones and the noble expression were not striking. Her profile was aristocratic, the nose prominent without being intrusive, and there was a feline pout to the small mouth. Her clear green eyes were prone to shine with intelligence and vitality, so it saddened Rathe to see them dimmed with grief as she stared up at him.

"He didn't do it, Anthony," she said. "You know Nicholas. He can't get rid of a spider in the house without releasing it alive into the garden. The idea of him... doing what they're saying he did is ridiculous."

"He was standing beside the body with blood on his hands, Caroline," Rathe felt compelled to say.

"Don't tell me you'd have no way of getting round that in Court."

"I don't practise any more."

"But if you did… "

Rathe paused for a moment, his mind contemplating the idea of being back at the Bar, standing in a Courtroom, his voice echoing around the room, commanding respect and attention. Once, the thought would have thrilled him and massaged his self-regard with all the oils and lotions of profound pride, but now his stomach baulked at the memory. The vision of his robes and wig, which once had been resplendent, seemed to him now to be visions of rags and decay. The wig had become cobwebs, the black robes shredded and tattered with neglect. The images came with their own curses: the face of Kevin Marsden, his pleas for mercy as he was taken down, the clamour of the press as they rushed to make their by-lines, and the animal howls of Kathy Marsden as her son disappeared from view. So vivid in his head, so heavy on his conscience.

"Do you think he did it?" Caroline asked.

"I can't say. I don't think I want to say."

Caroline lowered her gaze and, in that minute, Rathe felt an overpowering sense of disappointment. Not his, but hers; he had let her down in that moment and he felt that both of them were aware of it.

"Then you won't help us?" she said, her voice lowered to a whisper by the weight of her regret.

"I want to, Caroline," he insisted, "believe me, I do. But I don't know what you want me to do. I can't defend Nicholas because I'm not at the Bar any more. Even if I was, it would have to be at a trial, and that's a long way off. The best I can do," he added, after a heavy pause, "is tell you what I would say if you had approached me in Chambers, looking to instruct me. OK?"

"All right," she conceded. He tried not to think about the barely noticeable note of hope in her voice.

"I warn you, Caroline, it isn't good news," he insisted.

"Nicholas is found at a crime scene, beside a body. A candlestick is stained with the victim's blood and Nicholas has got the same blood on his hands because he says he touched the wound. In shock, yes, but nevertheless. What's more, he confesses that his fingerprints are on the weapon because he picked that up in the same state of shock. But his are the only prints on it. And he ran away from the scene before the police arrived, which makes him look like a man with something to hide. All that gives the police a fair bit to work on and it doesn't look good for Nicholas. Not by a long way."

"I know all that, Anthony, and I know how it looks. But you wouldn't be afraid of taking that on if you were acting for him, would you?"

He wouldn't, he had to confess that to himself. Certainly not if those facts and inferences stood alone, but they didn't. "When does Nicholas say he last saw Richard Temple?"

"A couple of nights ago. We'd been invited to dinner. Turned out Richard had too. If we'd known, we'd have made some excuse." She lowered her gaze. "Nicholas was drunk before we arrived. He had tried to sort things out with Richard. He just made a fool of himself."

Rathe sighed. "Do the police know that?"

"Yes. Nicholas told them all about it. You don't have to say anything, Anthony. I know a public argument between them isn't going to help things."

Rathe was pleased he had been spared the necessity of stating the fact himself. "Whose invitation was this?"

"Edmund Lanyon. You know him, I suppose. He's one of yours, after all."

Rathe knew the name, but he was not personally acquainted with the man. Lanyon was older than Rathe, a member of a different set of Chambers. There had never been any occasion, perhaps never any reason, for their paths to cross. "What about this motive the police say Nicholas has,

Caroline? You'd have to get over that hurdle too."

"I don't accept it is a motive. Not for murder."

"Richard Temple was about to ruin you, Caroline."

"All he did was sack Nicholas," she protested. "That's not a motive for murder."

"Nicholas had cost Temple a fortune. He'd been trusted to work with one of Temple's major clients and he made a mess of it. You've got a marketing executive worth millions trusting a new employee with an important contract and that trust Temple showed wasn't repaid. Instead, he ended up having to pay out a king's ransom to protect his reputation. Temple was talking about suing Nicholas for professional negligence, Caroline. That would have put you both on the streets. And that is a motive for murder."

Caroline had begun to shake her head in defiance of the facts. "Nicholas had been begging for another chance. And he would have made it up to Richard Temple, I know he would."

"That doesn't help him," Rathe said. "Because the police will say that if Nicholas did beg for forgiveness and Temple rejected him then Nicholas would be even more inclined to hatred and violence. Can't you see that?"

Caroline's eyes had filled with tears once more but it seemed to Rathe that this time they were tears of anger and frustration rather than pure grief and panic. "I still refuse to accept that my husband met Richard Temple in that church and battered him to death. I just don't believe it, Anthony."

She would have said something more, but the expression on Rathe's face silenced her. His brow had creased into a frown over those dark, austere eyes and his lips had pursed in confused concentration. It was as though some fact or some idea had been made clear to him but its consequences and inferences were disturbing to him. He began to pace the room, slowly, working out what it was which had occurred to him.

"Anthony, what's wrong?" Caroline asked.

"The church," he said. "Why were they in the church at all? It doesn't make any sense."

"What are you saying? I don't understand."

In truth, nor did Rathe, not at that moment. But when he turned his glare upon her, Caroline Barclay saw that his eyes had brightened and she thought she recognised something of her old friend's tenacity and determination, which had been so dimmed over the last few months, come alive inside them once more. Then, a smile crossed briefly over his lips and hope began to swell in her heart.

* * *

"I thought you'd buried yourself away somewhere dark and nasty to mope after what happened."

"I had."

"So what's all this about? You being here now?"

"I don't want you to make the same mistake I did, that's all."

Cook leaned back in his office chair and smiled. He stretched his arms behind his head and latticed his fingers. He wondered why he had felt compelled to grant the interview. It was not as though he and Anthony Rathe had any sort of bond of affection or friendship; quite the contrary, if truth be told. They had been professional antagonists: representatives of the two respective halves of the criminal justice system. The detective who collated evidence and sought punishment for a crime; the barrister who tested the evidence in Court and saw that justice was done. It was an ideal and both men knew it, but there was a tension within it, at least on Cook's part. He dealt with the violence on the streets, the blood and guts of crime, and the effects and consequences of it on the lives involved. Rathe's milieu had been the theatre of justice, the costume drama of the

Courtroom, where the crime was documented in ring-binders and where any number of intellectual tricks might be played in order to ensure that one side won and one side lost. For Cook, justice was a duty; but as far as he was concerned, for Rathe, it was nothing more than a professional game. Several times, Cook had seen known villains walk free because of some abstract parry or manipulation of events played by the defence team, in several cases by Rathe himself. Each time, the acquitted villain had offended again. Every man had a right to a defence; but every victim had a right to closure. There had been times when Cook wondered how Rathe and his ilk could sleep at night. When the Marsden case was laid bare and its tragic climax known, Cook had felt no emotion. When he learned that Rathe had walked away from his own life in disgrace, he had smiled.

"Why would I make the same mess you did?" he asked now.

Rathe remained motionless in his own chair, across the desk from the inspector. The office was sufficiently spacious for him not to feel claustrophobic, but he was close enough to Cook to detect the signs of a tired man. Long hours, bad food (if any), endless cups of coffee, functioning not on energy recharged by sleep but on adrenalin injected by the lack of it. He saw the broken veins in Cook's eyes and the stubble on the chin, but he also saw the shrewdness in that blue glare and the determination behind that day old beard.

"I don't think the Temple murder is as straightforward as it looks," Rathe said. "I don't want you to stop looking just because you think it's cut and dried."

Cook laughed but there was no humour in it. "Good of you, Rathe, but don't you worry about me."

"The evidence you've got is circumstantial."

"Who says?"

"I do. And you do, even if it's only to yourself."

"You don't know what evidence I've got."

"I know as much as his wife does. I'm a friend of the family," he added, as though compelled to explain the situation but the inspector showed no interest. "The motive is your best card, Cook."

"Only one set of prints on the candlestick, Rathe."

"Easily wiped off before Barclay arrived on the scene and picked it up."

"Barclay confesses to being at the scene."

"He can't do otherwise, not with the vicar being there too. What does he say about why he was there?"

Cook bit a fingernail. "He was worried about Temple's threat of a court case. He went to Temple's house to confront him about it but saw him going out. So, Barclay followed him."

"To St Augustine's?"

A curt nod of the inspector's head. "He watched Temple let himself in but he didn't follow. Not at first."

"Why not?"

"Got scared, he says. Crisis of confidence that he'd be able to stand up to Temple."

"That fits in with Barclay's character. He's not blessed with much backbone."

Cook ignored Rathe's personality assessment. "He knew Temple had lit some candles because he saw the light appear in the windows, so he thought Temple was going to be praying or whatever people do in church at night."

"Reasonable assumption."

Cook seemed to acknowledge the point. "So, Barclay walked away. Half way down the road, maybe more, he stopped, had a word with himself about being a coward, and he walked back. That's when he found the body. He says he wasn't in there alone more than two minutes before the vicar showed up."

"The church door was still unlocked?"

"Yes."

Rathe thought about this new information, calculating times and distances. "He saw no one else around?"

"Not a soul."

"Not even Healey coming to check on the church?"

Cook's eyes widened. "You losing it, Rathe, or was my last reply in French, or what?"

"So, if Barclay's innocent, there's a very short time frame between him and Healey arriving back on the scene for the murderer to escape. How long was he walking?"

"Barclay reckons he was no more than twenty minutes from leaving the church, wandering off, having a little debate with himself, and getting back."

"That's enough time for someone else to do it."

"In an ideal world," said Cook. "But we don't live in one of them. This playing about with time, it's all a bit shaky for me. Leaves too many people on the scene. Makes it all a bit busy."

"It's still possible, no matter how much it upsets you," asserted Rathe.

"Only if you accept it's true. Which I don't."

"That alters nothing. The motive is your strongest piece of evidence. The rest of it is muck-spreading."

"Throw enough shit and something sticks. You know that better than anyone."

"Meaning?"

"It's what these defence clowns do all the time. Toss some dung around an investigation which has been built up after months of hard work and see where it lands. Just so some rapist, some abuser, some killer can go and do what he does best yet again."

"They wouldn't be acquitted if the case was properly constructed," muttered Rathe.

"Sometimes the cases are constructed too well. Or, at least, presented too well. Innocent men get convicted, don't they?"

"That's when the system fails everybody."

Cook conceded the point, leaning forward with a smile. "But some innocent men shouldn't ever have been convicted, should they? It's only when he's faced with some fancy words from a man playing up to the press for a bit of publicity that those types are convicted."

"I didn't come here to talk about Kevin Marsden," said Rathe. His voice was controlled by ice.

"Those sort of men don't deserve to have the system fail them," continued Cook. "They don't deserve to slice their arms open in the showers because some bastard in a wig and cloak wanted his name showered in glory."

Rathe rose from his chair, but his eyes remained fixed on the detective. "Unless you get something more concrete against Nicholas Barclay, you're going to have to release him, Cook. You know that as well as I do. And when you release him, I'll be able to talk to him. Because I don't think he did it, but if you don't care about that, I'll have to care for you and find out what happened that night."

He held Cook's gaze for a moment longer before turning on his heel. He had opened the door and stepped into the corridor before Cook called his name. "What makes you think I'm making a mistake about Barclay?"

Rathe smiled. Cook had conceded some ground and it would infuriate him to have felt compelled to do so. It was a minor, petty victory, but Rathe found it satisfying nonetheless. "Let me answer that with another question. Why would Barclay – or anybody else for that matter – choose that church as the place to commit a murder? What's so special about that church?"

Cook shrugged, as disinterested as he could seem to be. "The vicar had given Temple a key, so he could get into the place any old time."

"But why there? He could get into his own house, his office, anywhere. The killer could have murdered Temple in any number of places more private than St Augustine's. So why did the killer choose there?"

Cook spread out his hands and shook his head. "No idea. I give up."

Rathe nodded, his lip twisting in contempt. "Exactly. But I won't, Cook. Not until I know the truth."

For several seconds afterwards, Cook did nothing but stare in anger at the closed door of his office. There was no sound but his laboured, frustrated breathing.

* * *

They walked through the cemetery, a slight breeze chilling their faces. The trees rustled and birdsong twittered around them. It was peaceful, calm, far removed from the sounds of the city. The purring of engines, the blaring of car horns, the rumble of trains, all sounds which seemed to have no connection with this area of tranquil stillness. They might have belonged to another world entirely.

"This is the second cemetery I've been to in as many days," said Rathe.

"For what reason?" asked the Reverend Thomas Healey.

"Personal ones."

"I did not mean to intrude."

Rathe waved away the apology. "The first visit was personal, at least. I was visiting the grave of somebody. Someone I once knew. Sort of."

"A friend or relative?"

Rathe shook his head. "Neither. Just someone I let down very badly."

"I'm sorry to hear that. We mustn't punish ourselves for our sins, not if we repent. And from your expression and demeanour, I take it you do repent."

"Every day."

"Are you a religious man, Mr Rathe?"

Rathe wondered about that. He didn't in all honestly think he could say he was. He never attended church, certainly, but he had a fascination for the idea of religion, an awe of its power and influence, and he knew that he found its architecture exceptionally beautiful. But as to whether he believed in God, the crucifixion and the resurrection, and the promise of paradise, he could not answer with confidence.

"Recently, I've become very fond of the special peace you find in churches," he said. Evasive, but true.

"Another man I knew briefly said a similar thing to me a few weeks ago."

"Was that the man who was killed here, by any chance?"

Healey turned upon his visitor with a saddened, almost betrayed expression on his face. "Is that why you have come here?"

"Yes."

"For what purpose?"

"I want to find out what happened."

"One man took another man's life by violence, and in sight of the Lord," hissed Healey. "That's what happened, Mr Rathe."

"I understand that, Mr Healey. But why? And why would anybody choose your church in which to commit murder?"

"I cannot imagine. I dare not imagine."

The old man wrung his hands with agitation as he glared at Rathe with a weary anger in his otherwise kind eyes. Healey began to retrace their steps back towards the vicarage, but Rathe continued to walk with him, regardless of whether Healey was now disconcerted by his presence or not.

"I believe Mr Temple had a key to St Augustine's," Rathe said.

"I gave it to him. How I wish I had not."

"May I ask why you gave him a key?"

Once more, his words stopped the vicar's steps dead. "The police asked me the same question. I could not give them a satisfactory answer, so I fear I shall not be able to do any differently for you, Mr Rathe. But, perhaps you will understand better than the detective I spoke to."

"I'd like to think so," said Rathe with a soft smile.

"You mentioned just now the special peace you find in an empty church," said Healey and the memory of Rathe's words seemed to soothe the old man. They continued their slow pace along the path. "And you are right, of course, there is such a peace when one is in the presence of God. It was that same peace which Mr Temple sought. I found him in the church one afternoon. I like to leave the door open some afternoons for individual prayer and personal solitude. Sometimes for my own, if truth be told. One day, this man Temple was sitting on one of the front pews."

"Did you speak to him?"

"Oh, yes. We had a long talk about the church and its history, its design, the size of the congregation. Matters of general interest. Mine can be a lonely life, Mr Rathe, and for someone – even a stranger – to take an interest in the church and my life within it can be a welcome distraction."

"I can well imagine."

A brief smile put an end to this personal diversion from the subject. "Two days later, he came back. The following day, he was there again. Over the following fortnight or so, it was a regular occurrence. Always in the later afternoon."

"And the key. Did you offer it to him, or did he request it?"

"He asked for it, a couple of days ago. It was then that he confided in me about his faith."

This time, it was Rathe who stopped walking, his hand

involuntarily reaching out for the vicar's arm. "His faith?"

Healey seemed troubled by the subject. "It was strange, looking back. Perhaps at the time I thought it was odd, I don't recall, but now it seems bizarre. He asked for the key because he said he might want to come to the church at unsocial hours, when he couldn't expect me to be awake to receive him."

"Did he say why?"

Healey clenched his hands together and his eyes roamed the perimeter of the churchyard. "I should have seen his trouble and offered some guidance on it."

"What trouble, Mr Healey?"

"Temple was a businessman, I'm sure you know that, just as I'm sure you're aware of the pressures such men face these days. Mr Temple had spoken to me of his own burdens and how they had preyed on his mind over the years. Building up his company, the long hours, the sacrifices, the risks. He was contemplating a civil litigation, he told me, but I did not ask for any details. He simply said that it brought its own anxiety. I got the impression when I first met him that he was a man with a great weight upon his shoulders and that he was carrying it by himself."

"Self-made men very often do," observed Rathe. "And Temple was still a comparatively young man, as far as I am aware. Barely forty years of age, I believe."

Healey nodded in agreement. "Towards the end of my time with him, I saw a change in him. I think talking about his problems had enabled him to relive them and see them for what they were. I don't think they mattered to him any more. I think he had found some way of dealing with them, of sharing the burden."

Rathe stared hard at the vicar. "Are you telling me that Temple had some sort of conversion?"

Healey gave a non-committal gesture. "I don't pretend to

have the authority to say as much, but how else am I to explain his sudden attachment to the church? He confessed to me that he had never been religious in the past but that recently, just prior to visiting St Augustine's, he had begun to see his daily trials as less significant than the prospect of facing evil in the world."

Rathe inhaled a deep breath of air. He felt he needed it, to purge the ramifications of Healey's information from his soul. "You think he asked for the key so that he could be close to God whenever he chose?"

Healey gave no direct answer. "He talked about sin, Mr Rathe. In particular, his own, and his wish to be absolved of it."

"Did you ask him what he meant by that?"

"Naturally, but his reply was only a faint smile and a shake of his head. 'It is a matter for me and those I have hurt'. Those were his words."

"Can you think what he meant by that?"

The old man bowed his head. "I have no wish to speculate. But his obsession with his sins, his wish to be close to God, his realisation that his personal burdens were insignificant compared to the larger issues of the world... I did ask him what he believed had happened to him and whether he believed he had found God."

"What was his reply?"

"That he had not found God, but God had found him. Now, in those terms, Mr Rathe, do you doubt that he had in some way been converted to a path of righteousness?"

Rathe was staring at the steeple of the church and his eyes never left it as he spoke. "Like you, vicar, perhaps it is wise not to speculate."

Internally, however, Rathe was doing just that. If some form of conversion had overtaken Temple, had his murderer been aware of it? If so, the killer might well have known where the most likely place to find Temple had been, which would explain why the murder had taken place in the church. Similarly, he might have found it easy to lure a newly converted man to his favourite place of worship. But it still offered no explanation to Rathe for the specific use of the church as a place to commit murder. Furthermore, what were these sins with which Temple seemed to have been so obsessed, and had he died because of them? Rathe had a sudden sense of the past bearing down on him and, for a moment, surrounded by the stone markers of demise which were scattered throughout the churchyard, he felt closer to death than he had ever done before.

* * *

It was late afternoon when Rathe managed to secure a meeting with Edmund Lanyon. The day was shifting into night, the skyline of the city darkening in the fading sunlight as the blues and greys of the daytime skies began to merge into the oranges of dusk before becoming the final blacks of night. Watching a sunset frequently reminded Rathe of Houseman's poem about that special phenomenon of the passing of the day and its words came back to him now as he sat on the South Bank overlooking the river, waiting for the barrister to keep their appointment. The river had begun to turn that special inky black which the Thames alone seemed able to take on itself and Rathe found himself wondering about the change in urban life which occurs when the hours pass. The replacement of sun with neon, the sound of traffic merging by the pulsating bass lines of riverside bars, the eventual peace of twilight.

There was that word again: peace. It had been peace Temple had initially craved from St Augustine's; the peace of his blossoming faith; the darker peace, however shattered, of his death. Peace in so many forms. It seemed to Rathe that so many people had found peace in some way or other but, for him, any sense of harmony seemed still so distant. For once, he did not have such thoughts in the context of Kevin Marsden's death, but in the death of Richard Temple, for it was that second, violent death which plagued Rathe in the present moment, and which prevented his mind from finding anything approaching its own calm.

"Mr Rathe?"

He was brought out of his thoughts by the voice, authoritative and direct, and looking up he saw the patrician yet stern expression of the man who had spoken. White hair was swept back from an intellectual dome of a forehead, and a pair of alert, grey eyes twinkled with arrogant confidence. The arched nostrils of the long nose flared in inquisitive interest at the purpose of this interview and Rathe rose to meet the expectation. His offer of a hand was ignored, being replaced with a slight bow of the head so that there could be no direct allegation of rudeness.

"Thank you for coming to meet me, Mr Lanyon," said Rathe. "I appreciate you could have felt no obligation to do so."

Lanyon demurred. "I rather think I did, Mr Rathe. Or are you so modest that you think your name would not be familiar to one of your own profession? As I understand it, modesty was never one of your virtues when you were in practice."

If Rathe had taken the comment as an insult, he showed no sign of any offence. "I'd like to think that I've learned something about modesty recently. Perhaps humility would be a better choice of word."

"And what have you learned?"

Rathe looked out over the river. "Not enough."

Lanyon stared at the profile of the younger man. He saw the obvious melancholy which was carved into the features and he recognised the abstract sense of sadness which loomed behind the man's dark eyes. His reputation as a barrister had preceded Rathe, as far as Lanyon was concerned, and the older man had some measure of regard for him in a professional capacity. However, Lanyon was not the sort of man who could understand any disregard of a sterling career on account of a single error of judgement.

But, Lanyon argued with himself, he did not know the full facts of the Marsden case. The newspaper reports of tampered evidence were known to him, of course; the media circus of one of the country's leading defence barristers making the leap to prosecuting Counsel simply, if stories were to be believed, for the sake of the challenge and the publicity; the eventual death of an innocent man by his own hand. These factors were known to Lanyon, just as they were to the rest of the country; but he could have no notion of the personal insights of the players concerned. His reaction to Rathe's predicament might well have been different, but he recognised the fact that it was not within his rights to judge the man on that basis. Whatever the truth of the Marsden case, it was clear from Rathe's own demeanour that if anybody felt he should be punished for any sin concerned with the case, he was standing there before Lanyon, gazing sadly over the mighty stretch of water which flowed beside them. And it was likewise obvious that the man's punishment was being dealt with by his own conscience.

"There's a discreet wine bar just around the corner," Lanyon declared. "I normally nip in for a glass after a strenuous day. Perhaps you'd care to join me."

It was not a question, nor was it phrased as one, so Rathe did not give a verbal reply. Instead, he followed the older man in walking through the throng of people moving towards them. Not for the first time, Rathe became aware of the sensation that everybody else in the city was going in the opposite direction to him, a tsunami of bodies heading towards him, moving in turn too quickly or too slowly for his own speed.

The bar was secluded rather than discreet, so much so that Rathe was not surprised that he had never heard of it before. Unlike many of the bars he knew, with their chrome fittings and loud music, this was furnished after the Victorian period. Panelled walls of oak, at least two large fireplaces with portraits above them, with unknown faces glaring disapprovingly down at the revelry below, carpets of a paisley pattern throughout, and large bookcases with ancient but now untouched volumes on a disparate range of subjects placed in them for effect rather than purpose. The place was filled with professionals, suits of greys and blacks, each with the same notion as Lanyon had of softening the edges of a difficult day with a glass of two of what proved to be the most excellent choice of wines. Rathe joined Lanyon in a large glass of the deepest ruby Merlot and they managed to find themselves a place in a darkened corner towards the rear exit.

"Perhaps you'd like to explain why you wanted to see me, Mr Rathe," suggested Lanyon in a brisk, business-like tone.

Rathe's summary of the situation was likewise a brisk, concise, and professional account. Lanyon listened with a blend of professional and personal interest but also with, it seemed to Rathe, some element of concern.

"And the police have arrested Barclay?" Lanyon asked. "I cannot say that I am altogether surprised."

"You sound convinced he's guilty."

Lanyon had a sip of the wine, giving an involuntary murmur of appreciation as he did so. "I've seen first-hand the animosity between them, Mr Rathe."

Rathe thought back to what Caroline Barclay had said about a public argument. "At your dinner party the other night?"

Lanyon smiled. "You're well informed. Why are you asking questions about Barclay and Temple, Mr Rathe? What is it you're after?"

Kathy Marsden had asked him a similar question in different circumstances not so long ago. For the first time, the possibility that idle curiosity about the Temple murder might not be his sole motive occurred to him. He did not dare to believe that it was true, but equally he found that he could not dismiss the idea completely from his mind. Temple had talked to Healey about the absolution of personal sin and he had sought such a reprieve in the comfort of his conversion. Was Rathe seeking something similar by immersing himself in a violent death? The suggestion struck him at once as being perverse, but it had occurred to him with such clarity that he knew it deserved further consideration.

"I just want to know the truth, Mr Lanyon."

Lanyon's eyebrows raised and he contemplated his guest for a few seconds. "If I had known the truth, perhaps I wouldn't have invited one or the other of them. I had no idea of this friction between them, not until that night. The two of them are only passing acquaintances of mine. I was not even aware they knew each other."

"Why did you invite them at all then?"

"My wife is friendly with Caroline Barclay. She said that Caroline and her husband had been going through some sort of money trouble and they needed something to take their minds off it. Temple, I knew through a solicitor friend of mine who had given some advice to him once in a while. I'd no reason to assume any connection between the two of them. Truth to tell," he said, dropping his voice to a whisper, "usually I'd say that if it had been up to me there wouldn't have been any dinner at all. Not my idea of a good time. But Mrs Lanyon loves the whole hostess thing and I find it's easier to avoid an argument."

Rathe smiled at this sudden intimate sharing of a guilty secret. He found himself warming to Lanyon, as though there was the suggestion of an affectionate and witty heart at the centre of the aloof exterior of professional marble. Rathe leaned back in his chair and enjoyed the wine. It was excellent, so much so that he found himself hoping that there would be time for a second.

"But I had no cause to argue this time," Lanyon was saying. "There was a reason for the whole thing, you see. It would have been my daughter's birthday, her fortieth. We felt it right that we marked it somehow."

"I'm sorry… "

Lanyon nodded. "Adele killed herself twenty years ago, Mr Rathe. It's not something I wish to dwell upon, as you can imagine."

"Of course not."

Lanyon was contemplating his wine. "If I'd known about those two men and their own private little war, I wouldn't have invited either of them and the evening might not have been spoiled."

Rathe leaned forward in his chair. "Tell me about this altercation between them."

Lanyon sniffed, gently but contemptuously. "If you want an opinion, it was Barclay's fault. Temple and I had been talking quietly in the corner of the living room. He had shown an interest in the collection of family photographs which we have set out there and I was showing him a photo of my daughter. Barclay came up and demanded to speak to him."

"That doesn't sound like the Nicholas Barclay I know, I'm bound to say."

Lanyon raised his glass of wine, swirling its contents. "He'd had his fill of this stuff, that was obvious. Before he arrived, by the look of him. I told him he was being a rude little bastard but he was adamant."

"How did Temple react?"

Lanyon frowned. "Oddly. When I'd met him in the past, I'd taken Temple to be a man willing to fight his ground, unafraid of the consequences or the challenges. You don't get to his level of success on your own by being afraid of either. Perhaps we both know something about that, Mr Rathe. The way Barclay was speaking to him, demanding his attention and making a show of himself, I'd expected Temple to put him in his place."

"But he didn't?"

"Not at all. He stared blankly at the floor, as though he was thinking about something entirely different. It was as though he couldn't hear what Barclay was saying to him."

"And when Barclay had finished ranting?"

Lanyon nodded. "Then Temple did speak, but he didn't retaliate. His voice was calm, quiet, almost inaudible. He said something about each man's sin finding him out and that it was important for everyone to recognise that sin within themselves."

"What did you think he meant by that?"

"I've no idea. Barclay hadn't a clue either by the look of him. I can only assume Temple meant that this mess Barclay had created by botching a new contract for Temple was viewed by him as a sin."

"Doesn't that sound rather tenuous?" asked Rathe.

"Possibly. As I say, I can't be sure of anything. But something had changed inside Temple, Mr Rathe. I'm sure of that."

The conversion, thought Rathe. That is what had changed; that was the fundamental alteration in Temple's character. And yet, the distance between Barclay's supposed sin of losing a large amount of Temple's money and the murder in the church seemed so vast that Rathe could not give it credence, even when accounting for the conversion. Something about the whole scenario still jarred in Rathe's mind. Until he could determine what that small point which did not sit right with him was, he felt there was nothing more he could learn about the night of the dinner. Not that he felt he had learned very much. He wondered for a moment whether he was any closer to discovering the truth of what happened that night in St Augustine's than he had been when he first learned of the crime. Perhaps all this, whatever he was doing, was a waste of effort.

Lanyon declined the invitation of a second glass of wine and, with a firm and commanding shake of the hand, he said goodbye. As he left, he turned back to face Rathe.

"Whatever it is you're trying to achieve, Mr Rathe," he said, "I suggest you think very carefully about it. Pandora's Box comes in many forms."

Rathe thought about the advice as he watched Lanyon disappear out of the rear exit of the bar. It might be good advice but, in order to understand it completely, Rathe felt he needed, not to say deserved, at least another glass of wine.

* * *

The following morning brought the threat of rain. Rathe had slept badly and the thought of moving through London in a heavy shower did not appeal to him. He was not a man who craved the sunshine, but he did not welcome rain. He preferred the golden beauty and the crisp air of autumn, or the fresh bloom of a spring morning. Summer and winter could leave him alone, but the remaining two seasons he found reviving and fulfilling.

A few simple enquiries had produced Hilary Preece's name. Caroline Barclay had told him that Richard Temple's only family, as far as she was aware, was a married sister living somewhere in the Oxford area. Several speculative phone calls, some embarrassing and some curt, had resulted in him tracing Hilary. Initially reluctant, she ultimately agreed to see Rathe for one hour only in a public place of her choosing, after which she wanted no further contact. Even if he had wanted to, Rathe would have been unable to refuse any of her conditions.

Perhaps predictably, she chose a country pub on a fine stretch of road bordered on either side by woodland and, beyond the trees, extensive fields. The pub had been a practical choice, it seemed to Rathe: neutral ground was sensible but a coffee shop would have been too noisy, too crowded, with the possibility of eavesdropping too acute for comfort. The pub's corner tables allowed privacy without the threat of seclusion. She arrived after him, which likewise struck him as an intelligent tactic, avoiding the vulnerability and embarrassment of a woman sitting alone in a pub, however well acquainted with it she might be.

She was pretty, with sharp blue eyes and very fine blonde hair, both of which contrasted with the red of her lips, but there was a hardness about the expression which suggested that any attempt to take advantage of this attractive blonde would end in disaster. She was expensively but not ornately dressed and the ring on her wedding finger was large enough to sparkle but tasteful enough to avoid ostentation. When she saw Rathe, she allowed him a small smile, which he felt unable to resist returning. She accepted a glass of white wine, insisting she would only have the one, and Rathe switched from the mineral water he had ordered to a glass of red.

"I think I ought to make it clear that I don't normally meet unknown men in country pubs," Hilary Preece stated.

"I should hope not," replied Rathe, smiling. "I can promise you that I'm not a pervert or anything."

Her smile broke into a small laugh. "I didn't think for a minute you might be. Certainly not judging by your voice on the phone. If you had looked like one when I peered through the window just now, I might have walked away. But you don't."

"I'm grateful for small mercies."

She gave him another smile and sipped some of the wine. "I suppose you think I should be in tears. About my brother."

"I don't know you, so I can't make that judgement"

"A lot of people would. The truth is that I don't feel sad at Richard's death. I don't feel anything other than surprise. I think that's the word. It feels strange knowing that he's gone, but I can't put it any higher than that."

"I presume from what you say that you weren't close."

She shook her head. "Not at all. We never were, really, but after my parents died things got worse."

"I'm sorry to hear that."

"Don't be. It was the usual story."

"Money?"

"More particularly, my parents' money and how it should be split. I won't bore you with the details but, by the end of five years' worth of arguing and fighting, I ended up with a far lower share than I deserved."

It was difficult for Rathe to tell whether this was bitterness or truth. Her eyes had gone cold, but her voice betrayed the fact that the subject still caused her some degree of pain. "And that was because of your brother?"

"All because of him. He was greedy, overpowering, and if he didn't get his way then he'd become just plain nasty. People used to say he was ambitious and that he had to be ruthless to succeed. Well, a ruthless businessman is one thing; a cold, heartless human being is another."

Rathe shifted in his chair. "I'm sorry, but I can't reconcile that with the man I've been hearing about."

"I don't understand."

Rathe contemplated her for a moment. "Was your family religious?"

She spat out a laugh. "Hardly. Dad was an atheist and Mum wasn't sure one way or the other so never gave it any thought. Why are you asking?"

He kept his eyes fixed on hers. "Your brother seems to have had some sort of religious conversion."

Rathe did not know what reaction she might have to his words, but he could not have expected the gentle shaking of her shoulders and the broad grin across her face. For a few seconds, she chuckled silently to herself, before seeming to become aware of the inappropriate nature of her response. She composed herself and returned her attention to him.

"Are you telling me Richard found God?" she sneered. As he nodded his head, she began to shake hers. "I can't believe that for a minute. You didn't know my brother, Mr Rathe, but I did, no matter how distant we were from each other. He was as far removed from God as you could get. Unless you're talking about the Old Testament, when God was full of anger and wrath."

"He had befriended a vicar in a local parish, Mrs Preece," argued Rathe. "He had been given his own key to the church."

She stared at him, dumbfounded. "I don't believe what I'm hearing."

"There was still a trace of the man you describe in him," confessed Rathe. "The man who is suspected of killing Richard had cost him a lot of money. Richard was in the process of suing him for professional negligence. It caused a serious rift between them."

She was nodding. "That does sound like Richard."

"But, I have to tell you," said Rathe, cautiously, "that there was a public argument between the two men. Richard talked about sin, particularly about absolving himself of it. And I can't reconcile that fact with the image you give of your brother."

She had fallen silent again, her eyes adopting a distant glaze, as though her mind had now travelled through time to a point in the past. Rathe sat in silence, watching her, knowing that it would be imprudent to press her to continue to speak before she was ready.

"Richard knew all about sin," she said at last. "Trust me, Mr Rathe, he was no saint."

"You might have to explain that," he said, quietly.

She took a moment to compose herself. "Richard had a difficult relationship with women. Maybe that's why he and I were never close, I don't know. He couldn't relate to them. It's hard to explain, but it was as though he was scared of them. Frightened, because he couldn't understand them."

"Didn't he have girlfriends?"

"Oh, yes, quite a few. He desired women all the time, but he couldn't cope with them. He had no idea how to handle them, not really. So, his answer to that problem, which was typical of Richard, was to try to control them. To make them into something which he could manage because they would be on his terms."

"I've known some men like that myself," said Rathe.

"There was one girl in particular," Hilary continued. "None of the girls Richard tried to dominate stayed around once they had seen what he was like, but they all tended to make some effort to conform to his ideas before they ran for the hills. But not Jane. She wasn't having any of it."

"And what happened?"

"She stood up to him," said Hilary, her voice flat, "and he knocked her down. Literally."

Rathe lowered his head. "He hit her?"

"More than once. What I'd call a sustained attack. Jane was lucky it burned out quickly. She might have had more than three broken ribs and a face full of bruises if it hadn't done."

Rathe sipped some wine in an effort to drown out the taste of filth which had formed at the back of his throat. "When was this?"

Hilary did a swift calculation. "A while ago. Ten years, perhaps."

"This Jane, where is she now?"

"I've no idea. As soon as she was out of hospital, she packed a bag and left. We never saw or heard from her again."

"But no charges were brought?"

Hilary shook her head. "As soon as he'd done it, Richard was penitent. He begged Jane's forgiveness, even volunteering to go to the police himself. He was really scared at what he'd done, really freaked out. So Jane thought Richard's conscience would punish him more than the law. From what you've said about this shift in faith, maybe she was right."

"Perhaps," murmured Rathe, his mind swiftly docketing this new insight into Richard Temple.

But Hilary had more to say. "Jane wasn't the only one. When Richard was at Lancaster University, something major happened. I think the memory of it was why he was so scared when he attacked Jane, because it brought it all back. I wasn't supposed to know about it and I never found out the full details, but something really bad happened."

Rathe leaned towards her. "What was it?"

Tears now brimming in her eyes, she drained her glass. "Families have secrets. Some of them are known by everyone, some of them known only by the people directly involved. Whatever he did at university was one of the second. Only mum, dad, and Richard knew the full story."

"But you knew some of it."

She nodded quickly, as though the knowledge of it was her own personal sin. "I don't know for certain. All I ever had were overheard snippets of conversation and whispers behind closed doors. I was too scared to talk about what I heard, Mr Rathe, but I know I got the gist of what my brother had done."

Rathe's voice lowered to match her own. Their words were barely audible over the crackling of the fire across the room. "Which was?"

She looked at him with those clear, blue eyes, but they were now blurred with fear and pain. "I think he raped and killed a girl… "

* * *

Rathe found himself back amongst the dead.

His journey back from Oxford had been uneasy, the implications of Hilary Preece's words making for sinister and intrusive fellow passengers. Looking back, he would realise that he could recall no details of the journey itself, although the information which Temple's sister had given him was clearly marked out in his mind. He had called Cook, his head pounding with thoughts, and it had taken no more than a few sharp words on his part for the inspector to cut short his cynical rants.

"I don't care right now if you think I'm interfering, inspector," Rathe had said. "I don't care if you want to spend your time plotting my arrest for wasting police time. I don't care about any of it. But I do care about the fact that when he was a student, your murder victim may well have committed a serious crime himself. And I care that you don't seem to be fussed one way or the other about that."

The voice on the other end of the line had been drenched in suppressed venom. "I don't give a rat's arse what you care about, Rathe, so don't think otherwise. But don't ever think I don't take my job seriously. Now, you calm down a bit, sonny, and tell me what you're on about."

And Rathe spoke, telling the whole story he had learned from Hilary Preece, ending his tale with a request that Cook find out what he could about Temple's university life. Cook had listened, grunting once or twice, before putting the phone down with a curt assurance that he would investigate. No thanks had been given. After the call, Rathe had felt at a loose end. He tried to accumulate the knowledge he had gained, but he couldn't separate it all into anything resembling a coherent whole. In the end, he had walked back to the dead.

He saw Kathy Marsden at the graveside of her son, tending to the flowers which she had replaced just before he arrived. He approached her quietly, his hands in his pockets, but she heard his footsteps all the same, turning round to face him as she got to her feet. Her eyes were saddened and her complexion pale, but he had the sense that she was as upset at seeing him as she was at the tragedy which had bound them together.

"You've still not forgiven yourself, Mr Rathe," she said.

"I don't think so." He looked down at the flowers. They were a splash of colour amongst the cold stones of the cemetery. "I've been trying to help a friend. I don't know whether I've been trying to ease my conscience by doing it. If I have, would that make me selfish?"

"I don't think selfishness is the problem," she replied. "I think it is something worse."

"Guilt?"

"Partly. But isn't your guilt mixed with self-pity?"

Her words struck him as brutal, but perhaps it was only the bitter sting of honesty. The church loomed in the distance, so similar in structure to St Augustine's but smaller, and free from its association with murder. "I want to make amends. That's all. To you, to Kevin. I just don't know how to do it."

"Kevin doesn't need you to make amends." She caressed the top of her son's gravestone. "And nor do I. It would be easy for me to blame you, Mr Rathe, because blaming my son for his own death is so very difficult to do. But he killed himself, he took himself away from me. If there is blame, isn't it on Kevin himself?"

"Do you believe that?"

She sighed. "I don't know what I believe. But what I know for sure is that you must learn to stand back from your own conscience. You must forgive yourself. Look, at the church over there, Mr Rathe. Isn't this the place for you to forgive yourself?"

In reply, she was greeted with silence. He did not speak for some moments and, when she looked at him to invite some response, she saw those dark eyes fixed ahead of them both. She had grown used to his expression of regret, so that she was taken aback when she saw the alert and exultant glare with which he had fixed upon the church. His lips had parted and his breathing had become shallow. She repeated his name several times, but he seemed not to hear her. At last, he turned to her, his eyes still widened in what she thought was nothing short of triumph.

"Forgiveness," he murmured. "Asking for forgiveness… "

Kathy Marsden shook her head. "I don't know what you mean."

His mobile chirped into life before he could answer. "Cook?"

The inspector's voice on the other end of the connection had lost some of its acidity towards Rathe. "I've got Temple's university record right in front of me. Confirms the sister's story. There was some trouble with a girl, but it looks as though it never went any further than an internal investigation. He was kicked out, but no criminal charges were brought."

Rathe was nodding. "No. That's the point, there wouldn't be. I'm starting to understand now."

"I think I might know who the girl was too, Rathe," said Cook, flatly.

"So do I. Was she in Temple's year by any chance?"

"Started on the same day. Same course."

Rathe closed his eyes. So, he had reached the end at last and the truth was known. "I'll see you in ten minutes. We should finish this together."

"Fine by me." And the call was terminated.

Kathy Marsden had listened to Rathe's side of the conversation with increasing confusion. "What's happening, Mr Rathe? What did all that mean?"

Rathe turned to face here, with what might have been salvation in his eyes. "Murder, Mrs Marsden. It means murder, committed in the face of absolution."

* * *

"I hadn't expected to see you again so soon, Mr Rathe."

"Nor had I."

"Would you like a drink?"

"No, thank you."

"Inspector Cook, a drink?"

"Too early."

"And you're on duty, of course."

"No, just too early."

They were standing in Lanyon's study. The barrister was standing behind his desk, his various legal papers scattered across the top of it, a collection of bankers boxes and lever arch files dotted across the floor. A working lawyer's study. To Rathe, who was standing in the centre of the room with his hands behind his back, it brought back memories of the professional life he had left in ruins. The recollection was unwelcome and uncomfortable. Cook was standing to one side, leaning against a fitted bookcase, one ankle crossed over the other, his fingers playing with a manilla file which he held in his hands, those crucial details of Temple's career at university hidden within it.

"Am I to assume that you are here in a professional capacity, Inspector Cook?" Lanyon asked now.

Cook grinned. "I'm here for the entertainment, Mr Lanyon. This is Mr Rathe's show."

Lanyon looked across at the younger man. "I'm afraid I'm lost."

Rathe walked over to the desk and took up a silver framed photograph of a young woman, no more than eighteen years of age in the image itself, the face of a woman with only a short time to live. There was no indication in those pale blue eyes and the brightness of the smile of the horrors which were to befall her, no suggestion in her blithe expression of the violence which was to come her way.

"Your daughter," said Rathe.

"I told you, I don't like to talk about her." Lanyon's voice was flint.

"You told me that the dinner party you held the other week was for her fortieth. That would make her of a similar age to Richard Temple."

"Would it?" Lanyon had no intention that his words should be taken as a genuine question.

Rathe replaced the photograph on the desk and fixed his gaze on Lanyon. "From the very beginning, I couldn't understand why Temple had been murdered in a church. I asked Cook the question: whoever murdered Temple, whether that was Nicholas Barclay or someone else, could have done it anywhere. So why in the church, specifically? You mentioned to me that you thought Temple had undergone some change of personality, after his argument at your party with Barclay. In fact, he had experienced some sort of religious conversion."

Lanyon held out his hands in acceptance of this explanation, sitting down as he did so. "There you are, then. If he'd found God, it's perfectly natural he should be in a church."

Rathe nodded. "But why would his killer be in the church? True, he might have followed Temple there, like Barclay had done, but I tend to think he didn't."

"Why?"

"You said it yourself," Rathe smiled. "Temple was looking at your family photographs with you when Barclay approached him. After Barclay's drunken outburst, you said Temple was restrained, disinterested in confronting Barclay and having the argument."

"He was." Lanyon looked across at Cook. "Does this nonsense have any point at all?"

Cook did not meet the man's gaze. Rathe turned away from the desk as he continued to speak. "Earlier today, a friend of mine was talking to me about forgiveness, specifically seeking forgiveness in church. That reminded me of Temple's words to you and Barclay about admitting one's sins and seeking absolution for them."

Lanyon scoffed. "I can see why it would."

"That's when the importance of the murder taking place in the church struck me. Temple was in St Augustine's because he wanted to confess a sin. The mistake I had made was in assuming that the murderer chose the location, that somehow he had lured Temple there, possibly on account of his conversion, but I was wrong. It wasn't the murderer but the victim who had chosen the church for an assignation. That was why Temple lit the candles, because he had arrived first and was preparing for his personal confession." Rathe turned on his heel, facing his quarry once more. "His confession to you."

Lanyon stared at Rathe with suppressed anger in his eyes.

"You'd better be sure of what you're saying here, Mr Rathe."

Rathe was defiant. "I am. Positive. Temple asked to meet you in the one church to which he could gain entry in private. There, he begged you for absolution and he did it before the God he had grown to worship. Your response was to take up one of the altar candlesticks and beat his brains out of his skull."

Lanyon's face flushed with rage. "Get out of my house. How dare you make such an accusation without a shred of evidence?"

Rathe remained impassive. "Because it is true."

Lanyon's fury intensified. "I'm warning you, Rathe. Get out or I shall make steps to throw you out."

Cook stepped forward. "I don't think so, Mr Lanyon."

The barrister looked from one to the other, suddenly aware that his route to the study door was blocked by the two of them. He was cornered, and his eyes grew wild at the realisation. "I refuse to listen to any more of this."

"Tough," snapped Cook.

"I spoke to Temple's sister," continued Rathe. "She told me of his peculiar attitude to women, his inability to deal with them and his fear of them. She said that his reaction to that social deficiency was to try to control women, to mould them into something he could understand. But his efforts could become violent. As they did with Adele, your daughter."

Lanyon's eyes remained fierce, but the tears which welled up within them were impossible to conceal. As they fell, his anger gave way to grief and he fell into his chair, sobbing, his head dropping into his hands. When he spoke once more, Rathe's voice was softened by compassion.

"Temple's sister thought he had raped and killed a girl. She was only half right. He had attempted to forge a relationship with Adele, when they were both at university together. But it had gone wrong, like so many of his attempts at a relationship."

Cook opened his manilla file. "This is a complete record of Temple's time at Lancaster University and the admission records for the year 1995, the year he started there."

"I asked Inspector Cook to obtain them this afternoon," Rathe explained.

Cook handed over one of the sheets. There were two damning lines of fluorescent green across the page. "I've highlighted two names."

"Richard Temple and Adele Lanyon," confirmed Rathe. "They were there at the same time, on the same course. Their paths crossed but Temple's character and his sexual immaturity came between them. Setting in motion all this grief and violence."

Lanyon took the page from Cook, but his face showed that he was barely registering the names he read. "She never said who it was. In all the months after it happened, she never told me his name. I don't think she could ever bring herself to say it."

"When Temple saw your daughter's photograph at your party that night, he recognised her at once," Rathe explained. "I doubt he would have said anything if it had not been for his new faith. That conversion caused a second tragedy, because it paved the way for his murder. He felt he had to confess his sin to you in order to achieve grace."

"But all he did was get himself killed," said Cook. "By you."

Lanyon was shaking his head. "This sister of his thought Temple had raped and murdered my daughter, but you say she was only half right about that. Let me tell you, you're wrong about that, Rathe. He killed Adele."

"She killed herself," Cook said.

"But only after what Temple had done to her," Rathe said.

The memory of Kathy Marsden's words came back to him, the recollection of Kevin Marsden dying because of what Rathe had done to him.

Lanyon seemed not to have heard them. "I found her, lying in the bath, the water tepid, but the steam on the windows showing how hot it had been at first. It is the blood I see most vividly. Staining the water, the tiles, her arms. Ever seen the effects of a razor against someone's wrists? All that blood she lost, all that blood I cleaned up alone… it was all on his hands."

"And it all came back to you, those images of Adele, when Temple tried to confess what he had done."

The anger was resurgent. "I don't care about his God, his beliefs, his hope to cleanse his own conscience. I don't care about it now and I didn't then. Not even when he turned to me with tears in his eyes. All I could see what his face over my daughter's, his sweat merging with her tears, his lust tearing apart her innocence."

"You took no weapon with you," murmured Rathe. "You didn't plan to kill him, because you didn't know what he had to say. You had no reason to connect him with what had happened to your daughter."

Lanyon's mind was not in the present but in the past, his eyes peering back through time to the moment of his own sin. "I don't remember hitting him. One moment he was turning his back to face the altar as he spoke, to face his God; the next, he was lying at my feet, motionless. I felt exhausted all of a sudden. I stared at him for some seconds, I don't know how long, and then I came to my senses. I panicked, I suppose, and wiped my fingerprints off the candlestick, desperate to be away from the place."

There was quiet, a harsh and unpleasant denial of words. None of them could have said how long it had lasted, none of them sure what the others were thinking. In the end, with an impassive glance to Rathe, it was Cook who spoke.

"Not much more to say, is there?"

The prolonged silence which followed spoke for itself.

* * *

"Do you feel any better?"

Rathe smiled, despite himself, unsure how best to reply. The sound of the tea being poured into his cup seemed to him to be as loud as a waterfall in some distant place of beauty. But he was in her small house, cheaply and vulgarly furnished, the distinct smell of an absent dog most prevalent in his senses. The tea was too weak, almost entirely milk and water, with only the vague suggestion of a brew of leaves. She had offered him cake, but he had refused. He was no lover of sponge and cream but, in any event, the slab of confection which she had put before him seemed too dry to be edible. He had refused with a smile which he had hoped was both gracious and apologetic.

"Not really," he said now. "Do you think I should?"

Kathy Marsden gulped her tea, rather than sipping it. "Yes. You identified a killer whom the police might not have spotted. Doesn't that matter?"

He looked down at the insipid brew. "Of course. I can see it does."

"So why don't you feel better?"

Rathe had no swift answer to that. He put the cup down on the tray and leaned back in the chair she had offered him, trying not to betray the discomfort he felt in it. "I kept thinking about something you'd said. About me not being responsible for Kevin's death. Lanyon said the opposite about Temple. He believed – no, knew – that Temple had murdered his daughter. By extension at least."

Kathy leaned forward towards him. "So?"

He forced himself to face her. "Why isn't that the same as me and Kevin?"

Her expression gave him a succession of responses: empathy, anger, frustration, regret, perhaps some emotions he had never experienced and could never identify. Rathe had never been a parent and he doubted that mix of gift and curse would be given to him now. Were there some sensations only those privy to the phenomenon of parenthood could feel?

"Because it isn't," was the only reply she could give him. He waited for her to offer him more words of reassurance, but she did not oblige.

"I should go," he said instead.

She walked him to the door and he stepped out onto her small driveway, suddenly becoming conscious that he might not belong here amongst the terraced houses and the small, inexpertly preened gardens, although his superciliousness seemed out of place in that specific moment.

"Bury your dead," Kathy Marsden said. Rathe looked back at her, uncertain how to respond. "You must bury your dead," she repeated.

"I thought I could," he replied at last. "By proving Nicholas Barclay innocent."

"You've done that. An eye for an eye, Mr Rathe. Kevin for this Mr Barclay. Isn't that enough for you?"

He waited there, too long perhaps, his own body pleading with him to move away but, stubbornly, refusing to comply with itself. What had he hoped to achieve by confronting Lanyon with his guilt? Justice? Rathe doubted such a concept existed. Redemption? If so, he felt none of it.

Bury your dead…

The words remained with him as he walked away from her house. He had no destination in mind and he gave no thought to any specific location. Simply, he allowed himself to move forward amongst the streets which stretched out before him, his head upon his breast and his thoughts alone with themselves. At last, he stopped outside St Augustine's, staring first at its steeple and then at its entrance. Memories both real and imagined flooded his brain but he dismissed them. He left the spire of that place far behind him as he continued to walk.

He thought about another church, a few miles down the road, but he shook his head. He would not visit Kevin Marsden's grave, not right now.

Whether he would ever again, he was not sure. Had his enquiry into the Temple murder made amends? He could not say. He did not feel it had, not especially, but he knew that he had secured justice, whatever the cost and however fragile. These thoughts and others began to collide within his head, with one idea in particular growing in intensity. That the Marsden woman had been right, that he had to find his redemption somehow, lay his ghosts to rest.

Whatever else he did and however he could manage it, Anthony Rathe knew now that it was time to bury his dead.

A Question of Proof

A Question of Proof

The verdict was greeted with different passions. The press roared in satisfaction whilst the public gallery cheered with a now-satisfied lust for justice. There were sobs of released tension from the grieving parents and hisses of dissent from the guilty man's supporters. Barristers, in turn, shook hands in congratulation and bowed heads in defeat; even the judge, as experienced in impartial stoicism as he was, seemed to allow himself a brief smile as he prepared to pass sentence. As he did so, the room fell silent once more. Afterwards, there was the excited bustle of movement accompanied again by the jeers and cheers of the assembled crowd, the sounds clashing with each other into a frenzied hum of voices. Amid it all, only two men remained in motionless silence, their eyes fixed on each other, their jaws clenched shut, prohibiting any reaction from either one of them.

Cook had expected the verdict. It would have been foolish of him to consider anything else. The evidence had been collected, tested, and examined again. The lawyers had scrutinised it, deliberated over it, and agreed to present it. Throughout all the processes of bringing the case to Court, to this moment, Cook had sat tight-lipped, his thoughts never given voice and his emotions kept locked within him. And even now, as he stared back at Harry Mackenzie and heard sentence be passed on him, Cook refused to show any sign of triumph. Instead, he remained seated, as people passed by him, eager to leave behind this arena of law and to go about their own personal businesses. Cook could imagine the plaudits at the station when he went back with the news. He could almost hear the inevitable praise, taste the first pint of success, and feel the arms around his shoulders. Harry Mack was off the streets for a minimum of 22 years, all down to

Cook and his team, and to those months of late nights and frustrated mornings. As though he, Cook, had saved all of London from its own worst nightmare.

Mack had stared at Cook during the verdict, its response, and his sentencing. Like the detective, the criminal had remained still, his eyes glaring into Cook's own despising stare. Cook had wondered, fancifully, if Mack had been able to read his thoughts, to know what was happening inside Cook's own head, and whether the man who had killed so many people without compunction or punishment might accept this particular penalty as recompense for all those other crimes which had gone unchallenged. Cook doubted it, in his heart of hearts, and Mack's eyes of defiance showed that the inspector's instinct was right. Cook felt as though he was looking at Mack for the first time, although his features were too well known to him. But it seemed to Cook that for the first time he was seeing properly those dark orbs in the hooded lids and the collar length black hair, too obviously dyed and swept back from the bulbous forehead, and that only now was he seeing just how cruelly twisted those thin lips were and how livid the scar which sliced through the left side of them truly was. It was foolish to believe Cook had not seen that face in his dreams and in his reality more times than he had wished to, but the idea was vivid in his mind all the same.

As Mack was led away from the dock, he shook his head slowly, tearing his gaze away from Cook only when it was impossible to retain it any longer. Mechanically, without registering the movement, Cook rose in deference to the exiting judge but he sat down once more, equally automatically, as soon as he was able to do so. For some time, he was alone in the Courtroom, seeing nothing but Mack's shaking head and fierce eyes. When the usher requested that he leave, he obliged, but his thoughts were still his own, still hidden from all but his internal self. Those ideas had not changed in all these months, not since he was first called to the scene of Lenny Voss's murder. From that moment to this, Cook's opinion about Harry Mack had not altered. If anything, after the verdict that morning, it had grown in intensity and now, Cook felt certain his instinct was right.

* * *

"I don't think he did it. I think he's innocent."

It seemed strange to hear his darkest fears said out loud, as though they were the thoughts of somebody he had never met, ideas which he could never have had himself. He drained his glass, the amber lager soothing his throat and twisting his vision. He had had more than he intended to have, he knew that, but he seemed to have been talking for hours and the drinks helped to ease him through his story.

By contrast, Anthony Rathe had said very little in the forty minutes they had been sitting in the bar. He had been surprised to get the call, if expressing it that way was not an understatement, and he wondered whether it was still that shock or his growing interest in what Cook was saying which was preventing him from speaking himself. It had been almost three weeks since they had seen each other over the St Augustine murder but, as ever, Cook looked exhausted, although his eyes were heavier now and Rathe knew it was nothing to do with the alcohol the inspector had consumed. His shoulders were slumped further under their strain than Rathe had known previously and the bitten fingers were red and sore. His cheeks were sallow, the day's worth of greying stubble standing out against the pale skin beneath it.

"When was the last time you ate something proper?" asked Rathe.

"What do you mean, proper?" barked Cook.

"Not fried or processed."

Cook sneered, although it might have been a grin. "I don't go to many fancy restaurants these days."

"You can boil a vegetable at home."

Cook grunted in irritation. "I didn't ask you here to lecture me about food."

"I know that. But you can't do any good to anybody if you put yourself in hospital with exhaustion or malnutrition."

"You're too dramatic." Cook conceded the point when Rathe gave no reply. "Do they do steak here?"

Rathe handed him a menu. "No fries. Baked potato and the salad."

"When did we get married?" scoffed Cook, but he said no more.

The food was ordered and eaten before Rathe would listen any more to Cook's problems. When he was done, Cook leaned back in his chair. Some colour had returned to his face, and he let out a satisfied sigh, stifling a belch as he finished. He had drunk a pint of water with his meal, which he felt entitled him to order another lager. Rathe ordered a second glass of Merlot.

"Right," he said. "Now, tell me about Harry Mack."

Cook's expression of fulfilment at the meal altered now to one of frustration, as though he had forgotten the reason he had called Rathe there at all. While he had enjoyed the steak, it seemed that Mack had been a bad dream which Cook had erased from his mind but which now, without any remorse, came barging back into his mind.

"I'm not asking you for help," Cook stated. "I want to make that clear, right?"

Rathe shook his head. "I didn't expect you to."

"It's just... " Cook began uneasily, shifting in his seat. "You look at stuff in a different way to me. Something not right with your brain, or whatever, but you look at stuff – upside down. Like with that Lanyon case. And I just want

58

someone to... " But he gave up trying.

"You don't think Mack murdered Lenny Voss, despite the evidence?"

Cook shook his head. "No. Simple as that."

"Even though you got that evidence yourself?"

"Right." Cook nodded. "Even so."

Rathe sipped his wine. "And you think a fresh point of view on the evidence might justify your conclusions. One way or the other."

"Something like that."

They sat in silence, an uneasy comradeship of sorts, neither one wanting to accept that this time they might need the other. Unlike Cook and Mack in the Courtroom, they avoided each other's gaze until, at last, Rathe leaned forward and placed his arms on the table, latticing his fingers. His brows were drawn tightly over his dark eyes and his lips were pursed but he nodded his head like a man who had reached a decision.

"All right," he said. "Tell me everything, from the beginning."

"I'm not asking for help," insisted Cook.

"I'm not offering it," replied Rathe and Cook nodded agreement with a smile.

He took out a paper file and slid it across the table to Rathe. "A summary of the case."

Rathe let the file sit between them. "Give it me in your own words."

"Lenny Voss, from the same pile of filth which gave birth to Harry Mack, murdered three months ago. He had been Mack's right hand man, his closest ally; the two of them were like brothers. They'd grown up together in the same neighbourhood, had each other's backs since they were kids. But recently, things had turned sour. Rumour was that Voss had begun to get sick of playing second fiddle. Felt he was being taken for granted."

"But these were just rumours?"

Cook shrugged. "Not so sure. Enough people have confirmed it and I got the feeling it was a bit more than Voss beating his chest."

"He was planning a revolution, looking to take over?"

"And looking to get Harry Mack out of the way. That was the story. You can imagine how that sort of thing goes down with someone like Harry Mack."

Rathe could well imagine. He didn't need to wade through the urban filth which Cook did in order to know that any sort of betrayal to people like Mack and Voss could only really have one outcome, assuming it wasn't dealt with swiftly and effectively before anybody lost their life. "So Voss's mutiny was your motive?"

"Seemed to be. But there's more."

Cook opened the file which lay between them and took out some photographs. He slid them over to Rathe. Post mortem images of a man lying on his back, close ups of the face mainly, those sallow cheeks and pinched features twisted by violent death. Lenny Voss hadn't been a handsome man in life if the photos were anything to go by, but in death he looked worse than horrific. His left eye showed signs of a beating, corroborating the story told by the livid purple marks on the thin, skeletal torso. Rathe returned his attention to the photographs of the man's face. There was a cruel, jagged gash to the throat, as livid as it was brutal, and on each cheek there were dark cuts, resembling the twin peaks of two mountains.

"Those marks on the cheeks, like inverted Vs," said Cook, pointing at each one. "Mack's trademark, his signature. As though he was carving his initial into his victim's face."

Rathe frowned. "A bit fanciful, almost theatrical."

"No one said Harry Mack was subtle."

"These marks were something else to point to Mack."

"We couldn't ignore them," was all Cook had for a reply.

Rathe returned the image to the file, not wanting to have them in sight for longer than necessary. "What about an alibi?"

"Over the past few months, Mack has been trying to get in with some big noise in Newcastle. Bloke called Frank Lovett, a proper case of the big guns. Drugs, extortion, prostitution, human trafficking, arms deals. All come as easy to Lovett as picking his own nose. But he's worse than that. For Lovett, it isn't just about home ground. He's international. Real serious stuff that makes some of our boys look like Girl Guides. From what I hear, it isn't just about money for him either, not even just about power and control. He enjoys it. It's fun for him, like playing football in the park."

"That was never fun," said Rathe. "How far had Mack got with this Lovett monster?"

"Not far enough. Lovett had shown no interest. Almost every meeting Mack arranged was snubbed, fucked off."

"Almost all?"

Cook nodded. "Lovett agreed to one meet, a week or so before Voss was murdered. Mack and Voss went. This was big news, a major breakthrough for Mack."

"I'm guessing it ended badly," muttered Rathe.

"Worse than badly. Voss put his foot in it, got riled because Lovett was looking down on them."

"Lovett, showing them who needed whom the most?"

"Something like that." Cook signalled for more drinks. "Lovett called time. A lot of talk about disrespect and flies on shit."

"Presumably you thought that might have been a secondary motive for Mack to kill Voss. Professional embarrassment, loss of opportunity?"

"It crossed my mind."

"But how does this Lovett business fit in with Mack's alibi on the night of the Voss murder?"

The drinks arrived. For the first time, Cook didn't begin drinking straight away. He seemed oblivious to the presence of the glass in front of him, his attention fixed exclusively on Rathe. "Mack claims that on the night Voss was killed, he got a phone call from one of Lovett's associates. An invitation, telling Mack to go to a certain place at a certain time."

"Where?"

"An industrial estate. That doesn't matter too much, but the fact it was in Newcastle does. Mack drove up there, thinking he was about to meet Lovett, all his hopes for a twisted partnership of dirt reignited."

"But Lovett never showed."

"Claims never to have ordered the meeting at all."

Rathe leaned back in his chair. "You traced the call?"

Cook lowered his gaze. "Mobile, pay as you go. Nothing came of it. But the call was made in London. Not Newcastle."

"But gangsters travel around, so there was no reason to think Lovett hadn't made it just because it wasn't from Newcastle?" Rathe nodded as Cook conceded the point with a shrug of his shoulders. "If the call was genuine, why didn't you accept Mack's story of the trip to Newcastle?"

"They said just because the call was made didn't mean he followed it up."

"If he thought it was from Lovett, why wouldn't he follow it up?"

Cook sighed. "That's what I asked. And I found Mack's car on the CCTV, bombing it up the M1."

Rathe raised his palms in surrender. "There you go then."

"Problem: there's nothing to prove Mack was driving it. He was well known for loaning out his cars to his lads for business reasons. When he couldn't be bothered doing that business himself, of course."

"They saw it as a fake alibi? One of the boys driving Mack's car, to make it look as though he was out of the way?"

Cook felt no reply was necessary. Rathe was silent for a moment, his mind turning fact upon fact, looking under the stones of the story for any alternative theories which might be scuttling underneath them. The evidence was circumstantial, nothing concrete to say that Mack was guilty of Voss's death, despite the motive, which to Rathe seemed to be the most compelling part of Cook's account. The business with the car sat uneasily with Rathe. He would have argued Occam's razor with that, taken it as a mechanism to say the case was closed on that principle. It was Mack's car, so Mack must have been driving it. But, he realised that it would have been set off against the rest of the evidence, however circumstantial.

Of that evidence, the trademark cuts to the cheeks were easily fabricated, especially if they were a well-known signature of one of Mack's own crimes. Alone, they meant next to nothing. They became more damning when placed next to the motive, however, and that motive was the spectre at the feast as far as the case against Harry Mack went. Professional pride was a special deal for this type of person, the need to save face and demonstrate control over your people, just as important as loyalty. Combined with the rumour of Voss's planned mutiny, Mack could be forgiven for thinking that his old friend had become a liability, a problem which had to be solved. But it wasn't proof that Mack did anything about it. Rathe had a brief mental image of himself in the Courtroom with Mack in the dock. He thought how he might have torn the prosecution's case to rags, almost involuntarily imagining the shake of the criminal's hand as he walked free, cleared of the murder of Lenny Voss. Rathe had the whiff of his old arrogance, that feeling of conceit that he was almost unbeatable. It struck him so strongly that his mind seemed to reel at the memory, a spinning vortex of recollection which inevitably came crashing down amid the ruins of defeat. Now, yet again, his mind was stalking around the remains of his life, after the devastating effects of the Marsden trial, his arrogance and superiority humbled, torn down and scattered like the crumbling remains of a lost wonder of the world.

As if to read his mind, Cook said, "His defence team didn't care. They could have driven a bus through the evidence, but it didn't matter to them. Any more than it mattered to us. Harry Mack has got away with murder, robbery, extortion, and all the rest for years. Nobody wanted him on the streets and nobody wanted him walking out of that Court. We all got what we wished for."

Rathe was shaking his head before Cook had finished talking. "That's not the point, is it? That isn't what justice should be about. Her eyes are blindfolded for a reason and that reason matters."

He raised his head to meet the inspector's gaze, finding the detective nodding at him as he did so. "Exactly, Rathe. Exactly. There's no easy way to say this, but I have to say it anyway. I put Harry Mack in prison, but I don't think he belongs there for the crime I got him for. He belongs there for a shitload of other offences, but not for the murder of Lenny Voss. I need to be sure I got it right. I need to know if my instincts about the conviction are wrong."

"I understand that," murmured Rathe.

"I don't want what happened to you to happen to me," said Cook, all the emotion drained out of his voice.

They said nothing else on the subject. But, as they drank together, their expressions said more than any words could have achieved and it was clear that, between the two of them, a deal had been done.

Shelly Voss must once have been an attractive woman. Her blonde hair might have glowed in an afternoon sun, her blue eyes might have been captivating in flickering candle flame, and her thin lips might have parted in an alluring invitation to a kiss. But now, in the cold grey of that autumnal morning, she looked as though time had been a cruel lover to her. The blonde hair was tied loosely at the nape of her neck, not so much golden sunshine as old straw; the eyes were heavy with the brutality of her life, not flickering with spirit but dimmed with sadness; and the lips were twisted into a sour pout of confrontation. As he introduced himself, she looked at Rathe as though he had come to judge her and she might need a strong defence against him. Privately, she told herself that she liked the look of him and a vision of a life which might have existed skidded into her vision. And out again. She knew it was a life which she could never truly have had, just as she could recognise quality when she saw it. She stayed motionless, watching him as he smiled gently at her. His clothes were expensive without being extravagant and he wore them well. The labels were an adornment of him rather than a fashion statement. She thought about Lenny, the way that he would have worn similar clothes, thinking he was sophisticated, when all he could ever do was make them look cheap and make himself look like a thug in fine threads. She felt a moment of emotion, taking it for sadness but thinking it was closer to regret.

Politely, in a voice which she might once have lay awake at night thinking about, he asked if he could come into the house. She stepped aside and gave him enough room to step into the hallway. She found herself wondering what he would think of the wallpaper, the furnishings, and the particular, individual smell which she knew all homes had. He gave her no clue of what judgement he had made, if any, but instead waited for an invitation to go further into the house. She led him into the kitchen, flicking the switch on the kettle and taking two mugs from a cupboard.

"Or would you prefer something stronger?" she asked.

"Nothing, thank you."

He said it as though she might be offended by it, which she found strangely compelling. The vision of that other, imaginary life drifted into focus once more. She moved a strand of stray hair out of her eyes, a reminder of her subjugated appearance which must mean that he looked at her with nothing but contempt or, worse, pity.

"Do you mind if I have something stronger?" she asked.

"Not at all."

Shelly smiled, but it was nothing more than a flicker of the lips. "Too early, right? You think I'm an alcoholic, a woman who needs a drink at half ten in the morning in order to face the fact that there's another day to get through."

Rathe shook his head. "I don't think anything, other than that you must be grieving. Everyone deals with that differently. For what it's worth, I'm sorry about your husband."

"Did you know Lenny?"

"I knew of him."

She smirked, again without any real trace of humour. She poured some gin into a tumbler, added lime, barely enough tonic to taste. "Lots of people knew of Lenny. I'm not sure I knew him at all. Not any more Didn't share the same bed, let alone each other's lives."

Rathe watched her neck muscles work with the gin. "I wondered whether you could tell me something about him."

She took a moment to savour the effects of the alcohol. A second measure seemed in order and she took care of it. Then, her eyes narrowing, she glared at him. "Who are you?"

"As I said, my name is Anthony Rathe and – "

"No. Who are you?"

"I used to be a barrister," he said, making it sound like a confession. "I represented a lot of men like your husband. Some were innocent, some were guilty. I never cared one way or the other."

She was glaring still, this time over the rim of the glass. "Why not?"

"It wasn't my job to care. It was my job to defend."

"That simple?"

"I used to think it was simple."

"Think what was simple?"

"Justice."

She sniggered, this time with humour, but it was a humour tainted with cynicism. "Was what happened to Harry Mack justice?"

Rathe crossed the room towards her, his face now close to hers. "Only if he was guilty."

Shelly Voss ran her tongue over her top lip, tasting the gin and lime which was left there. She liked him being this close, but simultaneously she hated it. His dark eyes were impassive, unreadable, but they seemed able to hold her heart in their gaze. Lenny had impressed her when she had first met him, but she had never found him impossible to resist. In a matter of a few minutes, this man, this Rathe, seemed capable of possessing her with those eyes and that voice, and she despised him for it. But she knew that she hungered for him, somewhere deep inside herself, in that place where all humans are still animals. Rathe had said she was grieving. Perhaps she was. Grieving: for Lenny, for what her life had once been, for what it was now, for what she had become, and for all the lost opportunities with which marriage to Lenny Voss had burdened her. All those opportunities which this man before her now seemed to embody.

"Are you saying Mack wasn't guilty?" she asked, feeling as though her heart might pulse out of her denim shirt.

Rathe turned away from her and her world seemed to grow smaller. "I don't know. I just want to be sure."

"Who doubts it?"

"A friend."

"Who?" she asked, hardly expecting an answer. She didn't receive one, other than a sly smile and those eyes turning back on her. "Fair enough. Then, why?"

Rathe shook his head. "Nothing tangible. A gut feeling."

"This friend of yours… he's not here himself."

Rathe frowned. Shelly's voice had hardened, as though she was insulted that Cook hadn't come to do his own dirty work, through what Rathe assumed she took to be cowardice or pride. Until that point, he had seen a woman crushed by circumstance, someone who might once have been alluring and intelligent but who had been beaten into submission by a way of life which she had either chosen or had been inflicted on her. He hadn't liked to speculate which it had been. But now, with those words spoken between the mouthfuls of gin, Rathe wondered whether in fact Shelly Voss was a woman who had argued with life from the beginning: a person not without those lost opportunities but, likewise, a person who blamed the world rather than herself for them.

"I just want to know the truth, Mrs Voss," said Rathe.

"For your friend?" It was a sneer.

"For myself." It was a rebuke.

She considered him for a moment, the only sound the gentle tinkle of ice against glass as she swirled her drink. She kept her eyes on him but gave a slight nod of her head. "What do you want to know?"

"What sort of man was your husband?" It seemed to Rathe to be as pertinent a question as any other.

A sadness crept into Shelly's eyes, replacing the hard scorn, albeit only briefly. "When I first met him, he wasn't like anyone else I'd ever met. He wasn't attractive, not looks-wise. He was always thin, a real bag of bones, and he wasn't full of brains either. But he was funny, with a knack for a quick one-liner. He was quiet in those days, used to let Mack do all the talking. But when Lenny did say something, you knew it was going to be hilarious, well worth the wait. I used to see him looking at me as he got himself ready to say something, making sure I was paying attention, trying to let me know he was hoping it was impressing me. Which it was. But, as time went on, he stopped trying. He'd got me by then, hadn't he? No need to keep fighting to impress."

Rathe let her remember better days for a short while. "You never cared about where the money came from?"

"Never cared what he was, you mean? Sometimes, you don't want to accept what's under your nose, do you? You're too busy enjoying the gifts, the jewels, the meals in restaurants you never dreamed of going to, the cars, the holidays. You don't think about where the money's come from, not at first. It's only when you get fobbed off with a couple of grand and don't see your husband for three days that you start to wonder. And regret."

Her talk embarrassed him. He thought about the number of times Cook must have stood in similar circumstances, having similar conversations, and somehow he knew that Cook would remain detached from the situation. It was his profession, his duty, his protection to remain disconnected and not worry about being in a stranger's house, listening to their most private thoughts. But it made Rathe feel like an intruder. He had no right to be there, listening to this woman bare her soul, delving into the pain of her past. He began to question what it was he was trying to achieve, whether this was another attempt to expunge his own regrets, atone for his own indiscretions. Shelly's voice pulled him back into the present.

"The truth is," she said, "that I never considered what he

did for a living, not at first. I had no feelings towards it because I never contemplated it. But once I began to question it, when I had opened my eyes and seen the devastation which he and Mack had caused so that we could have yet another new car or one more trip to the Maldives, I began to hate every penny which came through the door."

"Did you never think of walking away?"

She scoffed. "To what? To the family who cut me off because I married a man they despised? To the old, simple, but honest life I thought I'd always hated? I was just as trapped then, Mr Rathe, as a kid in suburbia, with life mapped out. It was still a prison, only more respectable than the one I swapped it for."

"We're all in our own private prisons," said Rathe. "The point is to try to escape from them."

She was unimpressed by his sententious attitude. "What's your prison like, Mr Rathe?"

He knew he had been unnecessarily pious, so the smile he gave her by way of an apology seemed inevitable. "Just as difficult to escape from as yours, Mrs Voss."

"That's your answer, then," she said, returning the smile. "Whatever he was, whatever I thought about him, I loved him. That can be the only set of chains you need, right? But I hated Lenny's work. And I hated Harry Mack for not letting Lenny leave it all behind."

"Would he have left it behind? I understood he was looking to take over Mack's business."

Before she replied, she walked out of the kitchen into the room next door. Rathe did not follow; he had not been invited to do so. She returned within a matter of moments with a framed photograph in her hands. He took it from her, looking down at the frozen moment of time which showed a fresh faced boy approaching his teenage years. Smiling, eyes screwed tight with excitement, a plastic gun clutched in his hands. Behind him, a younger, happier version of Shelly Voss. She shared the smile with the boy. He had inherited it from her, Rathe could see that clearly.

"Your son?" he said, handing the frame back to her.

"Danny. He's fifteen now. This photo was taken when he was eleven. When Danny was born, Lenny said he was going to give everything up. Get a clean job, no more dirty money."

"Just like that?"

"I told you Lenny wasn't bright. He knew every bad thing in the world, caused a lot of it in his own way. But he could be childishly naïve about some things. He was so proud of Danny. I watched him look with amazement at this tiny baby, as though he understood for the first time what life really meant. But Lenny had fads, impulses, opinions which mattered in that moment but which faded over time."

"The wonder of being a parent lost its hold?"

She nodded. "And I blame Harry Mack for that. He drew Lenny back onto the streets, back to the guns and the sleaze, by making him believe that it was about family. Mack convinced Lenny that they were like brothers, so they belonged together. After all those years, they were still closer than any real brothers could be. Such bullshit. But Lenny believed it and Mack knew that Lenny was bound to believe it, just because of who he was. And then, Mack began to manipulate Lenny."

"How?"

She was looking down at the photograph of her son. "By saying that Lenny could never give Danny the life he deserved working behind a bar or waiting on tables. By telling him that he could only give Danny a chance of a better life by accepting that his own life would only ever be by Mack's side."

"Lenny believed that?"

A single tear rolled down her cheek. "Completely."

"And, over the years," Rathe surmised, "Lenny began to think that if he took over the business from Mack, he could have more control and so… "

"And so have more of the money. For Danny."

Rathe nodded. The twisted, perverted logic of Lenny Voss's mind was easy to dismiss as naivety, as Shelly herself had done, but Rathe suspected it was more profound than that. To a man like Voss, it would have been a simple equation: he knew only a life of crime but he wanted his son to have better chances than his father had been given; so, he would forfeit his own life to ensure that happened. Rathe thought he could understand how that would make sense to a man trapped in that particular prison, especially with someone as persuasive as Harry Mack holding the keys to the cell.

Shelly was still talking. "Lenny couldn't see that the choices he was making were corrupting Danny instead of saving him."

Rathe frowned. "Danny is in trouble with the police?"

"Minor things. Shoplifting, criminal damage, weed, a few fights on street corners. But, little acorns, right? I never wanted Danny to be like his father. I hate watching him go like his dad. I hate my dead husband and his friends for influencing my son. I hate all of it."

The tears were coming now and Rathe felt that all he could do was to allow them to fall.

"I never wanted Danny to grow up thinking it was all right to cheat, steal, or worse," Shelly sobbed. "I just wanted good for him. Always. But Lenny Voss was his father. And I was his mother. What chance could he ever have had?" She looked down at the photograph in her hands. "This is the last time I remember him being truly happy."

Rathe moved closer to her, placing a hand on her forearm. Almost unwittingly, he allowed her to fall against him and then, almost without knowing it, his arms were around her. "I'm sorry, truly I am."

She looked up at him, her streaming eyes fierce with frustration and remorse. "It's not you who should apologise though, is it, Mr Rathe? It's Lenny. It's Harry Mack, all the others like him. Christ, maybe it's even me... "

* * *

Rathe wondered whether he had been right to insist on going there alone. Sitting in the small, windowless room, he began to feel a vulnerability which he had never experienced before. He had been in prisons in his professional capacity, but he had never felt this sense of helplessness which seemed to stir within him now. Perhaps it had been the armour of his robes and wig, or the protective shield of the legal arguments which had occupied his mind on those earlier occasions when he had set foot in such places. Perhaps now that those defences were gone, his mind had nothing to guard itself with and the fear and the horror of the compact and isolated space could work its effect upon him. He felt the urge to stand, but he resisted it, not certain whether it would help or not. Instead, he forced his brain to focus upon his purpose here and the questions which he was compelled to ask.

The meeting had been easy to arrange. Cook had ensured that Rathe would be given a private room for his interview, that the confrontation would be outside the normal hours for visiting. It had required several phone calls, but Cook had managed to arrange things as required. Rathe had promised to update Cook as soon as he left the prison, the promise being made after a series of insistent demands from the detective. Rathe wasn't sure whether it was a result of Cook's need to know what had been said or from his hope that he would not have Rathe's harm or destruction on his conscience. Whatever it was, Cook would not confess to either, Rathe knew that, but he had given his assurances that he would call and arrange a meeting with the inspector as soon as the thing was done.

It was not until the door opened that Rathe realised he had not known what to expect. How his presence there would be received was not something to which Rathe had given any consideration. With hindsight, perhaps it was better that he had not, for it meant that he had not had time to construct scenarios in his own mind. It had left him free from any perceived preconceptions he might otherwise have formed in his head, so that when the man stepped into the room, Rathe simply rose from his chair and met the man's glare with his own. They remained staring at each other for some time before slowly sinking to their chairs.

What impressed Rathe most about Harry Mack were his eyes, small pearls of blackness so deep that there was almost no white around them. They were looking at Rathe but there was nothing in them which he might have been able to call feeling. Rathe had the impression of a shark, to such an extent that he could imagine Mack's eyes rolling back into his head whenever he went in for the kill. His hair, collar length and luxuriant with grease, was a similar colour, so black it seemed to carry a blue tint, like the tail feathers of a raven. His expression was lifeless; his face had the features of a human being but nothing in them suggested anything approaching morality or emotion. Rathe might have expected cruelty or violence to be etched on Mack's face, but he could not discern even those and, somehow, the complete impassivity of the eyes and mouth was more horrible than either of them.

"Anthony Rathe," hissed Mack, his voice little more than whisper. "Rathe... Jimmy Morgan. You got him off when they tried to do him for Pete Beckett's murder."

Rathe nodded, remembering the case well enough. "I'm afraid I did."

"He reckoned you were a magician."

"He was wrong." Rathe lowered his head. "And Morgan was guilty. I knew it, he knew it."

Mack watched him, his eyes still seemingly disinterested. "Didn't stop you getting him off."

"That doesn't mean I have to be proud of it."

A slight shrug of the shoulders showed that Mack conceded the point. "I hear you jacked it all in. The court stuff. After the Marsden kid topped himself."

Rathe bristled. "I'm not here to talk about that."

Mack pounced, leaning forward across the table with a feral urgency. "Then why are you here?"

"Doing a favour," Rathe said. "For a friend."

"Who?"

"Doesn't matter," replied Rathe, shaking his head. "Nobody doubts you belong in here, Mack, but somebody thinks you shouldn't be in here because of Lenny Voss."

Now there was emotion, but it was a scornful, guttural laugh. "Tell that to Cook, the bastard." Rathe did not reply, but he gave no indication that Cook was the reason for the two of them talking together now. To do so would have been a mistake, and Rathe was aware of it, only too keenly. Mack continued to stare across at him. "Why send you? What's your part in all this, Mr Rathe?"

"I'm just helping a friend."

"Sounds to me like you can't walk away from it; from murder, from crime, from violence. No matter how hard you try, no matter how much you think you want to."

"I don't think you're in any position to analyse me, Mack. Even if you were, I don't think it would be your business to do so."

"I could make it my business."

Rathe could feel his heart banging in protest against his show of courage. The blood screamed in his ears at his refusal to feel intimidated. And yet, something in his brain convinced him that there was nothing Mack could do to frighten him. The man was barely human, a mixture of brutality and malice rather than flesh and blood, and it seemed to Rathe that to be afraid of something barely recognisable as anything normal was in itself ridiculous. It would somehow seem like a betrayal of himself. "I'm sure you could, Mack, but it wouldn't serve any useful purpose."

That thin, humourless smile once more. "Say your piece, Rathe. I'll try to stay awake."

"The police say your motive for killing Voss was this supposed mutiny of his."

Mack snorted. "Cook's a lazy bastard. He heard that rumour and couldn't see past it."

"Was it just a rumour?"

"Lenny had got too big for his trousers, know what I mean? Yeah, he made noises which I didn't like, but I dealt with it."

"That's exactly what the police say."

Mack began to trace shapes on the table. "No, I dealt with it. Put him back in line. But I didn't kill him for it. Know why? I didn't have to."

"Why not?"

"Because I sorted it. Taught old Lenny some of the old discipline."

Rathe's mind conjured up a memory of the mortuary photographs Cook had shown him. Those bruises on Voss's chest and stomach, the injury to the left eye-socket. "You did him over."

"Standard punishment."

"For insubordination?"

"Disrespect," corrected Mack. "Lenny was like a kid thinking he was bigger than he was. Kids need a slap to bring them back in line. Get what I'm saying?"

Rathe was barely listening. Instead, he was thinking about those bruises and, more particularly, about their implications. They had been recent abrasions, which meant that the attack had been no more than a few days before Voss's death. If Mack had beaten Voss back into submission, it would have been too soon for Voss to attempt to break away again; if he still planned a coup, he would have waited for the dust of the first attempt to settle. Rathe's mind went further: the beating was the end of the story as far as Mack was concerned. The disobedient child had been put back in his place, no more needed to be said about it. Either way, that beating seemed to Rathe to obviate any further action on Mack's part in relation to Lenny Voss's little bid for control. That, in turn, removed any backbone to the motive provided for Mack to have murdered Voss. Rathe sat back in his chair, his eyes adopting a distant glaze of deep concentration. He thought about Cook's doubts surrounding the case and, perhaps more acutely than before, he found himself sharing them.

Mack watched the former barrister sitting motionless in the seat opposite him. The silence which had descended was brief but it seemed to the criminal that it lasted an age. He thought Rathe was staring at him, and for an instant, Mack's natural fury began to rise in his gullet, but he realised soon enough that Rathe was seeing nothing beyond what was in his own mind. At last, Rathe looked back towards those cruel, dark eyes and appeared to remember why he was there at all.

"Frank Lovett," murmured Rathe, "what about him?"

Mack's head lowered, as though the name of the Newcastle monster was a source of pain for him. "Lenny screwed that up, no question about it. But don't try to make no motive out of it."

Rathe shook his head. "I'm not trying to."

"What no one can get into their heads, see," snarled Mack,

"is that Lenny might have been a dumb bucket of horse piss but he was still the oldest friend I ever had. He might have needed a slap every now and again but I didn't want his blood in my kitchen, you with me?"

"You did more than slap him."

Mack stabbed a yellowed, grubby finger in the air. "You're not like me, Rathe. You're not like any of us. It's a game to you, that's what crime is, but for people like us it's a way of life. Survival. For them like me, it's kill or be killed. For them like you, life's a game of bridge. Civilised, cosy, safe, something you measure in champagne glasses and fillet steaks. To me, it's a fight to the end, marked out with broken bottles and shattered bones. You're sophisticated, protected by the world because it respects you for being who you are, part of the pedigree. Me? Pedigree to me is a mad dog barking in the dark. I have to earn respect and it doesn't always come cheap. It's anything from a warning kick in the ribs to a bullet in the face to keep things under control. You've no idea about any of it, because the law and rules of life mean nothing to you beyond being a game you play. So, forgive me, Rathe, if I tell you that what you understand about lives like mine isn't worth a rat's fart. You say I gave Lenny Voss more than a slap, because you measure things to a different scale to me. You do it because you can. Because life fondled you with kid gloves. Well, life kicked me in the balls with steel-capped Doc Martens. You cuddled life but I had to fight it back. Lenny too, both of us had to. So, don't you dare think you understand what I did to him. I say I gave him a slap, because that's what I did. You might think it was more because it looks like more, but to me and to Lenny, it was a telling off and we both knew he deserved it. So he got it and we moved on. If I wanted him dead because of what he did, in my own backyard or with Frank Lovett, he'd be dead and I wouldn't have bothered with any form of kicking in the first place. He'd just be dead. Gone. Done. But you don't understand that, because we don't see the world in the same way."

"I'm grateful for that," murmured Rathe, unimpressed with the speech. "But, like I said, I'm not looking at what happened with Lovett as a motive for you to murder Voss. I'm asking because I want to know about that phone call on the night of the murder."

Mack's knuckles had whitened during his tirade but now he relaxed his hands, unfolding his fingers, and he leaned back in the chair as though the air had been expelled from his body. He gave a regenerative sigh and cleared his throat quietly, almost imperceptibly, before speaking again.

"You know about the meeting with Lovett, when me and Lenny went to see him. I don't need to go over that again, right? Right. I thought Lenny had ruined any chance I might have had of doing business up North. Lovett is a major player, partnership with him would have seen me and the boys right, but after Lenny's show, it wasn't going nowhere. So, I gave up hoping. But, out of nowhere, I got a call."

"From Lovett himself?"

Mack mocked the idea. "People like Frank Lovett don't do their own dialling, Rathe."

"So why did you think the call was genuine?"

"Because this kid, whoever he was, knew all about the previous meeting. Proper details, the sort of stuff only me and Lenny and Lovett himself would have known."

"Was anyone else at the meeting with Lovett?"

"Couple of his boys. No one else."

"So one of them must have made the call?"

But Mack was shaking his head. "No, they were big fellas. The sort who'd block the screen if they stood up to go for a piss in the cinema, get me? No, whoever phoned me was a kid. Soft voice, bit like a girl's. But nervy, like he wasn't used to setting stuff up. New to it all."

"So how could he have known what happened at the meeting, if he wasn't there?" Rathe's eyes had narrowed.

Mack shrugged. "The way Lenny carried on, I bet Lovett hasn't got tired of telling the story even now. Probably told all his lads what a pair of pearly clowns dared to try and play with the big boys."

Rathe was thinking once more, his eyes glazing over again, and his lips pursed. Something had been said which he knew was important, but it was eluding him. The more he tried to focus on it, the further away from him it drifted, like the litter on the breeze or a dream in the waking hours of dawn. "So, you believed the call and you drove straight up there, to Newcastle?"

"Too good an opportunity to miss."

"Even though the call had been made in London?"

"I didn't know that, did I?" hissed Mack.

Rathe paused. "And you thought it wise to go alone?"

Mack sniffed with derision. "Wasn't risking taking Lenny, was I?"

"Who knew you were going? Who knew about the call?"

A swipe of the criminal's hand emphasised the reply. "Not a soul. Didn't tell nobody."

Rathe cocked his head. "No one expected you to be anywhere else?"

"Had to cancel a date with a bird, but nothing else. Didn't tell her why."

"Didn't she ask?"

Mack's grin turned into a leer. "What they don't know don't hurt them, Rathe. Treat them like they deserve, get me?"

Rathe felt the bitter aftertaste of disgust at the back of his throat. "Who is this lady you left stranded, Mack? Anyone in particular?"

The yellow fingers drummed against the table. "Gentlemen never tell, yeah? It's called loyalty. And she's nothing to do with any of this, because she didn't know nothing about Lovett. She's nobody, just someone to help me unwind, know what I'm saying?"

"One of many, Mack?"

"Variety is the spice."

Suddenly, Rathe had every desire to be somewhere else. Somewhere whose air wasn't tainted by deceit, decay, and death. Somewhere, anywhere, where Harry Mack hadn't walked and had the opportunity to foul. He rose from the table and made for the door.

"I hope you're not the spice of the month in here, Mack," he said, unafraid and unaffected by the possibility of any physical comeback from the criminal.

There was no physical reprisal. Instead, Mack rose from the table and favoured Rathe with a crooked grin of spite. "More into the likes of you, I reckon, Mr Rathe."

"Goodbye, Mack."

"Before you go, Rathe… "

Rathe turned back to face him. He looked into the eyes of the shark once more, wondering about those lives Mack had ruined, the lives he had taken, and the damage he had done to the people who crossed his path. He thought about Shelly Voss and her fears for her son, the circle of violence which already seemed to be whirling around the boy. He thought about the countless other boys for whom pedigree would become that mad dog in the dark and for whom respect would be a kick in the ribs, or a bullet in the face.

"What is it, Mack?"

"Just one more question."

"Ask it quickly."

"Aren't you going to let me know what you say to this mate of yours, the one who sent you here?"

Rathe could hear those mad dogs barking. "No, I'm not."

* * *

"You should have told him it was me who sent you," said Cook.

"I didn't think he should have had that to use against you."

It was early evening, the time when people without murder in their lives begin to think about an evening meal. They were sitting in Rathe's house, expensively but subtly furnished, not ornate enough for Cook to worry about breaking anything but elite enough for him to be unable to consider it a home. Music was playing low in the background, a classical piece which Cook only knew as Mahler because the digital display on the music system told him it was. Cook had accepted a bottle of Italian lager, refusing the offer of a glass, and Rathe sat across from him in a luxuriant armchair with a glass of Burgundy. It had taken Rathe less than ten minutes to bring Cook up to date with the interview with Mack.

"You think I'm right then?" Cook said. "He didn't do it?"

Rathe sipped the wine. "Well, if he did, it wasn't for the reason put forward at the trial. I think both Mack and Voss, and all those associated with them, thought the beating was an end to the mutiny idea of Voss's. At least for the time being."

Cook was nodding. "And it couldn't be the Lovett fiasco. If Mack wanted Voss dead because of that, it would have happened that day, minutes after they were embarrassed out of Lovett's office."

"Yes, I thought that myself," conceded Rathe. "And there was no reason for Mack to think Voss had sent him on the wild goose chase to Newcastle, so he couldn't retaliate against him for that, either. Besides, Mack said the voice on the phone had been a young kid. Nervy, he said, softly spoken. Does that sound like Lenny Voss?"

"Not much," said Cook. "Doesn't sound much like anyone I'd put with Frank Lovett either."

"Perhaps not," said Rathe, but it was almost to himself rather than in any formal reply to the inspector.

Cook drank some of the lager. "If we're leaning towards Mack being innocent of Voss's murder, we have to accept that it was him driving his car on that night. That he hadn't lent it to some lackey for the sake of an alibi. Don't we?"

"I think so."

Cook leaned forward, warming to his theme. "Right, then, so Mack wouldn't have had time to do in Voss. By the time Voss was murdered, Mack was being caught on CCTV in his own motor chasing wild geese up the M1."

Rathe drank some wine with a smile. "It's good to know we're thinking along similar lines for once."

"I was never happy about that bloody car thing." Cook's words were spoken quietly, but no more forcefully because of it. "Goes to show I should always trust my instinct."

Rathe's gaze lowered. "It was a farce. The whole trial was a circus. When all this started, we talked about justice being blind. Perhaps she should always be blind, but she should never be stupid. You were right, Cook. People wanted Mack off the streets at any cost. It was never a question of proof. It was simply a question of convenience."

"It wasn't only justice which failed. It was me." Cook's eyes were staring ahead of him, blended with rage and regret. He stood up and paced towards the fireplace, as though he felt the confession would come more easily to him if he was moving. "I've been doing this for twenty years, give or take. I've never once knowingly done it wrong. Always tried to do the right thing, to get the result which meant the system could do its job. Never put away someone I didn't know was guilty; never once pursued someone I didn't think

83

was guilty. Not till now. The Lanyon case was different. I believed Nicholas Barclay killed Richard Temple. But when you showed me I was wrong, I accepted it, didn't I? And we got it right in the end. But this time, I was wrong. I knew there were holes in that case, I knew the defence team weren't pulling their weight, and I even knew the Judge didn't give much of a shit as long as Mack was put away. I knew all that and I just went with it. That makes me as bad as them."

Rathe stood up and moved next to Cook. They stood staring out of the French windows, across the expanse of lawn which stretched out into the fading sunlight. "It's not your fault."

"Isn't it, Rathe?"

"You weren't in charge of the enquiry, Cook. You didn't bring the prosecution's case, and you're not Mack's defence team, let alone the jury. It went wrong, yes, but not because of you and you alone."

Cook looked across at his companion. "And was Kevin Marsden because of you and you alone?"

The name, once more, struck Rathe's heart like a knife and he felt the glands in his throat tighten with the nausea of guilt. "Yes, I think so."

Cook drained his bottle. "Then you know how I feel, don't you?"

Rathe turned slowly to face the inspector. "Point taken."

"I told you I didn't want to turn into you because of Harry Mack."

Rathe's eyes glinted. "Then you have to do something about it. You have to find out what really happened and put it right. Through the correct processes. That's what you have to do."

"Can we do that?"

"Of course you can."

"No, Rathe, can we do that?"

And Rathe now recognised it for the plea it was, for the request for help that it had been, the unexpected display of vulnerability from Cook took him by surprise. He found himself nodding his agreement, not daring to speak in case his chosen words were misguided and he belittled the humility of the moment. Cook acknowledged the agreement with his own bow of the head and they turned back to look out over the lawns, allowing the shift in their relationship, however brief or understated it had been, to settle.

* * *

The girl eyed them both with suspicion, but it was for Cook that she reserved the majority of her dislike. She was young, barely in her twenties in Rathe's estimation, but the heavy make-up made it difficult to be sure. Her hair was bleached blonde, a longer and straighter version of Monroe; whilst the peroxide matched the paleness of the skin, it contrasted starkly with the heightened darkness of the lashes and the livid crimson of the lips. Beneath it all, Rathe thought she might have been naturally pretty; certainly, despite the harshness of her stare, the eyes were a delicate shade of green which he thought he could never remember seeing before, and the lips were naturally full beneath their clown-like adornment. The falsity of her cosmetics was all the more gaudy next to the natural beauty which lay beneath it.

"Tell me why I should say anything to you, Cook," she spat as he placed a Bacardi and Coke in front of her. "After you bloody well framed my Harry for murder. A right victim of yours, my Harry is."

He pointed to the drink. "Because I didn't frame him. And because that cost me a packet, Carla, and you don't often get to go to places like this."

She looked around the cocktail bar. "Nothing special. Harry takes me to places like this all the time. And he owns them all."

Cook raised a glass of whisky to his lips. "That right? Well, like I said, you don't get to go to places like this often. Because this one, see, is legitimate."

"You've always been a bastard, Cook," spat the girl.

"You're not old enough to know that for sure, Carla, so tell your mouth to drown its bullshit with some Bacardi."

It was later that same night. It had been after they had begun to go back over Mack's interview with Rathe that Cook had thought about Carla. It had been Rathe's comment about Mack standing up a girl in order to drive to Newcastle. Cook had known who Mack's current piece of meat was and they had sought her out without any difficulty.

"There's been loads of Carla Malones in the past," Cook had told Rathe, "and there'll be a load more in the future. Mack gets bored easily. Once he's satisfied himself with one girl, he moves on. To him, it's a business transaction rather than an emotional one."

"Don't any of them retaliate?" Rathe had asked.

"A girl retaliate against Harry Mack?" Cook had replied, the tone of his voice pouring scorn on the idea.

"So, what happens to the girls when Mack's had enough?"

"What do you think? If they can still earn money for him, he puts them back where he found them. The streets. Assuming they're lucky enough not to have bored him or upset him so much that he has them put in the ground or underwater instead."

"And if they can't earn any more?" Rathe had asked, hardly needing to hear the answer.

"Depends. If they didn't upset him but they can't work, they'll be plied with drink and drugs and told to enjoy themselves. Within two months, they won't recognise themselves or remember what got them on smack in the first place."

Rathe had remained silent for some time. "This Carla, she was from the streets?"

"Since she was fourteen. And she'll outstay her welcome soon enough, believe me."

Cook had known Carla would be in one of Mack's bars, because she was almost never seen anywhere else. She wouldn't let an inconvenience like Mack's imprisonment get in the way of her enjoying free drinks on the sole basis that she was invited into the criminal's bed every night. Mack wouldn't have minded her being out without him either, Cook knew that. If she was in one of Mack's clubs, he would have loyal eyes on her and any one of the punters would know who she was. There was no danger of her doing anything she shouldn't as long as she stayed in one of Mack's places, so he could rest easy. Which is why it had been difficult for Rathe and Cook to prise her away. In the end, it had been Cook's threat of arrest which had done it. He didn't care: there would be no reprisals if what Carla could tell them would help get Mack out. As he thought it, Cook felt a twist of repulsion in his stomach at the filthy obligation he felt on account of his personal instincts and conscience. The things he felt he had to do just so he could sleep at night.

Carla took a long drink, her eyes bulging at the taste. "Jesus, that's more than a double, isn't it?"

"No," drawled Cook, "but it's not watered down like Harry's probably is. So drink it slowly."

"Fuck off," she spat.

Rathe felt it was time to intervene. "Miss Malone, I think it's probably best if we don't take up too much of each other's time. It's pretty clear that none of us wants this interview to last longer than it has to."

She looked at him initially with the same glare of contempt which she had reserved for Cook, but his voice changed her expression and those green eyes became warmer. "I don't often hear men talk like you. Lovely, it is."

Despite himself, Rathe felt his cheeks glow and the hairs on his neck rose slightly. "There are just a few questions we'd like to ask," he said with an embarrassed grin.

"You could recite the bloody drinks menu and I'd get it on me," she drooled with a short, sharp cackle. "I bet you sound right seductive on the phone."

Cook hissed. "You wouldn't know what to do with him unless he slapped you about a bit first, Carla, so lay off."

The warmth in her eyes froze over once more. "I told you to fuck off, didn't I?"

This time, Rathe slammed the table with the palm of his hand. "You can both do that if you're going to go on like this. We're here with a common goal and that's to get the truth about what happened to Lenny Voss so that we can help Harry Mack. We can't do that if we're going to end up in the playground every time one of you speaks."

For a moment, it occurred to Carla that she might be able to make a joke about the eroticism of Rathe's fury, but she thought against it. His eyes had grown darker and his lips had tightened into a taught whipcord of anger. She looked across at Cook, who was now drinking to hide his own abasement, and she decided that whoever this man, Rathe, was, he ought to be kept on side. She had never seen Terry Cook cut down so quickly and so effectively before.

"All right," she replied. "Say what you've got to say and let me go."

Rathe took his time in formulating his questions. The bass line of the music of the bar drummed in his head and he seemed to be hearing it for the first time, as though his outburst had somehow awakened his senses, as if his explosion of anger had broken apart all the jumbled facts of the case in his head and now they were falling back into their correct places in time to that incessant, banging rhythm. And, in that moment, he thought he saw with the sharpest clarity to date, the truth behind the murder of Lenny Voss.

He became aware of them both staring at him and he realised that he must look like a simple child, unable to form words but making every effort to do so. "You were due to meet Harry on the night of Voss's murder, is that right?"

Carla nodded. "He was meant to be taking me to his new restaurant. Not even opened yet, but Harry wanted me to have the first meal ever cooked there. He's cute like that."

"I wouldn't say cute," Cook felt compelled to say.

Rathe ignored him. "What reason did he say for changing his plans?"

"Business," shrugged Carla, as though there was never any other reason for a change in Harry Mack's plans. "Something came up, something urgent."

"Did he say what?"

"No. Never does."

"So you have no idea what this urgent meeting was about?"

Carla rolled her eyes. "I've said, haven't I?"

"Weren't you angry, though?"

"A bit," she purred, "if I'm honest. I was looking forward to my dinner for one thing."

Rathe leaned forward. "And for another thing… ?"

Carla's eyes drifted from his to her glass, but the battle was short lived and Rathe's intense stare won the war. "Maybe I didn't like what sort of business Harry was talking about."

Cook sneered. "You know what sort of business Mack's into, Carla."

Rathe was smiling, but his eyes were filled with a dark understanding. "She doesn't mean business for money. Do you, Carla? You mean business for pleasure." A pause. "Who was she?"

Carla began to pick at one of her scarlet, false nails. "I don't know."

"But you have suspicions?" pressed Rathe.

"Sort of."

Rathe bent closer. For that instant, nothing in Carla Malone's world existed except for him. "An old flame of his?"

The girl showed her age in a petulant sniff. "Harry and me was walking through town one night, on our way to a club. All of a sudden, he turns me round and we start walking back the way we'd come. I didn't question it. You don't question anything with Harry, not really. You just go with it, get me? But I looked back over my shoulder and there was this sulky old bitch staring after us."

"Did you recognise her?" asked Cook.

"Sort of. I'd seen her sitting outside Harry's house a few times, just staring at it, like she was plucking up the balls to get out of her car and knock on the front door. She never did. Used to just sit there, staring, then drive off."

"But you don't know who this woman is?" pressed Rathe.

"Never seen her before."

Rathe looked over to Cook. The detective glared back, conscious that there was something in the younger man's eyes which suggested some sense of finality to the matter. Rathe's expression was strange, not exactly triumphant but not exclusively malignant either. It was a curious blend of the two, as though he was satisfied with his conclusion but furious that he had not seen it sooner. Cook kept his eyes on Rathe as the latter turned his attention back to Carla Malone.

"You were right, Miss Malone," Rathe said. "Your Harry was a victim. As much a victim of murder as Lenny Voss himself was."

* * *

Almost eleven at night and the only sound was the ticking of the clock which stood on the mantelpiece. Rathe stared at it for a long moment, wondering how it could be that the minutes continued to tick by when, in the room itself, time seemed to have stopped. He had declined the invitation of a seat, preferring to stand by the window as if to remind himself that there was still a world outside which was nothing to do with murder and violence or him. Cook had accepted the offer, however, sitting himself down in one of the leather armchairs placed in the corner of the room. Both men had refused a drink, so she helped herself.

"I don't know what you want me to say," Shelly Voss said as she dropped the ice into the glass.

"I want you to tell me the truth," Rathe said. "Just like I wanted when I first came here."

"Why you? Why not the policeman over there?" Shelly indicated Cook with a tilt of her head.

Rathe moved so that he was closer to her. "Because it's me that wants to hear you say it. Inspector Cook knows it's the truth, just as much as I do. He doesn't care if you say it or not. But I do."

"Why?"

"Because I think I understand." He looked into the blue circles of her eyes. "And I'm old fashioned."

Despite herself, she smiled. "Why didn't I meet you twenty years ago, do you suppose?"

Rathe did not return the smile. "Tell me the truth."

She filled the glass with gin, added so little tonic it was virtually redundant. As redundant as her refusal to speak, was the thought which occurred to Rathe's mind. Shelly looked up at him as she drank. "You think you understand? See if you're right."

He watched her cross the room and sit down, one leg draping itself over the other. He closed his eyes, wishing she was not forcing his hand like this, but knowing too well that every second her mouth remained closed was one more lost chance for her to do some good.

"All right," he conceded at last. "Have it your way. Perhaps I will have a drink after all."

A signal from Cook showed that no drink was required by him, so Rathe filled a tumbler with Scotch and began to pace the room, gathering his thoughts.

"Harry Mack was sentenced for the murder of your husband and nobody gave a damn about it. A world without Harry Mack free in it was a better place for all concerned. That was what everybody thought, except for that man sitting over there. The man who led the investigation into your husband's murder. If it hadn't been for Cook, Mack would have gone down in history as the killer of Lenny Voss and everybody would have been happy." He pointed a finger at Shelly. "Including you. Because you wanted them both out of the way, but for very different reasons. Isn't that right, Shelly?"

She drank some gin. "Keep talking, Mr Rathe."

"The more I listened to Cook, the more I began to think he was right," Rathe continued. "The evidence against Mack was almost unbearably weak, so much so that if he hadn't been who and what he is, the case would never have seen the inside of a Courtroom. The trial was opportunistic, a perverse charade of justice in action, but it was allowed to happen because Mack was an animal. And, in many ways that was the point."

"In what ways?" hissed Shelly.

"All in good time," replied Rathe. "Carla Malone was the crucial witness in this case. It wasn't until she accused Cook of framing Mack that I began to see the truth. She said Harry was the victim of a frame up by the police, by Cook in particular. But she was wrong. Harry was framed, yes, but not by the police. They simply drew the obvious conclusion which they had been led to draw. The marks on Lenny's face and the public argument between the two men were all indicative of Harry's guilt. But if Carla and Cook were both right, and if Mack had been framed, then whoever had done it must have had a reason, both to kill Lenny and frame Mack. And that person must have known Mack and Lenny well enough to be able to mimic Mack's murderous trademarks and know that he would have a possible motive to murder Lenny because of that fall out between them."

"Any number of their boys would have known that," said Shelly.

"True. But they would also know that Mack had taken his revenge on Lenny by beating him half senseless. You wouldn't know that. After all, as you told me, you no longer shared the same bed, let alone the same life. Do you remember saying that?"

"I remember," she spat. She got up to fill her glass.

"You knew enough about Mack and Lenny to mimic the tell-tale cuts and fabricate the motive; but you didn't know quite enough to know that the motive wasn't viable any more. And you didn't know because both men had abandoned you. Lenny had abandoned you for Harry Mack, in some sort of new-found loyalty to his childhood friend. And Mack had abandoned you… for Carla Malone." She remained motionless, but Rathe could tell from the whitened knuckles that his words had stung. "You and Mack had been lovers. He told me himself he had a string of lovers, the spice of variety in his life. I couldn't be sure but it didn't seem too much of a leap to suppose that you might have been one of them, Shelly. You'd be close to him through Lenny, through the same man who was ignoring you emotionally and physically. The same man you were growing to despise."

She shook her head. "I loved Lenny."

Cook had risen too, closing in for the kill. "But he was

taking your Danny away from you, wasn't he? You were watching your son follow Lenny's lead into crime. To drugs, to guns, to whatever else."

Rathe was behind her, his voice softer. "You said to me that Harry manipulated Lenny. Did he manipulate you into believing he loved you, that he would take care of Danny, that you were the one who mattered to him?"

Her tears now fell like autumn rain. "I knew what he was like. I knew what he was. But I just wanted someone to hold me, to tell me I was beautiful." She looked into Rathe's eyes and he felt his heart turn into ashes. "I wanted someone to tell me I was a woman. When your life has gone like mine, you take what little you can get. I don't expect you two to understand what that's like, but believe me it's true. And the little I could get was Harry bloody Mack. From Lenny to Harry, from muck to shit."

Rathe placed a hand on her shoulder, but she didn't fall into his embrace this time. She remained standing, crying. "If you knew about the argument over Frank Lovett, you could engineer the phone call to Mack which would get him out of the way. There was no reason for Harry to think it was you. A little softening of the voice and he'd never make any connection with you. He'd take it for granted, because that's what people are like. He took it as the voice of a young kid. But Lovett doesn't have young kids in his gang."

Cook was staring at Rathe, his attention seized by the younger man's words. "So it really was Mack in his car driving up to Newcastle?"

Rathe nodded, turning to the inspector. "You told me yourself that Mack was in the habit of loaning out cars for certain business trips he couldn't be bothered to make himself. The implication was that when the business was important enough, Mack would deal with it in person. He himself didn't deny making the journey north when I interviewed him."

Cook grunted in agreement. "After that mess of a first meeting, any call from Frank Lovett would be important enough to drag Mack wherever he was told."

"Exactly, in the hope of the possibility of renewed business between them," said Rathe, turning back to Shelly. "Again, the clue came from Carla Malone. She mentioned that she could find a voice… my voice… attractive on the phone. It made me think. The phone naturally distorts a voice to a small degree. If you disguise it as well… "

"It wasn't a young kid," Cook said. "It was a woman. You."

She nodded, the fight extinguished, the glass of her façade shattered. "I knew Harry wouldn't miss the chance. Why would he? He'd wanted to go into business with Lovett for months. And when Lovett denied fixing up the meeting, I was sure people would think Mack was lying about where he was."

"Which they did," confessed Cook.

Rathe was still holding Shelly by the shoulder. "What did you use? A knife from here?"

"I bought one. Standard kitchen knife." Now she did turn to face him. "I killed them both, Mr Rathe. That's what you want me to say, isn't it? That's the truth you want to hear because you think it'll make me seem less guilty in your eyes. As if confessing it will somehow wash away the fact of it."

Rathe shook his head. "No, Shelly. I want you to confess it because it's the right thing to do. Because, although Mack deserves prison, he doesn't deserve it for something he didn't do. That's not how it can be allowed to work. If we let it work like that, we're no better than the people we want to see put away. So, no, that's not why I want you to confess. I want you to confess because it's the only decent thing to do now. Because we have to show people that the right way can work. You have to show that to Danny. Lenny only ever showed your son how to live the wrong way. If you don't confess now, you're doing exactly the same thing. But if you tell Danny the truth and you accept what that truth means for you personally, you can teach your son a better lesson than any amount of murder or retribution can."

She smiled at him. Slowly, she removed his hand from her shoulder, raising her own palm to his cheek. "You're so naïve, Mr Rathe."

He smiled back. "Perhaps. But I can live with that, because I think I'm learning something else all over again."

"Such as?"

His dark eyes closed for the smallest fraction of a second. "Hope."

It was some moments after that before she turned to face Cook. The detective had been staring at his shoes, unsure where else he should look, but now, sensing her eyes on him, he raised his gaze to her.

"Inspector Cook," she said. "I'm ready to confess now."

* * *

As he had expected, Rathe found Kathy Marsden at her son's grave.

The morning was crisp, the air chill but not hostile, and the skies showed no threat of rain. The cemetery was deserted and it struck him once more how peaceful he found it. There was a serenity, a respectful silence about it which he found curiously comforting, as though he might only feel at ease with the dead. These thoughts hung heavily in his head, so that his chin sank to his breast as he approached her. She was on her knees, cleaning away dead leaves from Kevin's headstone, replacing the decaying flowers with fresh sprays of colour. She did not hear him walk up behind her and he startled her as he knelt down beside her and handed over his own small bunch of flora.

"I'm sorry," he said. "I didn't mean to alarm you."

She shook her head. "Too engrossed in what I was doing, Mr Rathe. Nothing for you to apologise for. They're lovely, but you needn't have," she added, taking the flowers from him.

"I know. I wanted to." The silence which he allowed to fall seemed, to him, rather awkward and he broke it as swiftly as he felt able. "I'd hoped to find you here anyway. I wanted to tell you something. I think it's important, and I wanted you to know."

"Oh?" She remained busy with her task, not raising her head to look at him.

"I helped a friend this week. The same policeman I told you about before."

"He's a friend now, is he?" she said. He thought she was mocking him, but he couldn't be sure.

"I don't know." He smiled. "I think so. In a way. But what I wanted to say was that I helped him find the truth about a crime. A crime somebody had committed and blamed an innocent man for. Well, when I say innocent… Of this particular crime, he was innocent. Am I making sense?"

Now, she did raise her head and her wind-rouged cheeks spread as she smiled. "Perfect sense, Mr Rathe. And it's good. What you've done, it is good."

"The man we cleared was evil, though. He was a killer, a drug dealer, a violent monster. But he hadn't done what he was convicted of. My friend argued that justice should be blind and I agreed."

"And?" she said, as she rose to her knees.

"Were we right?"

Kathy Marsden removed her green-fingered gloves and pushed a strand of hair away from her eyes. "Your eyes look brighter, Mr Rathe, than when I last saw you. How are you sleeping?"

He frowned, tilting his head to one side. "Fairly well."

"And how would you have slept if this villain you're talking about had rotted in prison, or died in prison, and you knew he was innocent but did nothing about it?" She waited for an answer but, in reply, he looked at his shoes. "How did you feel about Kevin, for instance?"

"Point taken."

She placed a hand on his breast. "What you feel in there is what determines if you are right. And you must learn to trust it, instead of allowing your head to cripple you with blame and doubt. I say this to you every time we meet."

"Perhaps I need constant re-assurance."

She laughed, louder than he had expected. "In that at least, Mr Rathe, you are not an isolated soul."

She allowed him to walk her back to her car. He helped her pack away the brushes and tools she had used to plant the new flowers and clear away the old. The bag of dead leaves and broken stems he placed in the waste bin provided, whilst she changed her Wellingtons for her comfortable, flat heeled shoes.

"What do you have planned for the rest of the day?" she asked.

He shrugged. "Nothing. A long walk perhaps. Enjoy the air."

"You need a hobby, Mr Rathe. A man should have a hobby if he cannot find a wife."

Rathe shook his head, smiling. "I can't imagine me being successful with either, somehow."

But his thoughts went back to Shelly Voss. He wondered what her life, and his, might have been like if she had met him twenty years ago, as she herself had asked. He wondered why he had wanted her to keep her palm on his cheek, to keep his own hand on her shoulder, to keep her close beside him. In that brief moment, he wondered many things, but he knew that they would only ever be intangible alternatives to his reality, moment of truth in a parallel world but nothing more than daydreams in this one. Goodbyes said, he watched Kathy Marsden drive away. He had not asked her what she was doing that afternoon and, almost as soon as he realised it, he felt rude and selfish.

He turned his head and looked down at Kevin Marsden's grave. His mind wandered through the corridors of his memory's prison, peering in through the open cell doors of recollection and regrets. A vivid image of Shelly Voss came into his mind, but her face was only partially visible through the bars of the jail he imagined her in. Kathy Marsden had said he had done the right thing; perhaps he had. But the associated pain was harder than ever to bear. He took one more look at Kevin Marsden's grave before he turned away and began to walk.

Ties that Bind

Ties that Bind

Rathe had begun to think of excuses to leave the party and go home when the woman began to talk to him. He had seen her throughout the evening, her lowered eyes and clenched fingers around the wine glass seeming to echo Rathe's own discomfort at his presence there, but she had made no previous attempt to attract his attention until she approached him as he stood in the corner of the room, forming half-hearted pretexts to escape.

Rathe recognised that he was being churlish. After all, the invitation from Cook hadn't been offered with any trace of insistence that Rathe accept, which meant he might easily have declined without causing offence, and so the fact that he had accepted surely meant that his present discomfort was, if anything, more of his own making than Cook's. The invitation had been offered in an almost perfunctory phone call the previous evening, in itself an unusual occurrence, and Rathe had known at once from Cook's hesitant voice that the call had been deferred several times during the course of the day.

"It's my wife's idea, this," Cook had said. "To invite you. I said you'd probably have something else on. Some opera you had to go to or something. Some art gallery you wanted to visit."

Rathe had smiled to himself. "When have I ever said I was interested in opera?"

"Took it for granted." Cook's shrug of the shoulders had been perceptible even over the phone. "Can't see you being into proper music."

"And your wife thought to ask me to come?"

"She suggested it. It's her birthday, so I suppose she can invite who she likes, right?"

Rathe had grinned once more. "I won't come if it'll embarrass you."

"No skin off my nose, either way. All I did was promise Andrea I'd ask you, which I've done. You do what you want."

"Where and when?"

Cook had paused. "You mean you're going to come?"

And it had been then that Rathe had forgotten the genial indifference between them during the call, displaced now with a stark question of fact about whether he would attend go or not. It had become now a formal decision to make rather than the simple catalyst for gentle mockery at Cook's expense. Which meant that when faced with it, despite himself, Rathe had felt unable to decline without seeming discourteous.

The evening had not been as tortuous as he had feared. He had been to more uncomfortable gatherings in his time. He recalled the endless Chambers functions he had been forced to attend, listening to sycophantic solicitors fawning over their latest victories whilst the egos of the barristers concerned were oiled with those platitudes of admiration. Similarly, he had watched as the clerks had poured wine and whisky down the throats of prospective new clients or rival barristers prime for poaching and he could remember listening to the banter between them which was no better than that between any used car salesman and his latest gullible customer. Those occasions had never sat easily with Rathe, even when he was on the receiving end of the plaudits. In those days, he had relished the applause of both his peers and those who had instructed him, but the forum of the networking drinks events had never appealed to him.

So, despite his unease, Cook's party was unlike any of those business evenings which Rathe had endured in his time. There were perhaps twenty people in attendance, none of whom Rathe knew, all scattered throughout the Cooks' home and spilling out into the back garden when necessary. It was a cool evening, not too cold to prohibit any time to be spent outside, and Rathe himself had welcomed the cool breath of the fresh air when he had stepped onto the patio earlier in the evening. The house itself was larger than he had imagined and he wondered whether it was an innate snobbery inside himself, of which he should be ashamed perhaps, which had presumed that a policeman of detective inspector rank might only have been able to afford a small, modest house. It was a neat home, tastefully decorated, although Rathe assumed that the furnishings and the style were Mrs Cook's work rather than her husband's. It seemed a house which was proud of its feminine touch and there was no sense of the moral dirt through which Rathe knew Cook walked on a daily basis, as though the tidiness and the gentility of the house were a refuge from, or an antidote to, that cruel and lethal world which Cook's job demanded he inhabit. It was a home which spoke of hard work and self-sacrifice, the dwelling of people who had grown up with very little but who had striven to have better in their adult lives. There were no silver spoons in the Cook household, but there was a fine dinner service which had been bought and paid for by grit and determination to succeed. Rathe had thought back to his own upbringing, to the privileges he had enjoyed and the luxuries which his background had afforded to him, and he had felt at once that something important in his own life had been missing as a result, something which Cook knew and understood but which he, Rathe, might only ever be able to see in others.

He had been introduced to Andrea Cook upon his arrival, having handed over the bottles of Merlot and Pinot Grigio to Cook. He hadn't been sure what food was being served, he had explained, so he had thought it best to take no chances.

Andrea herself was impressed by his thoughtfulness and she had smiled at him with what he took to be genuine gratitude. She was attractive, understated but natural, with dark hair which he suspected she had had styled for the occasion. She had shaken his hand with warmth and showed him into the living room so that he could help himself to a drink.

"Terry's talked about you a fair bit over the last couple of months," she had said, "so I thought tonight would be a good excuse to meet you."

Rathe had been embarrassed by her revelation and, as he looked over to Cook, he had seen his discomfort reflected in the detective's face. "It's very kind of you to invite me, Mrs Cook."

"Andrea, please. And you're… ?"

"Anthony."

"Like Hopkins," she had sighed. "One of my favourites. Such a lovely voice he's got – and so have you. It's so… "

But the words had failed her, so Cook had taken advantage, thrusting the bottles of wine in her hands. "Let the man get a drink, Andrea, and you go sort these out, eh?"

She had bustled off with a coy smile back at Rathe and a cold glare at her husband. Cook had waited until she was out of the room before he had opened a bottle of lager and handed it across to Rathe. "I'm sorry about her. Drank a bit of fizz before everyone turned up. Always sends her stupid."

"It's her birthday," Rathe had replied. "Let her be stupid."

Cook had smiled, drinking some of his own beer. "You can come and deal with her in the morning, then, when she can't get out of bed and wails that she's never drinking again."

It was thoughts like these which had been replaying in Rathe's head when he began to think it was time to go home. He had not seen Cook for some time, the duties of host extending beyond private conversations with Rathe, and he had not made any special effort to cultivate new acquaintances. He was not socially inclined to do so at the best of times and he felt certain that any connections he might make that evening would be transient only. Rathe had no need or desire for such passing friendships. At last, he had decided that he would have one more drink and then be on his way. It was almost as soon as this decision was made and the final bottle opened that he saw the woman approaching him.

She was perhaps Cook's age, certainly no older, but her dark hair was prematurely grey and her blue eyes heavy with unease. Rathe could never have thought her attractive: she was too thin, her features too stern, her lips too compressed, her stare too wild for such a consideration, but he had a distinct impression of vulnerability which he felt it was impossible to ignore. She drained her glass of wine as soon as she was beside him and she began to turn the empty glass in her hand. It took a moment for Rathe to grasp her unspoken invitation.

"Allow me," he said at last, pouring more wine into her glass.

"Thank you." She waited for him to stop pouring and then sipped at the drink. He doubted she wanted it in all truthfulness. "You look about as happy to be here as I am."

Rathe smiled. "I'm not very good at parties."

"I don't think I've ever seen you around. You've not been to one of Andrea's things before, have you?"

He shook his head. "First time."

"I thought so." She looked around the room. "You don't know anybody here at all?"

"Only... Terry." It felt strange to him, using Cook's first name, but he doubted the usual use of the surname alone would be appropriate.

The woman turned to him, her eyes now blazing with a different emotion than anxiety. Rathe frowned involuntarily at the intensity of what he took to be desperation in those blue eyes, as though they were screaming silently for his help. "I hoped you'd say you knew nobody. Sometimes, you see, it makes it easier, confessing something to a stranger. Do you know what I mean? There are no preconceptions, nobody dismissing you as paranoid."

"I'm afraid I don't understand… "

She closed in on him, her long fingers like talons closing around his wrist. "I want you to understand. I want someone to understand."

"I'm not sure I can help you, Miss… ?"

"Elizabeth Newsome."

"Anthony Rathe," he returned, by way of obligatory introduction.

"Ask anyone here about me, Mr Rathe, and they'll tell you I'm mad. They all think I am losing my mind. I know they talk about me behind my back and I can live with that, but only because I know what's really happening. I know the truth."

Rathe had the sudden desire to be anywhere but in the Newsome woman's company. His mind filled with places from his past, both distant and immediate – his former Chambers, the Old Bailey, his parents' front room on Christmas morning, family holidays by Mediterranean shores, Cook's office, the headmaster's office, the Marsden grave, the arms of any one of the beautiful girls there had been – all of them preferable to the presence of this woman. Her fingers around his wrist were as tight as they were unwelcome and, when she spoke, he could smell the stale wine on her oppressive breath.

"That man over there, by the window," she was hissing. "He's my husband. Edward."

Rathe followed her glare and saw a tall, austere man in his late forties, straight-backed and impressive, with luxurious black hair swept back from an intelligent brow and cold, angular features enhanced by a neatly trimmed beard. There was something sneering about his expression, an arrogance which Rathe found both irritating and distasteful. His suit was expensive but the man wore it like a uniform, as though it was a symbol of his importance rather than of his deference to elegance.

Elizabeth Newsome shook Rathe's wrist, turning him away from her husband. "Don't let him see you staring, Mr Rathe, please. I don't want him to realise that I know."

"Know what, Mrs Newsome?"

She glared at him once more, her eyes now a frantic blend of nervousness, malice, and fear. Despite himself, Rathe was unable to turn away from her, those eyes demanding and holding his attention with their hypnotic allure of horror. "I know what he's planning, Mr Rathe. I know what he wants."

Her spell temporarily broken, Rathe looked back over to Edward Newsome, who was nodding in agreement with some point made by his conversational companion. "And what does your husband want, Mrs Newsome?"

She clenched his wrist once more, forcing his eyes to return to hers. She held his gaze for longer than he felt was comfortable before releasing her grip on him. "I'm so sorry. Please, forgive me, Mr Rathe. Ignore me. It's just me being stupid, take no notice."

But he knew she didn't believe a word of it. And, somehow, that knowledge seemed to taint his own views and he found himself doubting that her feeble denials were justified. "Tell me what your husband wants, Mrs Newsome."

"I shouldn't burden a stranger with my troubles. It was wrong of me."

Rathe leaned in closely to her, not so much intimidating as persuasive. "Tell me."

He felt a slight tremble in her thin fingers as they touched his arm once more. Their nervous shuddering seemed to him to complement the hesitancy of her voice when she replied, so softly he had to strain to hear her.

"Murder."

"I'm sorry, what?"

"My husband wants me dead, Mr Rathe." She pleaded with her eyes for his belief. "He wants to murder me… "

* * *

Rathe found Cook in the garden, sitting on a small bench, staring into a fish pond. The water rippled gently in the night breeze, illuminated by the small lights which lined the perimeter of the pond. As he approached, Rathe could see the slivers of silver and gold flitting through the dark pool of the water, their movements nothing less than mesmerising in their fluidity. Overhead, the trees extended towards the moon, generating a further layer of silhouetted privacy to this secluded corner of the lawn. The noise and bustle of the house seemed further away than the length of the garden itself, incapable of intruding on the tranquillity of this part of the garden, to such an extent that it could have been in a different place altogether.

Cook was sitting back, his hands in his lap and his legs outstretched. His attention was fixed on the pond, his eyes following the fish as they made their aimless way around the depths of the water. Rathe did not sit down for want of an invitation, but he stood facing Cook without obscuring the view of the fish.

"You come to tell me I'm neglecting my guests?" murmured the inspector.

"No. I don't think anyone's noticed you've gone," replied Rathe. "No offence."

It was difficult to tell by the minimal illumination of the pond lights, but Cook might have smiled. "Andrea loves hosting parties. I can't stand it. The noise, the mess, the small talk. I'd rather sit here and look at my fish."

Rathe glanced down into the water. "Do you often sit down here?"

"It's my space, for my time." He glanced up at Rathe. "For when everything else gets too much and you just want the world to disappear for a few minutes."

"I know that feeling."

"So, I come here and look at my fish. What do you do?"

Rathe shrugged, bowing his head. "Brood, mostly."

"You shouldn't. It's not healthy. You should find something to do. Like opera."

"I'm not getting into opera just to please you."

"Please yourself, but you need to find something. For the times when you want the world to vanish too."

"A hobby is supposed to pass the time, not fill it." Rathe raised his eyes to the moon, pausing for a moment. "How well do you know the Newsomes, out of interest?"

Cook's eyes shifted from the fish once more, narrowing as they turned to Rathe. "Why are you asking?"

"Just curious."

"What's Elizabeth been saying to you?" Cook's voice was guarded, as though he was afraid of the answer. "Whatever it is, ignore it."

"She told me people would say she's paranoid."

Cook nodded. "She is, that's why."

"Does she have reason to be?"

For a moment, Cook looked as though he was going to tire of the subject of Elizabeth Newsome both quickly and irritably. He bunched his fists in his lap and tightened his lips, as though preparing himself to launch off the bench and grapple Rathe to the floor simply for having the temerity to mention her name. However, the fury was not to come; instead, Cook exhaled loudly in a frustrated sigh, and leaned forward, putting his elbows on his knees. The fists remained in place.

"Let me ask you this about Elizabeth Newsome," he said. "What did you think of her, first impressions and all that?"

Rathe put his hands in his pockets and leaned against the trunk of a tree. "Nervous, anxious. Frightened."

Cook nodded. "I remember when she was funny, full of life, ambitious. I remember when she had a comeback for everything and a one-liner for anybody. But I also remember seeing her disintegrate, fall to pieces, and wither away. Until she was that ghost of a person you met tonight. Elizabeth Newsome has turned into a very sad woman, Rathe."

"What happened?"

Cook chewed his lip, preparing himself for what he thought might be a long story. "Her and Ed have got a son, right? Good lad, called Sean, must be getting on for sixteen now. They had him later than most couples, because they were both in their thirties when she fell pregnant with him, but he's grown up to be a strong and decent lad." He paused, the memories stirring in his mind. "About six years ago, by accident presumably, Elizabeth found out she was expecting again. She went full term and gave birth to a daughter. They called her Jane. Straight away, it was obvious things weren't right. You can imagine the signs. Long story cut short, the girl died before she was two."

Rathe was nodding his understanding. "And Elizabeth never got over the loss?"

"Worse than that, she blamed herself. During all the doctor talk about mortality rates, sudden infant death syndrome, heart failure, brain malfunctions, and all that, it was mentioned that women who conceive later in life run a higher risk of losing the child. Elizabeth's mind latched on to that one point. Couldn't see past it, ignored everything else."

"The poor woman," muttered Rathe.

"Over the last four years, she's let her grief and guilt consume her. At one point, Andrea tried to help her and get her to see things differently, but it didn't work. I told her it wouldn't, but she wanted to do it anyway. That's typical of her. But, in the end, it was harder on Andrea than on Elizabeth."

"Meaning what, exactly?" Rathe's voice was without emotion, as though daring Cook to justify the words.

Cook recognised the challenge with a heavy sigh. "Sounds cruel, but I don't think Elizabeth wanted to be helped, not then and not now. I reckon she's so used to the feeling of guilt that it's all she understands. But because she won't let go of it, it's twisted her view of the world. She sees things differently to everyone else, misreads things. Misinterprets what people mean."

"You're saying she's delusional?"

"I don't know these fancy words like you, Rathe, so I can't say. But Elizabeth's got no lights on in the attic. I'm no expert, and don't pretend to be, but I don't reckon she's grieved properly. She's let it all fester and you know as well as I do that grief can twist your insides into knots."

Rathe nodded, sadly. "It can… so can guilt."

Cook shrugged, as though his point had been made. "Elizabeth Newsome died when her daughter died. The person you spoke to isn't the woman I knew. Not any more."

For a second or two, they remained silent, the tragedy of Elizabeth Newsome's daughter hanging between them like an unspoken secret yet to be confessed. At last, Rathe took a step forward and turned back on his heel to face Cook.

"What about the husband?" he asked. "What's he like?"

Cook rolled his eyes, sniffing with distaste. "Cold, difficult to get to know. I'm not a fan."

"How did he take the death of the child?"

"Who can tell? He doesn't let you know what he's

thinking. Ed's one to keep himself under wraps."

"Secretive?"

Cook shook his head. "Private. He handled his grief like he'd handle some bad news from the bank, as just something to be dealt with. Elizabeth went into meltdown; Ed just formed another layer of ice."

"I can't imagine it being a happy marriage." Rathe forced himself not to look at Cook.

The detective raised an eyebrow. "I don't think it's any sort of marriage. They just exist together."

Rathe examined a fingernail. "Would Edward Newsome ever be violent to her?"

Cook's eyes narrowed and he took a step closer. "What's all this about?"

For a moment, Rathe wondered whether he should respond. Standing there in Cook's private corner of peace, with the stillness of the night around them, the melodramatic suspicions of Elizabeth Newsome seemed outlandish and ridiculous. Rathe was suddenly aware that repeating them there and then might make him seem as foolish as people assumed Elizabeth Newsome herself was. But the question had been asked and, for better or worse, he knew it required an answer.

"Elizabeth thinks her husband is planning to kill her."

Cook made no immediate response. It seemed as though hours were spent processing the information and Rathe felt compelled to stare down at the flagstones beneath their feet, almost embarrassed by the words he had said.

"Did she say why she thinks that?" asked Cook at last.

"She didn't get the chance. Edward began to walk towards us, so she wouldn't say any more. But she begged for me to help her. And I mean she begged me, Cook."

"Why you?"

Rathe licked his lips awkwardly. "Easier to talk to a

stranger, she said."

Cook turned back to the pond and dipped his fingers gently into the water. The soft trickle of the disturbed water seemed to soothe the air around them. "Have you come out here to ask me if it could be true?"

"I just wondered what you'd think of it," Rathe said. "You know them both better than me, obviously, but there was something about her eyes and her expression which seemed so earnest, so desperate to be believed. And she told me people thought she was mad. She confessed that straight away."

"So?"

"So it made me think she might not be. How desperate do you have to be, after all, to approach a complete stranger and say something like she did?"

Cook looked back over his shoulder. "But she is desperate, Rathe. Which is why you can't take what she says seriously. I might not like the uptight bastard, but Ed Newsome is no more capable of murder than one of these fish. He's not got the balls for one thing and he's too self-possessed for another. Trust me, he'd walk away from any sort of confrontation before he let himself get so hot under his shirt that he'd kill someone."

Rathe remained impassive. "So you're sure there's nothing to what she said?"

Cook stepped away from the pond and brought his face close to Rathe's. "I'm sure. I know you've got something in you which feels the nced to try to save people and I think I understand why it's in you. But, this time, there's nothing to be done about it."

Rathe ignored what he took as a cynical reference to his own psyche. "You didn't see the look on her face."

Cook shook his head again, but with a smile, as though he had scored another point. "Not tonight I didn't, no. But I'll have seen it a hundred times before, because it's always there. It's the memory of her daughter carved in her face and it never leaves her. The only thing to change is the fantasy she spins to explain it. I told you before, but I'll say it again. Elizabeth Newsome is a sad, depressed, and broken woman. But that doesn't make Ed Newsome a murderer."

"Perhaps not," conceded Rathe.

Cook clapped a hand to Rathe's shoulder, as though that sealed the agreement between them that there was nothing more to be said about Elizabeth Newsome or her suspicions of impending death. As the two of them walked back to the house together, Cook spoke about something unrelated but Rathe barely heard a word of it. His mind was elsewhere, recalling with a vivid intensity those pleading eyes and trembling fingers of the woman who had suffered in life and, it seemed, who may yet suffer in death.

* * *

The following morning dawned with a clear sky and the diurnal promise of the sun. It was one of those mornings which a painter might have striven to capture in his waking moments or which a poet might have manipulated immediately into a metaphor for the refreshing and clarifying virtues of sleep, just in case that crispness of the forthcoming day was so pure that it could never be expected to last its course and might never be replicated. It was a morning when the city seemed eager to proceed, where no problem appeared to be insurmountable, and when the river was blue with hope as opposed to black with menace. And yet, as he looked out over that same river of ambition and across the same skies of optimism, Anthony Rathe knew that his own mind was in turmoil.

The two conflicting conversations from the previous night lingered in his memory and he knew that he had spent much of the remainder of the preceding twilight hours fluctuating between them. On the one hand, he could understand Cook's almost rational explanation of the Newsome woman's hysteria, especially when he took into account the immense grief which she must have experienced and which, according to Cook, she had not confronted. And yet, conversely, Rathe found it impossible to ignore the deep entreaties of Elizabeth's expressions and words when she had spoken to him. His brain compelled him to side with Cook's realistic analysis; but his heart and his instincts clasped hands in solidarity with Elizabeth Newsome's alleged paranoia.

By the time he and Cook had gone back inside from the garden, the Newsomes had left the party. Andrea Cook was less than impressed that her husband had not been around to say goodbye, but Cook had shrugged off the admonishments with a roll of his eyes and the sharp fizz of a new bottle of beer being opened. Rathe had permitted himself no more to drink and he had made his excuses. At the end of the driveway, Cook had issued a reminder to forget the Newsome woman and her claims, advising Rathe to turn his mind to something more profitable.

"Like opera?" Rathe had quipped.

"If that's your bag," Cook had grinned, turning his back and walking away.

But Rathe's mind was not for ignoring the possibility that the woman was in danger. He found it impossible not to think that, if he ignored her and those fears became a reality, his own conscience would break under the strain of her life hanging on it alongside that of Kevin Marsden's. The thought was impossible to entertain. By contrast, if he could satisfy himself that Elizabeth's fears were delusional and there was no danger from Edward Newsome, Rathe felt he would have lost nothing but his own time, but that loss was nothing compared to the peace of mind which he would gain because, of course, he had all the time in the world to lose.

An internet search which was both quicker and easier than he had anticipated provided details of a number of Newsomes in the immediate area, but only one with a third occupant in the property by the name of Sean. The address was across London, involving a change of Tube and a cab he feared, but it would be easier than driving and the journey would give him time to formulate his thoughts. He drank a cup of coffee, contemplated a bagel but discounted the idea, and left the house.

He could recall very little of the journey itself when he arrived at the Newsomes' property. His mind had been elsewhere, planning and rehearsing his words and imagining her reactions and responses, and so he had not noticed the collection of underground stations through which he had passed and the change of trains had been completed in a mechanical haze. He seemed to remember a crying child on the second train, but that had only made him think of the dead Newsome baby, Jane, and the effect her passing had had on her mother. He remembered checking directions on his phone and deciding that what seemed to be only a short walk through a leafy suburb was preferable to a cab journey through the same district. But, as he stood at the gates of the property, the walk itself now seemed to be from another time and place altogether.

The house was set back from the road, the driveway a long path of flagstones, bordered on the one side by a fence and overhanging trees and, on the other, by a finely decorated and carefully maintained garden. The front door of the house was hidden by an arched portico which hung over the front steps. There was a bay window downstairs and three large windows on the upper floor, seemingly peering out from the shadows of the gables above them. An extension was to the left of the house, built onto a sizeable garage and, whilst impossible to see for certain, Rathe had the impression of a large garden at the rear of the property, no doubt as well cared for as its front counterpart. The area was quiet, tranquil, far away from the general noise of the city, and Rathe felt like something of an imposter, intruding on this peaceful solitude, as though the purpose of his journey was a stain on the serenity of the place.

Elizabeth Newsome responded to the ringing of the doorbell as promptly as might have been expected and her initial look of surprise at a visitor was quickly intensified when she saw Rathe standing on the threshold. A momentary confusion passed over her face whilst she tried to place him in her memory, but it was a second only before she recalled his face and name, changing her expression from surprise to gratitude.

"I never expected you to... " she stammered. "You believed me? Last night, you believed what I said?"

Gently, he pointed inside the hallway. "Perhaps I could come in?"

Flustered, unable to comprehend his belief in her, she muttered an apology and let him in, closing the door rather louder than she might have intended. She led him into a cosy sitting room, which was newly decorated but which betrayed an old fashioned taste, as though the house were desperate to return to how it looked in happier times. Elizabeth offered him coffee, which he accepted, sitting down in an armchair at her invitation, whilst she tottered out of the room to make the drink. Rathe looked around the place, unengaged by it until he saw the photographs on the sideboard. He saw a collection of images of the family. In some, Elizabeth seemed to be a different woman, her face full of humour and eager vitality, and Rathe remembered what Cook had said about her manner before the death of the baby. Here, as large as life, was that energy and liveliness facing him behind the glass of the frame. But next to it, in so many of the images, was the same dour expression which he had seen on Edward Newsome's face the previous night. The man was smiling for the camera, but the twist of the lips was forced and uncomfortable, as though his body were present at the occasion but his mind and spirit were somewhere far away, somewhere where his smile would not be forced and his manner not reserved. There were photographs of the son, Sean, sometimes between them and sometimes alone, but always with the same expression of happiness and freedom on his face. He was a good looking boy, his features a perfect blend of Elizabeth's old good humour and Edward's self-control. In age, across the photographs, he ranged from perhaps four to sixteen, no older, but it was clear from the projected maturing of his face that nature would continue to mould him into a handsome and impressive man.

Above the sideboard, there was a crucifix. Rathe found himself staring at it for some time, and the sound of the coffee being made in the kitchen appeared to slip away from him. As fanciful as it sounded, even in his own head, it seemed to him that the image of Christ on the cross had been placed above the photographs of the family deliberately, and the small hole in the opposite wall, where a nail perhaps had once protruded, suggested that the crucifix indeed had been moved recently. Stretched out in front of the photo frames, too, he saw a rosary. It might have been a coincidence, the beads placed there when Elizabeth went to answer the door, but they were laid out neatly, not dropped in the urgency of a moment, and Rathe had the distinct impression that these two symbols of the family's faith had been set down purposefully, in order to protect the family from further sorrow. Almost unwittingly, he remembered again that people thought Elizabeth Newsome was paranoid and delusional, if not mad, and the apparent deliberate placing of those trappings of worship seemed to confirm it, so that suddenly Rathe had a crisis of faith in his own instincts and he wondered whether he had made a mistake in coming here.

But he had no time to allow those doubts to fester, because no sooner had they sparked into life than she was back in the room, carrying what he suspected was a tray of the best china which surrounded a silver plated coffee pot. It may not have been her intention to be fulsome, but Rathe was at once embarrassed at the idea that her display of sophistication had been for his benefit alone, perhaps as an overstated gesture of gratitude for his taking her distress seriously.

She poured the coffee as she spoke. "I thought you'd ignore what I said to you, Mr Rathe. I wouldn't have blamed you. I'm used to people dismissing me as a neurotic fantasist."

"I'm afraid I was told to do just that," he felt compelled to confess, accepting the coffee with a smile. It was good: strong, black, bitter.

She was not offended by his words. "When you hear something consistently, you either begin to believe it or you become immune to it. But I refuse to believe that I am what they say."

Rathe shifted in his chair. "You'll have to accept, though, that people won't take what you say about your husband seriously if you have nothing to back it up with."

She looked across at him, an eyebrow raised not in defiance but in hope. "You came here today, so you must believe me."

He lowered his gaze from hers. "I came here because I wanted to ask you to support what you said. I haven't necessarily said I believe you and it'd be wrong of me to allow you to think so until I've said it outright."

"Of course, I understand that," she said, sipping some coffee but making it seem as though she were distracting herself from the instinct to weep.

"Why would your husband want to harm you in any way, let alone to… ?" He felt unable to finish the sentence, as though the words required were so outrageous that they could never make sense.

She did not look back to him. Instead, she replaced the coffee cup on the tray and placed her hands in her lap. "Why? You ask why he wants me gone?"

"I think I have to," replied Rathe.

Now she did look at him, her eyes dampened with sadness, but her voice hardened with bitterness. "For love, Mr Rathe. It's all for love."

He was fully aware of the implications of her words, his mind making connections and forming suppositions with a speed which in retrospect even he found startling, but the simplicity of his next words belied his understanding of the situation. "I don't understand, Mrs Newsome. If your husband loves you… "

She rose from the settee, as though his apparent stupidity had offended her. "It isn't me he loves, Mr Rathe. Not any more. I am sure that at one point he did love me and I will never believe it wasn't true once. But I know that it's no longer true. To say otherwise would only be lying to myself. Do those sound like the words of a woman under a delusion?"

Rathe shook his head, feeling something close to shame. "No."

She pointed to the crucifix and rosary. "They give me peace, comfort, and hope. Without faith perhaps I would lose my mind. It isn't very fashionable today to be sure of the existence of God, but if there is no such thing as His comfort and grace after death, then the lives we lead now are all there is to the world. Don't you find that a depressing thought?"

Rathe remained silent. She gave him a brief, unhappy

smile of what he thought was disappointment that his own beliefs must seem to her to be no different to the majority of lost souls she had referenced. She did not press the point. "I say that faith and the rosary give me comfort and peace. To Edward, they are nothing less than chains around his ankles. To him, they're an unbreakable tie which binds us together in misery."

"Because your faith forbids you to divorce?"

"Marriage is a promise made to God as well as to each other."

Rathe got up from his chair and walked towards her. This honesty she had demonstrated, the sensitivity of her words and emotions, had tipped his balance back into believing that she was far from mad. He could not accept that someone who was deceiving themselves into unfounded ideas of murder could be so honest as to confess what she had done. He was no psychologist, but it seemed unlikely that a person could be so detached from reality in one respect yet so clearly aware of it in another.

"Tell me more about your husband, Mrs Newsome," said Rathe, his voice gentle and trustworthy.

Elizabeth appeared not to have heard him. "Her name is Michelle Leverton. I don't think I've ever said her name out loud before, but it has burned in my mind constantly for six months. I don't really know anything about her but I despise everything there is about her. Perhaps that does make me sound like a lunatic."

"No," muttered Rathe. "I think it makes you sound human."

She thanked him silently, with a smile which showed appreciation and gratitude. "I'd suspected something for a long time. You don't share your life with somebody for almost twenty years and not learn enough about them to know when they are keeping secrets from you."

"What made you suspicious?"

She lowered her head, as though the memory and its recollection were two distinct sources of physical pain which she was forcing herself to suppress. "Late nights at work, sudden weekend conferences, never letting his phone out of his sights. Silly lies which he contradicted without knowing it. The way he looked at her at the company Christmas party last year, even when she was throwing countless glasses of Bacardi and Coke down her throat and dancing like a maniac. How he would talk about her, saying what an asset to the firm she was, how clever she had been on this account or that contract. Taken on their own, they don't mean infidelity, but when you put them together they turn your suspicions into certainty."

"Did you confront him?"

Elizabeth gave an adamant shake of her head. "I wasn't so direct, Mr Rathe. He had gone in the bath, but left his phone in the bedroom. I found her number in it and I changed it to mine. You don't think to check the number of the person you're calling on a mobile, do you? The next text he sent to her came to me."

Despite the tragedy of her situation, Rathe found himself impressed by her ingenuity. It had been a simple but effective ruse. Deceitful and underhand, certainly, but no less devious than Edward Newsome had been and Rathe felt Elizabeth's actions had not been entirely unjustified. Once again, he found himself doubting that a woman capable of such a trick was in any way as feeble minded as Cook and the rest of their circle of friends labelled her. "You confronted him after that, surely?"

She nodded, biting her lip in remembrance of the sting of betrayal which she had felt so prominently. "He didn't deny it. You probably think he had no way of denying it after the way I had caught him and perhaps you're right about it. But

I prefer to think that not denying it was a small shred of respect which he still had for me. Lying to my face after what I had done would have been one insult too many. Do you think I'm foolish for thinking that way?"

Rathe held her gaze. "I think you're anything but foolish."

She continued to stare at him for longer than felt comfortable for him. "You're a kind man, Mr Rathe. It seems a long time since I felt kindness."

He did not feel it prudent to reply directly to that. "How did your husband react when you said you could never grant him a divorce?"

She rolled her eyes to the ceiling. "You don't know Edward or else you wouldn't ask that. He acted exactly as Edward would be expected to act. With solemn resolve and a complete lack of anything approaching emotion. Edward is a distant man, Mr Rathe, dispassionate and aloof. Once, I thought it was an attractive quality, his ability to remain unflustered by the world. His composure seemed to me to be a strength. But, as time has gone on, I have come to think of it as almost inhuman. I'm not sure I wouldn't have preferred him to shout in my face, call me every name he could think of, or even sobbed on his knees and begged me to let him go. I think sometimes I might have preferred that to his cold, arrogant acceptance of the situation. As though he were the victim in this and he was bearing his suffering with dignity."

The tears had welled up in her eyes as she had spoken and now they fell without apology. She took a handkerchief from her sleeve and clutched it to her face, muffling the sound of her weeping into a distorted version of itself which was somehow more terrible than the reality. Unsure of how he should respond, Rathe remained motionless. He doubted that she required any physical comfort from him and he thought that an arm around the shoulders might be an invasion of her privacy. If he had changed his mind, however, he would not have been able to offer any comfort in any event, because she composed herself in a matter of moments, the burst of sobbing burning which such intensity that it exhausted itself almost as soon as it began.

"I'm sorry," she muttered, as much to herself as to him. "Sometimes, it just comes over me."

"You have no reason to apologise for that," Rathe replied. "Certainly not to a stranger."

She looked back to him. "I don't think of you as a stranger somehow. Is that presumptuous?"

Rathe did not know how best to respond to that, so he lowered his head and allowed the moment to pass. "What you said to me last night... Do you think it's true solely because of your husband and this Leverton girl?"

"Isn't it reason enough to want me out of the way?"

"But if your husband is, as you say, willing to accept the situation for what it is, that would remove any suggestion of motive, wouldn't it?" Rathe spoke carefully, so as not to appear offensive.

"I didn't say he was willing to accept it," she replied with a harder edge to her voice than he had heard before. "I said he didn't argue with me about it."

Rathe rolled his tongue across his bottom lip as understanding seeped into his brain. "You're saying that, privately, he might try to come up with another way of ending the marriage but, publicly, he would want to avoid any form of unpleasantness."

She nodded. "Wouldn't that be a sensible plan, if he did intend to do something horrific to me? As you've just said, if he could make people believe that my refusal to divorce him didn't matter to him, it would look as though the idea that my stance on divorce and his feelings about Michelle Leverton were groundless."

Rathe nodded. It was the thought he had formed himself

in the last few seconds of their discussion. He knew it was inevitable that a detective like Cook would suspect Edward Newsome as a matter of routine in the face of the murder of his wife, especially if there was a vivid and unshakeable motive for the crime. But if Edward Newsome had said that the question of the divorce was of no importance to him or Michelle Leverton then that would seem to dilute the power of that motive, sufficiently perhaps for the purpose of a skilful defence Counsel. Rathe had a series of swift but intense images of what havoc he would cause to that motive at a trial with the assistance of Edward Newsome's reticence.

"There are such things as still waters and they often run deep," he said.

"More coffee?" she asked, as though it was an invitation to celebrate her victory on the question of motive.

Rathe declined the offer. "Do you have any other reason to suspect your husband is planning what you think?"

She was pouring more coffee for herself, but she stopped doing so as soon as the question was asked. Rathe sensed her discomfort, her sudden tightening of her shoulders and tense straightening of her spine, as though she feared that her next words, unless chosen very carefully, would drive him from the room and her life and any hope of his help would drop through her fingers like falling sand.

For a moment, he mistook her anxious hesitation for reluctance to speak. "I've got to ask, Mrs Newsome, you understand that."

She nodded violently, dismissing his words. "It's not that I don't want to tell you, Mr Rathe, it's that I'm afraid you'll dismiss me. And I think, so far, you're sympathetic to my situation. I don't want to lose that sympathy."

"But if you say nothing else about it, I won't know the full story, so I can't be fully on your side or not," he argued.

She looked up at him now, her eyes once more damp with

sadness and despair. "When I met Edward, he was with someone else. It wasn't serious; at least, he's always claimed it was never serious. But as soon as he got with me, any memory of his previous girlfriend was gone. Thrown out. All the photos, the clothes she'd chosen, and books or films which reminded him of her. Everything, gone. As though she was never a part of his life at all. I wanted to go to Rome for a weekend many years ago, but Edward wouldn't go because he'd been there before, with her. Do you understand what I'm saying?"

"I do," confessed Rathe, "but it seems an extreme view to have."

"But it's Edward all over. When he moves on, he moves on completely. But now, with me, with a marriage, it isn't that easy, is it? You can't erase twenty years like you can six months. Half of everything is mine. So, he has to do it some other way."

Rathe began to pace the room, clasping his chin in concentration. "Are you telling me that this side of his character is so strong that you think he'll turn to murder in order to satisfy it?"

"I know it sounds ridiculous," she said, "but it's easier to know I am scared of him than to explain why properly. Like explaining two and two makes four. It just does, it's a fact. And it's a fact that Edward will want to remove himself from his present life completely so that he can have a new one with her. But this time, it's not throwing out old shirts and CDs because there is too much history to throw away. But he can do one thing, Mr Rathe" – she held up an index finger – "just one thing which will erase all of that time at one go."

"That's not proof of intent, Mrs Newsome," Rathe had said, almost hating himself for it.

"What about sleeping pills? Are they proof of intent?" She made the phrase sound ludicrous to his ears, as though it were something he should be ashamed of saying, and her eyes remained defiant, daring him to contradict her.

"Sleeping pills?"

"Edward has never had trouble sleeping. Never." Her voice was becoming hysterical without rising above a hissing whisper. "But I found a whole load of sleeping tablets and prescriptions for more of them in the bathroom cabinet. Edward's no insomniac, Mr Rathe, so what is he doing with those tablets?"

He would have replied, but he became aware suddenly of the presence of another person in the room. There had been no sound of the living room door opening, not that he remembered at least, and yet his attention was diverted now from Elizabeth's eyes to the young boy who peered from behind the door, his brow creased in concern and his eyes dimmed with confusion. A shock of dark hair fell over one eye and there was a faint glow of nervousness about the otherwise pallid cheeks. He had aged since the photographs on the sideboard but it was unmistakably the same child who stood in front of Rathe now, having taken yet a further step on the path to maturity. His clothes were casual but smart, the jeans as loose around his waist as the T-shirt was tight against his chest, but he wore them with an easy confidence which suggested that he knew he was handsome and so there was no reason to draw attention to it. Elizabeth Newsome stood up and went to her son, her arms going around his broad shoulders in an instinctive display of maternal protection.

"I'm sorry, darling," she drawled, "did we disturb you?"

"You been crying?" asked the boy, his suspicious eyes flickering from his mother to Rathe.

Elizabeth dabbed away whatever remained of her tears. "It's nothing. Honestly, Sean, it's fine."

"Who's this?"

The stranger stepped forward, holding out his hand. "Anthony Rathe. I'm a… friend of your mother's."

Sean looked back to Elizabeth, ignoring Rathe's outstretched hand. "What's he doing here?"

"Don't be rude," hissed his mother. "We're just talking, that's all."

"Dad at work?"

"Of course he is. Where else would he be?"

"Anywhere these days." Sean Newsome looked back at Rathe. "Does Dad know he's here?"

Rathe knew that his welcome had been outstayed and he found his presence there now to be an embarrassment. He stepped forward, rubbing his hands together as though the action might wipe away the uneasiness which had overcome him. "Look, I don't want to intrude any longer and I should let you get on with your day."

Elizabeth held out a hand to stop him. "Honestly, Mr Rathe, you don't have to go."

"I think he does," muttered Sean.

"Don't be so rude," his mother hissed again, a flame of unease bursting onto her cheeks.

Rathe was now at the door himself. "No, really, I do have to be going. I've stayed too long as it is."

Elizabeth followed him out of the room, leaving Sean alone in the living room, his head bowed and his fists clenched.

"I'm so sorry about Sean," Elizabeth said at the front door, her hand perched on the handle.

"Don't give it a second thought." Rathe moved her hand away, as though he might never escape the house if he did not make his own move to do so. He had opened the door and stepped into the porch before she spoke once more.

"Do you believe me?" she asked. "About Edward, about everything?"

Rathe lowered his gaze to the stone steps beneath his feet, trying desperately to find a suitable answer. Did he believe her? It was difficult to be convinced, he knew that, but he retained that reasonable doubt which he had striven to demonstrate so many times in his professional career. Elizabeth Newsome might not be the paranoid mad woman people said, but she struck Rathe as being far from straightforward. He found her intense, plausible, persuasive; but, simultaneously, he found her fears hypothetical, melodramatic, and unsubstantiated. She was looking at him with those pleading eyes once more and he felt unable to give her any satisfactory answer.

"Do you believe me, about Edward?" she asked once more, leaning against the door-frame like a defeated woman, who knew his answer without him giving it.

Despite himself, and notwithstanding her conviction that he did not accept her fears, he looked at her in those desperate eyes and spoke words over which he had no control and from which there was no return.

"Yes, Mrs Newsome," Rathe declared. "I believe you."

* * *

After his assurances, Elizabeth Newsome had been more than willing to give Rathe details of her husband's place of business and mobile phone number. Arranging to meet the man had not proved as onerous as Rathe had anticipated and he wondered for a moment whether it was because Edward Newsome had no reason to be afraid of meeting Rathe or whether he was curious why a stranger was requesting a meeting at all. Newsome had simply asked what the purpose of Rathe's request was, to which Rathe gave a suitably vague response, and what time and venue Rathe would prefer. Not wishing to jeopardise his position when Newsome had been so amenable, Rathe left the details of the meeting to him.

"I normally have a glass of wine and a late lunch at

Marcello's," Newsome had said. "Do you know it?"

Rathe was well aware of the small Italian bistro off Northumberland Street, so he agreed that he would see Newsome there at two that afternoon. It was close enough in time not to seem as though Newsome were putting off the interview, but far enough away for Rathe to question what he hoped to achieve by it. Rathe doubted he could simply come out and ask the question directly and, furthermore, there was the difficulty that any question he asked might seem to be both intrusive and offensive. But, as the morning lapsed into the afternoon, Rathe decided that what was said between them was of less importance to him that the opportunity of engaging with Newsome himself and assessing the type of man he was. There was often nothing like personal experience and, as his mind lingered on the point, Rathe began to grow impatient to meet the man who he had been told was devoid of emotional responses and yet who may or may not be contemplating murder.

Rathe was punctual for the appointment, but Newsome was already waiting outside the bistro when he arrived. The man greeted him with a smile, admittedly brief, and a handshake which was firm and authoritative. Rathe could tell at once that his suit was not bespoke but it was expensive enough to give the impression of it and the matching tie and handkerchief at least carried the suggestion of sartorial etiquette. His eyes were attentive behind the wire-framed spectacles, never once leaving Rathe's own probing glare, but there was no warmth in them and the small, trim beard could not disguise the pursed aloofness of the mouth once that brief smile had vanished. He was shown to a table in the far corner of the restaurant without any prompting, confirmation of his regular presence there, but it did not strike Rathe as being done with any intention of exhibitionism. Any display of egotism from Edward Newsome struck Rathe as unlikely from the outset. It was simply a routine task between waiter and diner which was carried out every day of the week, whether there was company present or not.

They ordered a Chardonnay each on Newsome's recommendation, Rathe preferring a red wine but not wishing to insult his host, and waited for the drinks to arrive before they began to talk beyond superficial conversation about the restaurant and their previous respective visits and the contents of the menu. When the wine arrived, Newsome leaned forward in his chair and clasped his fingers together. It seemed like a natural stance for him to take, a sign that the meeting could commence now that he was ready for it to do so.

"I've heard of you, Mr Rathe," said Newsome, his voice gentle, almost feminine. "There was a time when one couldn't open a newspaper without seeing your name somewhere in it."

Rathe looked anywhere but into those expressionless eyes. "It's not a time I like remembering."

"No, I can imagine it isn't. After what happened to that young man who killed himself… "

The reference seemed to make Kevin Marsden appear before Rathe's eyes, as though the dead, decayed boy himself had walked in to poison the genial and sophisticated atmosphere of the restaurant. Rathe concentrated on the glass of wine, on its subtle smell of flora and the delicate taste of citrus fruit, hoping that both combined would wash away the bitter, foul stench of the unwanted memory.

"I didn't come here to talk about Kevin Marsden or what happened to him," Rathe said, refusing to apologise to this man about any of the past.

Newsome sipped some wine. "No, I dare say you didn't, but then I can't imagine what you did come here to talk about."

"I appreciate this must seem a little strange to you."

"I'd say that was putting it mildly."

Unbidden, Cook's words about Edward Newsome came back into Rathe's brain. Cold, he had said, difficult to get to know: Rathe could understand that point of view, even after so little time in the man's presence. There was something odious about his quiet tone of voice, his patronising manner and cool politeness, all made the worse for those dead eyes which drifted around the room and back to Rathe's face with a tired regularity.

"It's only because I believe you're a friend of Terry and Andrea Cook that I agreed to meet you at all," Newsome was saying. "Otherwise, I prefer to lunch alone. It's my private time."

Rathe smiled, not too slyly. "Do you always lunch alone?"

Something in his expression captured Newsome's attention. "I'm sorry?"

"Don't be," said Rathe. "I was just asking whether it is entirely unheard of for you to have a lunch companion."

Newsome lowered his hands to his lap and leaned back in his chair, as though his understanding of Rathe's implied meaning had forced him backwards. "I saw you last night talking to my wife at the Cooks' party, did I not? I see she has been talking to you about certain matters."

"Is any of it true?"

"Those matters are private, Mr Rathe. They are not your concern now and there is no reason why they should be your concern in the future."

Rathe drank some wine, suddenly desperate for some cleansing of the dryness of his mouth. "Your wife is in great pain, Mr Newsome, and it's a pain you're causing her."

My wife is indeed in great pain, Mr Rathe, but the root cause of her pain is not my fault."

"She has told me about Michelle Leverton."

If Newsome was surprised or unnerved by the news, he did not betray it. "She had no right to do so, since it's private business, but as long as she has confided in a stranger, I see no reason to deny it."

"But you don't think it's any cause of pain for your wife?" Rathe pointed out, his eyes fixed on Newsome, refusing to allow the man any sanctuary from his close examination of his reactions.

"I didn't say that, Mr Rathe. I said that my relationship with Michelle is not the root cause of Elizabeth's depression."

"I presume you're talking about the loss of your daughter," Rathe said, his voice softening when his eyes would not. "I'm sorry for that."

Newsome did not acknowledge the gesture of condolence. "You cannot take my wife at face value, Mr Rathe. Grief has twisted her point of view to such an extent that reality and fantasy are too easily blurred for her. Whatever she has confided to you is true only in her own head. I have tried to convince her of it, to make her see sense, but I've failed. I've asked her to get help, professional therapy, which I would have paid for, but she throws it back in my face. I may have fallen out of love with my wife, Mr Rathe, and you may condemn me for that, but I have not stopped caring for her and seeing her drown under the pressure of these paranoid imaginings of hers is as painful for me as it is for her."

It was the closest Rathe had come to having any form of sympathy for the man. He was right: finding a new love did not necessarily mean depriving all feeling for the lost one, particularly where there were children involved. Rathe was not a father, and never expected to be one, but he felt that he was empathetic enough to understand that special bond in others and he felt sensitive enough in his own self to know that such a bond might transcend almost every other emotional tie imaginable. And yet, it had been said that

Edward Newsome was a man who felt the need to erase all memories of his past life once he moved into a new phase. How could he, Rathe, reconcile what appeared to be two contradictory versions of the same man? Perhaps the answer was obvious, one which had to be put down, perhaps, to Elizabeth Newsome's potential distortion of the truth.

"I haven't got over Jane's death but I have come to terms with it, Mr Rathe," Newsome was saying, bringing Rathe back out of his labyrinth of thought. "I can think about it without tears at least, if not without any sadness. Elizabeth can't do the same, as I have said, and it has driven me away. Whether you accept it or not, that's how I see things. Yes, I fell for Michelle and I want to be with her more than anything in the world, but, in many ways, Elizabeth's reaction to Jane's death has acted as a catalyst for those feelings. And now, on top of all that misery, there's this lunatic idea of murder."

"You're saying you and Elizabeth need to share equal blame for what has happened?"

Newsome nodded. "But I can live with the pain I feel as a result of all this. I can do that because I have to. But Elizabeth refuses to accept any complicity in it. Instead, she accuses me of wanting rid of her. Can't you see this pre-occupation she has with death? It's all to do with Jane, it all stems from us losing her, I understand that; but Elizabeth can't see the upset and pain she's causing to others by allowing herself to be consumed by it."

"The upset she causes to you, for instance?"

Newsome shook his head. "No, not to me. I've said I'm as much to blame as her. I mean to our son, to Sean. He's the only innocent in this, Mr Rathe, and he shouldn't be allowed to suffer for any of it. Michelle, Elizabeth, me, we all have our roles to play in the present mess we call our lives, but Sean has never caused anybody any sadness. Elizabeth is so blinded by her own paranoia, she can't see what she's doing to the only child she's got left."

Rathe had begun to frown, partly because he himself had not thought of the surviving Newsome child or his reaction to the breakdown of his parents' marriage, and partly because of the sudden display of emotion from this aloof, austere man. He wondered how long Newsome had kept those feelings beneath his proud mask of noble stoicism and, further, how often he had come close to saying those same words to his wife. Perhaps he had thought they would be ineffectual or maybe, like his wife, he had found it easier to say to a stranger, even one whom he had shown no predilection to respect or to trust.

"Does Sean know about you and Michelle?" Rathe asked.

"With Elizabeth raving about it almost daily, how could he not?"

"What about the accusations of murder?"

Newsome did not answer straight away. His eyes flickered behind the lenses of his glasses as he fought with his internal battle for privacy and honesty.

"Tell me the truth, Mr Newsome," urged Rathe. "It has to be said at some point, so make it now."

Newsome looked at Rathe, as though seeing him for the first time. "He overheard us, arguing, a few days ago. We had no idea he was there. He does that. Appears from nowhere in the room behind you, not making a sound. As a child, he would have nightmares and creep into our room, wanting comfort but not daring to wake us. So, he would kneel beside one of us and stare at us, willing us to wake up. When we did, we saw him, glaring at us, with fear in his eyes. But he was so silent, so quiet, we never heard him come into the room."

Without hesitation, Rathe recalled the way Sean Newsome had appeared in his mother's living room that morning.

"What did he overhear that day?"

"Elizabeth was blind with rage," Newsome recalled. "She had found a prescription of mine, sleeping tablets. All this bitterness with her, with Michelle, with all of it... I haven't been sleeping, so I got pills for it. Elizabeth thought I was going to use them on her."

"She said you were stockpiling them."

Newsome shook his head, laughing in desperation. "It's nonsense, you have to believe that."

"She says you've never had trouble sleeping before."

Now, a flash of the old repressed anger returned to the eyes. "I've never been under this sort of stress before."

"When she found the pills," Rathe said, ignoring the small outburst of emotion, "she confronted you, right? Did she ask point blank what you intended to do with them?"

Newsome was shaking his head before Rathe finished talking. "She didn't ask anything. She accused. Outright."

"And Sean overheard?"

Newsome had regained his composure. He removed his spectacles and cleaned them on his handkerchief, as though wiping away the mist of upset which had temporarily clouded his vision and betrayed the heart beneath the stone. "Every word of it."

"Presumably you told him it was his mother's hysteria," said Rathe without any trace of denunciation.

"Of course, I did. But she has told him the opposite. God knows what he believes." They fell silent for a moment, whilst each of them regained their thoughts and considered how best to proceed. It was Newsome who spoke again first, his voice once more laced with the cool arrogance which had struck Rathe at once when they had met. "Let me ask you a question now, Mr Rathe. I presume my wife has shared with you these fears she has of me trying to murder her. I assume that is why you are sitting here talking to me right now."

"Yes, she has." Rathe saw no reason to deny it.

"Speaking as a barrister, a lawyer, did she offer you anything which you might feel able to accept as conclusive proof of her accusations?"

This time, Rathe saw no opportunity to deny it, even if he had wanted to. "Not in a legal sense, no."

Newsome considered Rathe for a moment, curious about the slight sense of evasion about the answer. "But she gave you some cause to believe her?"

"Do you think I'd be sitting here if she hadn't?" Rathe asked, serving the question with more ice than it required.

Newsome conceded the point. "Perhaps we'd best stick with the idea of legal proof, then. She offered no physical or tangible evidence that I might be trying to murder her. No example of an attempt which failed, for example?"

"None."

Newsome leaned forward for emphasis, his voice constricted into a hiss of fury. "Because there is no proof. None!"

"You do have a motive for murder, if you were inclined that way," Rathe felt duty bound to say.

"My wife's religion makes life seem like a prison, I won't deny that."

"She said the rosary is a tie which binds you to her forever."

"Till death do us part?" Newsome was scornful. "Perhaps I do see it like that. But what I feel for Michelle is strong enough for religion not to be a problem."

"You're saying you can wait for nature to take its course and free you?"

"Yes."

"Is Michelle willing to make the same sacrifice?"

More emphasis: "Yes."

Rathe smiled and sipped some of the wine. It was

excellent. "Forgive me, but isn't that a little idealistic, not to say naïve?"

Newsome's eyes narrowed. "Only to a cynic."

"Or a realist."

For a moment, there was a silent impasse, one of them unable to think of a suitable riposte, the other feeling no more words on the subject were required. For Rathe at least, although he suspected it applied to Newsome, it was a relief when the waiter came to take the food order. Newsome took the menu in his hands and Rathe noticed the slight shake of the fingers as he did so, the last dying remnants of the man's display of suppressed emotion. When the menu was put before him, Rathe declined the offer.

"Thank you, but I have very little appetite," he said with a smile. He rose from his chair and offered his hand to Edward Newsome. "I know you prefer to eat alone."

Newsome took Rathe's hand and gave it a cold, feeble shake. "Perhaps it is best."

Rathe left money for the wine, despite Newsome's prosaic objections, and left the restaurant. Outside, he leaned against the wall and drew deep breaths of the cold, cleansing air into his lungs. For several moments, he remained there, his mind wandering without fixing on any one, single thought. As he walked away at last, his brain refused to settle and he felt as though he was as far away as ever from understanding what was happening between Elizabeth and Edward Newsome and whether or not their lives were in fact destined to end in murder.

* * *

It was early evening before Rathe was able to make contact with Michelle Leverton. She had refused to allow him to come to her home, stating a preference for neutral territory on the grounds that people couldn't be too careful when dealing with strangers. Rathe had bowed to her caution and allowed her to choose whatever rendezvous she thought best. She had given him the name of a small wine bar near Westminster, one which he did not know, but he had assured her that he would be there. Seven o'clock sharp.

"Give us both time for something to eat, unless you want to buy me dinner too," she had said.

"I'll see you at seven o'clock, Miss Leverton," Rathe had replied, with no smile on his lips or in his voice.

He had made sure he was early for the appointment, but she was there before him nevertheless. She would not have been difficult to identify, even if she had not told him she would be sitting at the far edge of the bar. The place was filled with couples or parties of friends, so that the solitary woman drinking without company but looking almost pathologically at her watch then towards the door was an obvious social juxtaposition.

Michelle Leverton was pretty rather than beautiful. He guessed she was ten years or so younger than Edward Newsome, but he knew that he found the age of women from their looks alone to be deceptive. Her hair was a dark brown, tinged with artificial red, which contrasted with the deep blue of her eyes. Her lips were glossed but not ostentatiously so, and her clothes suggested elegance rather than openly personified it, as though she took the view that a gaudy show of wealth or sophistication was an ironic misunderstanding of the nature and allure of either. She wore minimal jewellery but what there was betrayed the same appreciation for an understated stylishness. She had had a drink already, the empty glass to her left with its melted ice and washed out lemon at the bottom testifying to the indulgence. A replenished glass was in front of her but, as he introduced himself and took the seat beside her, he offered as a matter of politeness to buy her a third.

"Bacardi and Coke, please," he was surprised to hear her

say. "Thanks."

He ordered the drink and a Merlot for him, conscious that her eyes were on him and had not left his face from the moment he had approached her. He felt the crimson shame of unease creep along the back of his neck and into his cheeks and, for a fleeting moment, he wondered how high on her lists of priorities Michelle Leverton had placed fidelity. The idea was followed at once by a sense of regretful inevitability that at some time in the future Edward Newsome might find himself alone and deprived of love from either of the women who sought to claim him as their own.

"You spoke to Edward this afternoon, Mr Rathe," Michelle said now, as he handed over the money for the drinks. "He said you'd been fishing for Elizabeth."

He was irritated rather than disgusted by her seemingly confrontational manner, which seemed at odds with her attractive and tasteful appearance. "If I was doing any fishing, Miss Leverton, I was doing it for myself."

"Why?"

The eternal question which Rathe had asked himself so many times before. Why did he get involved in matters which weren't his concern? An image of a hanging, innocent man and the gravestone which Rathe visited so often flashed across his mind, as though it was the obvious answer to the question, but Rathe could not believe that what drove him into these situations was something so transparent. But when he tried to find a more complex answer, his mind refused to co-operate.

"I have my reasons," was his reply.

"I don't see why the lives of people you don't know would have anything to do with those reasons."

Rathe turned round on his stool and faced her. "If someone told you they thought they were about to be murdered, would you walk away just because they were a stranger?"

She gave it almost no thought. "Probably. I'd tell them to go to the police and move on."

She saw it as a sensible option; Rathe could only see it as evidence of the difference between the two of them, although he felt no need to say so. Instead, he sipped some wine but it did nothing to sweeten the sour taste in his mouth.

"I know the answer to this, Miss Leverton," he said, unable to keep the regret from his voice, "but do you think Edward Newsome wants to kill his wife?"

She drank some of the Bacardi, not quite draining the glass, and looked at him out of the corner of his eye. "Of course not."

"Is that an honest reply, or a biased one?"

"Honest," she declared, with perhaps more emphasis than it required. "You've met him. Do you think he could kill someone?"

Rathe raised his eyebrows, taken aback by the question which he had not anticipated and, more crucially, which he had not yet considered. Now, he thought back to Edward Newsome and tried to imagine him sliding a knife between Elizabeth's ribs, or placing a gun to her temple, his hands around her throat, his silk tie around her neck, a pillow across her face, crushing her skull with the nearest object to hand. No, he could imagine none of those things. That was the truth of it, now that he confronted the question. But, in equal measure, he could envisage Newsome grinding up a bottle of sleeping pills and stirring them into a warm drink or a glass of wine. He could imagine that without any difficulty.

"I think so," he said, with his eyes drilling into hers. "Yes. Unfortunately, I think I can imagine anybody doing it in the right circumstances."

"Even yourself?"

"Possibly."

She smiled at him and drank some more. "What a sad way

of looking at the world."

"Perhaps it's just that I see the world differently to you." He sipped some of his own wine. She was already nearing the end of her drink and he had barely begun his. He saw no reason to try to keep up with her. "Are you going to tell me why you think I'm wrong about Edward?"

"It's just impossible to believe," she said, in a tone of voice which sounded as if she was tired of having to repeat it, making Rathe wonder how often she had had to say it to herself before she was convinced of it. "How well do you know him, Mr Rathe?"

"I only met him briefly at a party last night," he confessed. "I spoke to him for the first time at lunch today."

She sneered at the confession with a sly grin. "People think he's uncaring, unfeeling, cold. Did you think that when you met him?"

"I can understand why people might think it."

"That's because you only see what he shows you. We all do that, don't we? We're different people to our lovers than we are to our colleagues, or even to our parents. Edward doesn't show you the love, tenderness, intelligence, humour that he shows me because he's got no reason to. He isn't a man who wears his heart on his sleeve. I look at you and I see what I think is a sadness in your eyes. You've got the look of a man who lives under a heavy burden. I don't know what it is and I don't want to, but Edward would never give any hint of it if he was carrying it instead of you. Just because a man doesn't display his emotions, and keeps them private for himself, doesn't mean he doesn't have them."

Rathe nodded, despite himself. "Fair point, duly accepted. So are you telling me that he's too sensitive to be able to commit murder?"

She drained her glass and ordered another, Rathe waving away the offer of a second. "It's much easier to believe that his wife is delusional. You know about the loss of their child, of course. She's never got over it. You only have to speak to her to know that."

"People do seem to think she has some sort of obsession with death because of it, which is fuelling these fantasies of murder."

Michelle stirred the ice in her new Bacardi. "I don't say what she suffered isn't tragic. And I don't say I'm proud of what Edward and I have done to her. But she needs help with her grief, Mr Rathe, and her refusal to do anything about it has driven Edward away."

"Cause and effect, is that it?"

She looked at him, her expression daring him to contradict her. "Put bluntly, yes."

"So, if their daughter hadn't have died, Edward wouldn't have wanted to leave Elizabeth for you?"

"If she'd got help when he asked her to, he might not have. But who can tell for sure? Perhaps when we met, we would have happened anyway, even if the death of their daughter hadn't been a factor one way or the other."

Rathe was silent for a moment before he made any further comment. "Forgive me, Miss Leverton, if I say that sounds like a callous and cynical attempt to absolve yourself of any blame at all."

Her eyes flashed fire. "Who the hell do you think you are, you sanctimonious bastard? Wading into people's lives without knowing the first thing about any of them and making judgements like that about people you've never met? What gives you the right?"

Rathe did not look at her during her outburst. He was conscious of other people's attention turning to him but he ignored the temptation to return the stares, disregarding the burn of embarrassment on the back of his neck.

"What gives you and Edward Newsome the right to

indulge in your own selfish desires and justify your actions by blaming a broken woman's personal grief?" His voice controlled his anger, but it was far from easy. "What give you the right to sleep at night under the blanket of assurance that you have done nothing wrong when the one woman who truly has done nothing culpable lies awake in turmoil, grief, and fear? Don't pretend to me that you're insulted by what I say, Miss Leverton, and don't presume to be possessed of any sense of moral cleanliness. Because you don't have the right to either response to what I've said."

He rose from his stool and pushed away his half-drunk wine. She had offered no reaction to his words but she had had the affront to continue to stare at him whilst he delivered his judgement on her. He had expected, perhaps even hoped, that he might shame her into looking away, but he had failed. Even now, standing over her as he was, she was not prepared to avert her glare from him.

"If I thought for one moment I'd succeed," he continued, "I'd do my best to convince Elizabeth Newsome to divorce her husband so that you could have him. Because, for me, you deserve each other. And if I'm any judge of character, even if you did get him to yourself, I'd say that sooner or later Edward would be left alone, once your interest in him waned. And I think that would be pretty quickly. But it's academic, isn't it? Because I doubt Elizabeth will divorce him under any circumstances. And why do you think that is, Miss Leverton?"

He had leaned forward so that his face was only inches from hers. The sudden claustrophobia of the situation choked her but, simultaneously, it seemed to compel her to reply.

"Her bloody religion," she spat with a gasp. "That's why."

But Rathe was shaking his head. "No, you don't understand at all. It's not so much the religion, Miss

Leverton, but the strength of character in Elizabeth Newsome which drives her to preserve her faith when it would be so much easier to betray it. Ask yourself whether you'd have the same fortitude as that in similar circumstances, to be able to live with a clear conscience, even at the price of your own sanity and happiness."

Michelle Leverton set her jaw in defiance. "Of course I would."

Rathe gritted his teeth in contempt, hissing out his reply. "Really? Then do the right thing for all concerned and walk away from the Newsomes and don't look back. Let them mend and heal, even if it means you're temporarily broken. Try to find half the dignity and courage this so-called delusional woman has and do what you have to do to make this situation right. Why don't you get yourself another drink, Miss Leverton, and have a think about that?"

Even as he walked away from her, Michelle Leverton couldn't take her eyes off Anthony Rathe. Once he had disappeared in the crowd and she had seen the bar doors swing open and closed, she still stared at the space where he had been, as though she could still see him sitting there in judgement of her. His words echoed in her brain, even when she tried to use the hum of camaraderie and the background music of the bar to drown them out. In the end, she realised that she might only silence his words in her head by drowning them in more Bacardi. She finished her drink and ordered another, disregarding the quickening of her pulse and the stares of strangers which bore into her, seemingly from all directions.

But she could deal with the staring and the increasing sense of drunkenness. She might have another drink after this one, and another after that, if she felt like it, and screw them all. Let them stare. She didn't care; but she did care about the fact that it was easier to swallow more drink than it was to admit to herself that Anthony Rathe had been right. She knew what the right thing to do was, just as she knew that she could never do it, because it would mean accepting defeat. And she never lost.

Yes; Rathe had been right about her. Somehow, even in that short space of time he had known her, he had got the measure of her and she was shocked by it, perhaps even terrified by hearing it said so bluntly and so honestly to her. So she ordered another drink without starting the one she had, because she knew that the only way to bury the truth he had hissed at her was to silence it in those endless cold glasses which seemed to stretch out in front of her, waiting to do their job.

* * *

Three days later, Rathe's mobile delivered a summons. It was a call from Cook: short, terse, and tinged with suppressed anger. "A car's on its way for you. Be ready in 10 minutes." Nothing more, nothing less. The journey seemed to last for ever and it had nothing to do with distance or time: it was the unease which Rathe felt in every pore of his body, an ominous sense of tragedy which was complemented by the anxiety within him at Cook's brusque, hostile tone of voice.

He was driven to a modest but respectable house in one of the northern suburbs of the city. The details of the house and the area were to some extent lost on him, because he was distracted by the initial procedural trappings of murder. The flashing blue lights, the ghoulish spectres of the forensic officers and their soulless protective suits, the lengths of official tape cordoning off the house and its small, neatly trimmed lawn. Sitting in that taciturn, junior detective's car, Rathe felt as though he was being delivered back to the scene of a crime he had himself committed, but the notion was a ludicrous and momentary fantasy, brought on by the confusion of his situation and the rapid series of thoughts which were hurtling across the landscape of his mind. He had feared murder as soon as Cook had called, but this house was not the place he had expected the crime to have been committed. This was not the house he had been in three days previously; it wasn't the house in which he had talked to Elizabeth Newsome about the fear of death and the cruel depths of grief. This place, this home which had been converted into a crime scene, was a house Rathe did not know.

He was led up the garden path, his mind silently laughing at the irony of the fact. He wondered how many of those paths he had been led up, and down, over the last few days. As his brain regained some of its control over itself, he began to think that he knew whose house and whose murder he had been summoned to discuss. If he was right, he knew that there would be an easily identifiable suspect and, if guilty, he wondered how far down how many garden paths that apparently delusional woman had taken him. He had believed her; unable to explain why, but he had believed her. And all the time, he thought now she had been laughing at him, manipulating him, drawing him into her net of deceit and revenge. And he had fallen for it, tumbled down to his knees in the face of her pleas for help, guilelessly accepting her version of events whilst she sniggered at his unwitting co-operation in her plot, setting him up as a character witness in the hope of some sort of insanity defence. It was all so clear, so obvious, but he hadn't seen it until this moment. By the time he reached the front door of the murder house, Anthony Rathe had almost no thoughts beyond his own fury, not only at his own gullibility but also at Elizabeth Newsome's treachery.

Cook was in the hallway when Rathe walked through the front door. For a moment, the two of them looked at each other as though they were strangers, two gladiators awaiting a tournament with dispassionate apathy for the other's life.

"Where is she?" asked Rathe.

"Who?"

"Michelle Leverton." Rathe rolled his eyes around the hallway. "This is her house, isn't it? She's in here somewhere, lying dead. Right? That's why I'm here."

Cook shook his head. "You're here so I can tell you to your face what a bloody fool you've been. What do you think you're doing, Rathe? You got lucky on a couple of cases over the past few months, I'll give you that. But that doesn't give you the right to play with people's lives."

I'm not playing with anybody's life," countered Rathe.

"I told you not to have anything to do with Elizabeth Newsome," barked Cook, his spittle flecking Rathe's cheek with scorn. "I warned you. Christ, I came close to begging you. But you couldn't help yourself, could you?"

"I'm not responsible for whatever's happened here," snarled Rathe. "I refuse to be held accountable for it. Not this time, not again."

"You've stirred up the shit and a girl has died." Cook pointed to the living room door. "In there. She's dead. Because you couldn't keep your nose out of someone else's business. That's the reality of what's happened here, Rathe, and if that's not your fault then I don't know whose it is."

Rathe straightened his back, his eyes refusing to betray how much the words had stung. "Is that why you brought me here, Cook? To tell me that?"

"Yes." Cook turned his back. "You can go home now."

Rathe grabbed the inspector's shoulders and spun him around. There was a look on the detective's face which was a strange marriage of surprise and anger, but Rathe ignored it. "No. I'm going into that living room, Inspector. I'm going in there to do what I can to prove that Elizabeth Newsome is a killer, because somebody has to do that while you stand out here whinging about me trying to understand something which was dumped in my lap without me wanting it or asking for it."

Without giving any of the official detectives a chance to stop him, Rathe threw open the door and was inside. Almost at once, his eyes were drawn to the ugly creature which lay sprawled in the centre of the room. He knew that it had been a woman, even an attractive one, with whom he had had an uncomfortable drink only a few nights ago, but now it was nothing but a tangle of motionless limbs and cold, dead flesh. What had once been Michelle Leverton was dressed in a set of silk pyjamas, which had ridden up her forearms and shins, revealing the once delicately pale but now unnaturally white skin. Her dark hair had fallen half across her face, so that only one of her deep blue eyes glared up at him, like the eye of an old doll in a Victorian story of the supernatural. Her hair had been dyed a slight red, Rathe remembered, but the most distinctive red about her now was the blood which had seeped from the wounds to her abdomen and arms, spattering her face and throat. The knife which had inflicted them was lying by the door, a long teardrop of blood sobbing from the tip of the blade. He had not liked the woman on instinct, but Rathe could not help but view the scene with sadness at what could only be described now as a waste of life.

Rathe felt Cook at his shoulder before the inspector had uttered a word. "Probably best I keep an eye on you while you're in here. Make sure you don't bugger up anything else."

Rathe smiled, briefly and privately. "I'll try not to make your job any harder than it is already, Inspector."

"How did you know this was Leverton's house?"

"The tone of your voice when you summoned me here suggested something significant had happened and you weren't happy about it. Wasn't too hard to say that it had to involve the Newsome woman in some way, especially since you and I haven't spoken to each other since the night of your party. In that whole scenario, only Elizabeth or Michelle could be considered likely victims of murder: Elizabeth by her husband, Michelle by Elizabeth. This house isn't Elizabeth's, so... "

Cook considered that for a minute. "So, it was a guess."

Another brief, private smile passed over Rathe's lips. "I suppose there's no doubt Elizabeth did it."

Cook walked past Rathe, into the centre of the room. The dead girl lay between them like a guilty secret. "Not in my head. Part of the reason I was so angry with you. Never nice knowing you've got to arrest one of your personal friends."

"Happened before, has it?"

"Once." But Cook was not about to give any more details of that part of his past. "She must have finally snapped and let out all her grief about her daughter and the affair. That accounts for the number of wounds to the body."

Rathe had been counting them. "There's more than a dozen. Some don't seem as deep as others."

"Doctor reckons that's down to the struggle. Some of the blows won't have made any discernible contact if Leverton was defending herself and trying to deflect the blade. I'm quoting him there, more or less."

"Time of death?"

"About eleven last night – the medic's turn to guess. He'll confirm when he's had a look inside her."

"No witnesses, I suppose?" asked Rathe.

Cook shrugged. "Not yet. Door to door's under way, but nothing worth getting worked up about yet."

"Someone came in, unseen, and did this... "

But, as he spoke, Rathe felt a familiar sensation along his spine, as though an invisible spider of doubt was crawling up his back. He was looking around the room, not seeing things which he knew he should be seeing. The details of the place passed before his eyes, none of them telling him what he wanted to know. The bookcase filled with the classics – Austen, Hardy, Collins, Dickens, the Brontes; the smaller set of shelves filled with poetry, both Romantic and modern; the extensive and diverse collection of CDs; the empty bottles filled with small stones and shells which adorned the mantelpiece and the small window sill; the vase of lilies which stood to the side of the marble hearth, their crisp whiteness so apt in the face of violent death. But none of the things he saw helped him understand what it was which seemed so wrong about the room.

"No sign of any break in," Cook was saying. "So she knew her killer, obviously."

"What's in those glasses?" Rathe asked, pointing to two large tumblers which were side by side on a small side table.

"Waiting to be analysed, but it looks like Coke."

Rathe walked over to the glasses and knelt down. Carefully, as though to touch them might signal his own death, he craned his neck so that the tip of his long nose was only a hair's breadth from the rim of the glasses. He sniffed each one, his brows furrowing in confusion as he did so. He sniffed the contents of the glasses again, paused, and then repeated the action one last time. He rose to his feet and began to pace the room.

Cook pointed to Michelle's body. "Stab wounds, remember? Lots of them. No reason to suspect any poison, so why are you going round smelling stuff?"

Rathe turned to face him, his thoughts seemingly so far away that he could barely register Cook's presence in the room. "That night, at your party... Elizabeth Newsome was drinking wine."

"Drinks too much of it," muttered Cook. "Doesn't help much with her head trouble."

Rathe wasn't listening. "Is there any wine in this house?"

Cook shook his head. "Not found any. Loads of rum though."

"Bacardi… " Rathe's eyes brightened and seemed to come back into focus and he looked around the room as though seeing it for the first time. Now, the shelves of books, the CD collection, and the stone-filled bottles sang to him like the choruses of those operas Cook seemed so desperate for Rathe to like. "Bacardi, the wounds, and the furniture in this room. These glasses on the table."

Cook was looking around him, his lips curled in confusion and his eyes widened in misunderstanding. "What about them?"

"There are witnesses after all, Cook, crucial witnesses," Rathe said. "And they're all in this room. We were wrong about Elizabeth Newsome. She isn't a killer."

"What are you on about?" hissed Cook, stepping forward to confront the younger man who stood now with a look of clear perception on his face.

"Edward Newsome was never plotting murder," Rathe said. "All that really was in Elizabeth's mind. You were right about her and I was wrong. But we've both misunderstood what happened here last night."

Cook put his hands in his pockets, if only to stop himself from shaking Rathe into talking sense. "And you reckon you understand it all now, do you?"

"I think so," replied Rathe.

"Any chance of telling me?"

Rathe moved towards the door. "On the way."

"On the way where?"

"To get the truth." Rathe pointed around the room. "Although it's all in this room, Cook: all the truth is in here. And these books, these ornaments, those tumblers on the table, the wounds to the body – they all prove it beyond reasonable doubt… "

* * *

Elizabeth Newsome sprang out of her chair, an expression of defiance on her face. "No. It's not true. I won't believe it."

Rathe turned to the broken figure huddled in the chair next to him, limbs shaking and head bowed, sobbing softly. "Tell her it's not true. Tell her you didn't kill Michelle Leverton."

Sean Newsome lifted his tear-stained eyes from his hands and looked up at Rathe first and then across to his parents. Elizabeth was still standing, her hands clenched to her lips and her glare fixed in a terrified plea with her son to convince her that the nightmare was not real. His father had remained seated, leaning forward with his hands on his knees, his lips clenched against the horror of it all, the only sign of visible emotion being the tears in his eyes glistening against the lenses of his spectacles. Sean looked to the rough policeman, standing with his head tilted back, daring the boy to lie; then he looked at the altogether kinder face of the man who had done most of the talking. His eyes were calm, soothing, and his voice held Sean in a blanket of assurance that the truth could be told without fear.

"Just tell them the truth, Sean," Rathe said. "It's the only thing we have left now and it needs to be said. Trust me, please, and tell us what happened."

Sean faltered, swallowing his fear, before lowering his head once more. "I've not done anything wrong."

Rathe sighed quietly at the lie, as though accepting that his efforts so far had been in vain and it was time to withdraw any chance of mercy. "If you don't do it, Sean, I'll have to do it for you. And that isn't what I want to do."

"I haven't done anything wrong," the boy repeated, his voice muffled by his hands and tears.

Rathe walked towards the boy's father. "I owe you an

155

apology, Mr Newsome. I took your wife's fears at face value, because I couldn't believe that she would approach a stranger with such a serious allegation if it wasn't true. What I had underestimated was just how deeply her grief over your daughter's death had overwhelmed her. I can see now that you were right when you said she had a pre-occupation with death and I understand that it has clouded her view of things. I did believe you at first," he continued, turning to Elizabeth, "but the time has come now for the truth. Your husband doesn't want you dead. He may not want to be married to you, but he doesn't want to harm you either. You have to accept the help he's offered you in the past. You have to deal with your grief over Jane."

Elizabeth forced herself to look from her son to her husband. "I was sure you wanted to kill me."

Newsome rose from his chair is a flurry of distress which seemed to overwhelm him without warning. "And look where that certainty has got us, Elizabeth! Look at the state of us all now!"

Elizabeth cowered at the words, raising her palms to her face as if in an effort to block them out. Cook put a hand on Newsome's shoulder and eased him back into his chair. Rathe waited for the room to fall silent once more before taking any further action. He walked across the room to the sideboard which he had seen on his first visit to the house. He pointed initially to the crucifix on the wall and then he picked up the rosary which was laid out in front of the family photographs. He turned them around in his fingers as he spoke, the beads clicking in an irregular rhythm.

"You despise these as much as your father does, don't you, Sean?" he asked. "The ties of faith that bind your family together are the same ties which are forcing your family to fall apart. Isn't that right? Because without your religion, your parents could just divorce. But, because of that religion, you see your mum going mad and your dad living in misery, hating her and his life here more and more each day. And seeing these beads and that cross on the wall just reminds you of the truth of that situation every passing day, doesn't it, Sean?"

The boy didn't reply, but his tears grew in intensity which was, perhaps, the only answer Rathe needed.

"Your dad told me about the time you heard your mum accuse him of trying to kill her," Rathe said, his voice gentle once more, "after she'd found the sleeping pills. He told me about how you have a habit of walking into a room without anyone knowing it. You did just that when I was here the other day, remember? But you hadn't just walked in, had you? You'd been outside for a while, silently listening to us. You'd overheard me talking to your mum, just as you'd overheard her accusing your dad. And you heard her telling a stranger about her fears that your dad was going to kill her. Didn't you?"

This time, the boy fought for his voice. "Yeah… "

Rathe replaced the rosary and moved behind the chair in which Sean was sitting. He leaned over the back of it, his voice soft against the boy's ear, the same sense of assurance of the safety of truth coming back into it. "How did that make you feel, Sean, hearing what your mum was saying to me? And what she said to your dad that time?"

Sean twisted in his seat like a snake under attack. His eyes flashed fire at Rathe and his lips were curled back in a snarl of bitterness. "Hate. All I felt was hate. For her… for the bitch who'd screwed everything up."

Rathe looked across at the Newsomes. Elizabeth's eyes had grown wide with shock, her jaw dropping open in mute and fearful disbelief. Edward rose from his chair and turned his back on the scene, his hands raised to his head in frantic but futile pain.

157

"Her name was Michelle," said Rathe.

"I know what her fucking name was," hissed Sean.

"She recognised you when you went to her house, let you in, offered you a drink?"

"Can of Coke. It was all she had. I hate Coke."

Rathe almost smiled at the petulance of the detail. "She drank it with Bacardi. I could smell it in one glass on that table, but there was no trace of it in the other. That one just had... Coke, pure and simple. Your mum drinks wine, but Michelle had none of that to offer. So, if it had been your mum there last night, with no wine to drink, would Michelle have offered her Coke? I don't think so. She'd have offered your mum a coffee, I reckon. An adult wouldn't offer another adult a soft drink if no stronger drink was available. But a kid... ? When there was Coke in the fridge... "

Cook felt it was time to speak. "And then there were the wounds to the victim. Some deep, some not. The pathologist took that as evidence of a struggle, the shallow wounds being inflicted as the victim was trying to swipe away the blade."

Rathe interjected. "But the bookshelves and the ornaments in the room were all in place. Nothing had been knocked over, spilled, or disturbed. There wasn't any struggle, was there, Sean? You stabbed Michelle once, deeply, and as she fell to the floor dying, you took out all your anger on her. But you wore yourself out quickly and, at your age, you're not as strong as you think you are."

A long, tragic silence fell over the room. After some moments, the sound of crying became evident and Rathe knew without looking across the room that the last piece of Elizabeth Newsome's world had come crashing down around her. He put his hand on Sean Newsome's shoulder, but the boy flicked it away with a twist of his body.

"I just wanted them to be happy again," Sean said. His

voice had lost much of its fear. It was as though he had found some new form of strength once he had been forced to confront his own guilt. "Mum and Dad – I just wanted them to be happy. Wanted things to be back how they were, at first. But then, I just wanted them to be OK and it didn't matter no more if they weren't together, just as long as they were happy."

"I can understand that," said Rathe.

Sean glared at him. "You don't understand shit. I hated that bitch for everything, yeah? She was taking my dad away from my mum and me, right? And I hated her for it. I wish she'd just leave us alone, leave my dad alone, and let him see that really – deep down – he loved my mum and not her. But she wasn't going nowhere, was she?"

Edward Newsome turned to face his son. "She loved me, Sean. Can't you understand that?"

The boy raged in his chair, his knuckles whitening under the pressure of his fingers clutching the arms rests. "No, I don't understand it! Why did she have to choose you? Why couldn't she have someone else, anyone else? Why you?"

Elizabeth Newsome made a move towards her son, her instinct now to protect and comfort him, no matter what atrocity he had committed. Her eyes and arms and heart reached out to him, but they were stopped in their tracks by Sean's arm lashing out towards her, his finger pointing at her like the accusatory sword of judgement

"Don't come near me!" he screamed. "Don't you understand yet, Mum? I hated that woman for what she'd done, yes, but I hated you for not letting Dad go! She wouldn't leave us alone, but you could have let him be happy. You could have let him walk away and be OK. We could have managed that, couldn't we? You just made it worse. You and your bastard religion made it worse. Because it was more important to you than any of us being happy."

Sean had got up from his chair and gone to confront his mother. Rathe, uncertain what was about to happen, had felt compelled to follow the boy, in case he was obliged to pull Sean away from his mother. Rathe could see that Cook had had a similar thought, because he moved behind Elizabeth, ready to catch her if she moved unwisely. Edward Newsome remained motionless, the situation beyond his control.

"If we couldn't be happy together," Sean was saying between choking, rasping sobs, "we could have been happy apart. Why couldn't we have just been like that? But you wouldn't let it happen, Mum. It was because of you!"

Elizabeth reached out a hand, tentatively, but withdrew it almost at once, as she saw the venom and hate spill out of her son's eyes, nose, and throat. To anyone else, she thought stupidly, all that malice might look like tears of sadness.

Rathe held out his own hand towards her, forbidding her to move any closer to her son. Now, he was between them, like a bridge between hatred and grief. "You hated Michelle first, Sean, and then you hated your mum's faith. Between them, they ripped your family to pieces when really it should have been putting itself back together after Jane's death."

"The way you saw it, son," Cook said, "the girl and the religion were both to blame."

"But you knew you couldn't hope to destroy one," Rathe concluded, "so you murdered the other."

"Right." Sean looked across at him and then back to his mother. "Right… "

Elizabeth dropped her hands in defeat. Her eyes drifted around the room, barely making sense of it all, before they came to rest on the crucifix on the wall. Through her tears, she managed to find the words which she knew she should not say but which she likewise knew she could not keep inside.

"Sean, I can't betray God… "

The son she had lost lifted his head and glared into her face. "There is no God, Mum. If there is, I hate Him."

* * *

Rathe and Cook were sitting at the bottom of the garden, looking at the fish. There was a bottle of single malt on the stone flags between them. Each man cradled a generous tumbler full of the stuff, but only Rathe's was tempered with a single, large ice cube.

"Have you heard from either of them?" he asked.

Cook nodded. "Edward's staying with Elizabeth. She offered him the divorce, but he knew she didn't mean it, so he refused. Reckons they've got a reason to stay together now."

"Meaning Sean?"

"Need to be there for him, that's what they say." Cook sipped the whisky. "If it weren't for them both… "

Rathe listened to the ice in his glass crack under the influence of the amber liquid. "Edward told me that Elizabeth never thought about the impact her delusions had on Sean."

"And he was right."

"Do you think he thought of the effect his affair with Michelle Leverton had on the kid?"

Cook considered the question for a few seconds in the stillness of the night which hung around them. Finally, he decided that the best answer he could give was no answer at all. Rathe thought he might know what the reply was which had formed in the detective's head and, for a reason he could not define, Rathe felt certain it was the same negative answer which had taken shape in his own mind.

"Maybe they are both to blame, then," said Rathe. "Perhaps none of them were ever truly innocent."

"We're only ever responsible for ourselves. No one else."

"Do you believe that?" asked Rathe. He lifted his glass and

161

drank. "Or is it this stuff talking?"

"No idea," mumbled Cook, drinking some of his own whisky.

They remained in silence for a little longer, neither one knowing what to say, but both wanting some words to be spoken. They allowed a few more seconds to pass, watching the fish move amongst the darkness of the water.

"It would have happened anyway," said Cook, at last. "Michelle Leverton's death, I mean... Sean Newsome would have killed her even if you hadn't gone poking about in the mud. Right?"

"I expect he would, yes."

Cook exhaled some air. "It's thoughts like that which make me glad I've got my fish."

Rathe nodded and drank his whisky. "It's thoughts like that which make me glad I don't like opera."

The Quick and the Dead

The Quick and the Dead

Anthony Rathe had been sitting alone with his memories for the last half an hour. He had been provided with the glass of Pinot Noir which he had ordered but he had not tasted it as yet. He had hardly registered the waiter placing it down in front of him, although he knew that he had mumbled some words of gratitude. The people who passed his table barely glanced at him, as though the sight of a man drinking alone in a hotel bar was something so common that it failed to arouse anybody's curiosity. Whether that said anything about the modern world or not was a question which Rathe might have enjoyed debating at any other time in his life, but now he gave it even less attention that those same people gave him. His mind was elsewhere, drifting back over time, taking reminiscences and reliving them as though they were his reality of this moment, as though months and years had not drifted away since the events which he now remembered had actually taken place.

It had been the phone call which had started it, a call which he had had no right to expect and certainly no reason to anticipate. Her voice on the other end of the line had brought Rathe's past crashing into his present with such a fierce tidal wave of memory that he almost failed to under-stand anything she had said to him. He had stammered questions about why she was phoning him after all this time, about what she wanted from him, about whether she had known how much he had missed her, or how deeply she had affected him when they had spoken last. But she had not been prepared to discuss any of it. The call had to be brief, she said, and all it could be for now was a request she had to make of him which he would either accept or reject. The call was to be that simple. No more, no less. She had asked him

165

to meet her that afternoon in the Artesian bar of the Langham Hotel at three and, as he reflected now that he always would have, he had accepted the invitation without hesitation.

The choice of bar was no accident. The first time he had taken Alice Villiers out for a drink, he had taken her to the Artesian. Eager to impress, with all the arrogance of those days demanding that nothing less than extravagance would do to demonstrate his worth, he had ordered cocktails and led her to the mauve settees which were placed beneath the grand chandeliers which descended from the high ceiling. He and Alice had stayed there for hours, their plans to move on for food or a different bar were soon forgotten. They had drunk, they had chatted, they had laughed. They had forgotten that outside the long, broad windows of the hotel bar, London had a life which it was living still, despite them, no matter how much they might have thought that they were the only people alive at that moment. How much champagne they had drunk, he could not remember now; but he could recall Alice's horror at the bill and his casual, yet drunken superiority as he shrugged off the three figure sum with an easy smile and pompous glint in his eyes.

Those days seemed so far away. He sat now with the solitary glass of wine in front of him. The settees were still mauve and the chandeliers were still grand, but the Anthony Rathe who sat in their company would have been unrecognisable to the conceited version of himself who had blithely paid that tab and walked out of the bar with the girl on his arm and the world at his feet. Now, the settee seemed pale when once it had seemed so vivid. The chandeliers were ostentatious, rather than magnificent. And the wine sat untouched where once the champagne had flowed.

He was watching the entrance to the bar, scrutinising every face which passed through it, half-afraid that he might

166

not recognise her when she walked into the room, or that he would be so pre-occupied with his memories that his brain would not process her face in time and that she would see the blank, soulless shell of the man she once knew and turn on her heels and vanish from his life once more. As it was, the moment she walked in, scanning the room for his face, Rathe felt every other patron of the bar, every other person in the room with him, fade away into nothing. For a split second, he forgot once again that London had a life which it lived for itself, a life which had nothing to do with him, because in his world there were only two people alive.

Rathe felt that he had changed in the six months since she had last seen him. Mentally, he was sure he had. The Marsden disgrace had stripped his soul bare and left it to rebuild itself. It had done just that, but it had never been the same. It had lost the bravado, the self-belief, the innate confidence that water could be turned into wine with a clever twist of words and flash of legal trickery. It was a change for the better, Rathe knew that, but with it he felt sure there had been a change in his physical appearance. He felt his dark eyes had become heavier, weighed down by something he might have told himself was regret, the spark of confidence extinguished in them. He felt his lips had become perma-nently pursed, the external display of an inner pain. He felt that with the loss of his arrogance, a fire had gone out of his cheeks, leaving them paler, more sallow, as though his entire expression was a ghost of its former self.

If he had changed, two things struck him at once. Firstly, Alice had not noticed any change in him, because when she spotted him sitting there facing her, she smiled at him and began to move towards him. Secondly, if he had altered in any way over the months which had passed, it was clear to him immediately that those same months had left Alice Villiers entirely unaffected. Her blonde hair still hung over her shoulders, bouncing as she walked, like a field of wheat in a summer breeze. Her features were still curiously feline, not conventionally beautiful but undeniably alluring, their attraction being not in the way they were designed but in the manner in which they held your attention. Her eyes were a vivid green, alert and inquisitive, but with a certain spark of mischief which Rathe remembered would intensify with wine. Her smile now was brief and uncertain, but it brought back to Rathe's mind the almost childish shyness of her full smile, always accompanied with a dip of the head, as though the act of laughing was something for which she expected to be mocked. There had been a small gap in her front teeth, not so wide as to be noticeable, but pretty enough to be heart-breaking when she was forced to display it.

He rose to greet her, uncertain whether he should shake her hand or bend to kiss her cheek. One was too agonisingly formal, the other too obvious a temptation to go further. In the split second before she took the decision out of his hands and offered her cheek for the kiss, Rathe had a foolish, momentary fear that he did not even know what to call her. For all their time together, she had been his Ally, but the past six months had turned them into strangers and such a familiarity seemed in that instant to be unwarranted.

"Thank you for doing this," she said, sitting down and placing her handbag at her feet. "I've no right to ask it of you."

Rathe had no reply, so he pointed to the bar. "Can I get you a drink?"

"Please," she said. The sudden awkwardness of the situation she had forced them into struck her, seemingly for the first time, and she looked around the room, at the bar, and the other guests, just so she didn't have to look Rathe in the eyes. "Wine. White. Any kind."

"Right," he replied, making a move towards the bar.

"Thank you, Anthony," she said softly, and Rathe thought he heard the sound of ice breaking.

The drinks brought, he sat down once more opposite her, conscious that he felt still that her proper place was beside him, but knowing that it was a thought which could only be known to him. He had no idea why she had contacted him now, without any warning, and he had forbidden himself to hope. Instead, he sat in silence, waiting for her to explain, his eyes never once leaving her face. She drank the wine, composing herself, but she found it difficult to look at him. Perhaps, he wondered, his face had altered after all.

"I'm sorry about what happened," Alice said. "I couldn't cope with it."

"I don't suppose I made it easy."

She shook her head. "It wasn't just you. It was the papers, the phone calls, the prying questions."

He knew what she meant. After Kevin Marsden's suicide, Rathe had been approached for comment, the most frequent question being whether he felt any guilt about it. He had responded with typical disdain at the idea. His words were in most of the newspapers and in almost every legal journal. Rathe's fame at the time had made it inevitable that the media would hang on every one of his misjudged, conceited words. When the internal enquiry into the case revealed that Marsden had been innocent, that the evidence had been fabricated as well as circumstantial, Rathe had understood that it had been his own advocacy alone which had made that false and unstable evidence seem undeniable and complete. It was his own rhetoric which had driven the boy to his end and, once he saw the truth of it all, those same condescending words of arrogance came back to haunt Rathe. After that, the requests for comments were made with sneers, the plaudits had become condemnations, and the frailties of the criminal justice system were painted as being

orchestrated by Rathe alone, as though he had been responsible for the police, the jury, and the sentencing simply
because he had made a public display of switching from
defence to prosecution in an effort to win yet more public
glory. The policemen who had fabricated the evidence never
seemed to be approached for any explanation, paid off with
early retirement or premature death by alcohol consumption,
their faces never appeared on television, in print, or online.
That privilege was reserved almost exclusively for Anthony
Rathe.

"You have to do something about it," Alice had said. He
could hear the words now, as clearly as he had heard them
then.

"Do what? What can I say to make them understand?"

She had been intense in her reply. "I don't know, but
anything is better than nothing. Because we can't keep hiding
away from it. You have to get up and do something."

"And if I can't?" he had asked.

"Why can't you?"

And then he had said the words which had given life to a
belief which he felt now that he might never dispel. "Because
maybe they're right. Maybe I am responsible for what
happened to him… "

It had been the beginning of the end. Alice had been
unable to live with his defeatism, his increasingly internal
existence, his deepening sense of shame and regret. When
she had left, he had not blamed her. She had a choice not to
live with his guilt; he had no such option.

"What did you do with yourself?" Alice asked now. "After
I'd gone?"

Rathe shrugged, running his index finger along the rim of
his wine glass. "Drank. For a long time, I drank. Ignored any
phone call that wasn't you."

She didn't need him to say that he must have ignored

every phone call he received then. "We couldn't have survived it, Anthony. Not how we were. How you were."

He didn't have to accept that, but he knew that she was entitled to have her own point of view, so he simply said, "No."

She looked down at her lap. "Has there been anyone else? Since… ?"

He waited for her eyes to return to his before he replied. "No."

She heard the tone of voice, as though the question need never have been asked. "Nor for me."

For a moment, Rathe thought he should reply, but in that same fragment of time, his mind abandoned him and he could think of nothing to say.

"Do you still think it was your fault?" she asked, instead. "What happened to the Marsden kid?"

In the pause which followed, she saw from his expression that the core root of their shattered romance was still alive inside him. As if to register his disapproval, as well as her refusal to try to convince him otherwise, she drank some more of the wine.

Rathe, for the first time, did likewise. "Is this why you asked me here, Alice? To go over all this again?"

The truth was that they had never really gone over any of it, not with any honesty on either side about how it had all made them both feel. Alice had wondered more than once whether she should contact him, but something had always held her back. She had never known precisely what it was, but she had a feeling that it was her own personal sense of shame at abandoning the man she had professed to love at the time when he needed her most. Was that not something about which she should feel guilt? And had that guilt stopped her from confronting the fact that she had walked away from him when he was at his lowest because of some selfish sense of preservation? His tone of voice now made it clear that he did not want to discuss it any further if he could help it. Perhaps his remorse was so profound that it would never leave him; if so, she thought that each day must be a battle for him, an effort to evade his own sense of injustice, so that any reminder of what it was he was trying to bury in his subconscious would be unwelcome.

"No, it's not," she replied, shuffling forward in her chair. "I wanted to talk to somebody about something and I... And I didn't know who else I could trust with it. I suppose you don't think I've any right to say that."

"What is it?" Rathe asked. He remained motionless, resisting the temptation to move closer to her, as she had moved nearer to him.

"The other day I had a phone call from a man called Roger Gilchrist. Ever heard of him?"

"No."

Alice reached down for her handbag and drew from it a folded piece of A4 paper which she handed to Rathe. He took it from her and opened it. He was looking down at a screenshot of the home page from a website. Rathe didn't know much about technology, but he could tell that the site wasn't anything fancy. Its purpose was practical rather than aesthetic. There was a Google map image showing an address near the British Museum, a photo of the London skyline at midnight, and a series of services provided by the company. Several phone numbers and links to Twitter and Facebook. Across the top of the page, there was a series of tabs: "Services"; "Fees & Charges"; "About Us"; "Contact Us"; and so on. Above the tabs was a name: RPG Investigations Ltd.

Rathe handed the paper back to Alice. "Private detectives?"

She nodded. "Gilchrist is the owner, the top man."

"What does a private detective want to speak to you about?"

"He wouldn't tell me," she replied. "He said it was too delicate to talk about on the phone. But he said it was important, personal and private, and he had to see me as soon as I could arrange it."

Rathe frowned, drinking some wine whilst his mind began to stir. "Are you sure it was really him, really Gilchrist?"

Alice nodded. "I said I'd phone him back on the main number on the website. I asked to speak to Gilchrist and my call was put through. When he answered, it was the same voice."

"Did you arrange to meet him?"

"Tomorrow at seven."

"Where?"

"A bar near Westminster Bridge. I wanted a public place."

Rathe nodded, acknowledging the intelligence of her actions. "And you want me to come with you, is that it?"

She smiled, awkwardly. "Moral support."

"Why me? After all this time, Ally, why me?"

She lowered her gaze once more. "I know it's a lot to ask. And it's taking advantage, I can see that too… "

"Then why?"

She looked back to his dark eyes. She never remembered them looking this sad. "Because Gilchrist said it was personal and private, whatever it is he wants to talk about. And nobody knows me like you do. No one ever has."

Rathe felt he ought to try to take her words as flattery, designed to prick his vanity so that he would feel compelled to agree to help her, but he could not bring himself to do it. There was something honest in her eyes, in the delicate tinge of shame in her cheeks for daring to ask him to help her, that he could not accept that she was being manipulative and not candid. Just as he had known he would accept her invitation to the Artesian, he knew that he would accept her plea for support in meeting Roger Gilchrist.

"Of course I'll come," he said, so quietly that she almost didn't hear it.

She fell back into the comfort of the chair, as though the relief at hearing his agreement had exhausted her. She gasped a word of thanks to him but he shrugged it off with a shake of his head. He pointed to her glass and said, "Another?"

She looked back at him and smiled. This time, there was no awkwardness in it, and a measure of warmth had come back into her eyes. Rathe wondered whether there was a similar softening of his own gaze.

"Yes," she said. "But let me buy."

She was on her feet before he could protest. As she walked towards the bar, he held out a hand to stop her.

"Alice, if a private detective gets in touch with you out of the blue," he said; "and I mean you specifically, not just anybody, and if he says he needs to talk to you about a personal matter, and he says he can only do it in person... "

She stared into his eyes, giving a small nod of her head, as though he had put into words the same thoughts which danced around her head and which had given her more hope than she had dared wish for.

"Alice, I think he's found Kirsty... "

* * *

Kirsty Villiers: missing since Christmas 2012. Twenty-two at the time of her disappearance, last seen walking towards the Devil's Gate nightclub in Kensington. Officially still a missing persons case, no body having ever turned up, but nor had there been any new leads. Appeals, campaigns, television interviews, newspaper stories, magazine articles, but all with the same negative result.

Kirsty Villiers on a festive night out one moment;

swallowed up the next by the city which was supposed to be her home.

Rathe had never known Kirsty. She had disappeared three years before he and Alice had met, but it hadn't been long into their relationship that Alice told him the family's darkest sadness. She had kept her summary brief, confining it to dates and basic circumstances, and following that with a dismissive overview of the little which the police had managed to achieve. Rathe had listened with a dutiful concern, but he had not felt any emotional engagement with the facts. Not then. He hadn't known the girl, so it had not been difficult to assure himself that it was neither his loss nor his place to do anything about it. If he remembered correctly now, he had listened and allowed Alice's tears to flow, remaining silent whilst she composed herself, and then changing the subject. When he had met the parents, he had barely registered any sense of grief or loss which they might be feeling. He had been too eager to ensure that he made a notable first impression and that Alice's parents were aware of his past achievements and his future prospects. Beyond his talk about himself, however, the details of that first meal had been hazy even on the following day, let alone three years after the event.

Today, he was a changed Anthony Rathe, he felt sure of that, and it was this alternative version of himself who wondered whether he would approach the subject differently now if he were hearing it for the first time. Would he be more sensitive to the sadness of those photographs which he had once seen in the Villiers's household? Would he recognise the sense of loss which the parents must feel whenever they looked at Kirsty's face, framed in silver or wood? He felt sure he would. Rathe wondered whether the uncertainty of not knowing if a child was alive or dead was not, in its own way, a crueller torment than having to accept that a child is dead, violently or otherwise. He did not feel qualified to give an opinion on that himself, but he knew that in those past years it was a question which he would never have asked, let alone tried to answer.

The memory of himself in those days before the Marsden case were capable of turning him sick.

It was these thoughts, and imaginings like them, which had occupied the majority of his afternoon and evening once Alice Villiers had left his company. They had remained in the Artesian for the duration of that second drink, but they had not mentioned either Kirsty or Roger Gilchrist again, not once Rathe had assured Alice for a final time that he would accompany her to meet the detective. Rathe had taken details of the bar which Alice had chosen for the rendezvous and they had arranged to meet each other outside it at ten to seven.

"I'll be there for quarter to," Rathe had said.

Alice had not replied, but within her she felt something approaching her initial attraction to the man. He was the same, but different. He had changed, certainly, lost his easy confidence and magnetic swagger which once she had found so irresistible, but it had been replaced by an uncertain introspection, an almost awkward sensitivity which impressed her just as deeply but in a different place in her soul. She had the impression that he felt he had let her down in the past and that he could not bear for history to repeat itself. As soon as the thought occurred to her, her mind recalled the name of Kevin Marsden to her and she made a sudden connection between Rathe's approach to the dead boy and her request for help.

He had walked her out of the hotel bar, where she had thanked him again. She had reached up to his cheek, drawing him down slowly, and she had kissed the place where her hand had touched. He had made no response, and she had not expected one, but if she had turned back at any time as she walked away towards Regent Street, she would have seen him standing looking after her, as the world went about its business around his motionless figure.

Rathe spent his afternoon in lonely consideration. He ambled across London and had a look at the offices of RPG Investigations. He was not overly impressed but neither was he appalled. The premises were not exclusive but, likewise, they were not so squalid as to suggest incompetence or unreliability. He sat in a coffee house with a strong, bitter Americano, scrolling through his phone's Google search results on Kirsty Villiers. The images of her face which had been used in all the media coverage confronted him at once. He was not surprised to find that his memory of Kirsty had been woefully inadequate. Her hair was dark, where Alice's was blonde, but the eyes shared that clear, emerald intensity. She was attractive, Rathe was in no doubt about that, but her appeal was different to Alice's. Kirsty was more convention-ally beautiful, her lips more prone to pout as well as smile, and her habit of looking at the camera almost side-on suggested some aspirations for the screen or the catwalk. Alice's attraction was in her subtlety, her diffidence, and her inability to see that she was beautiful. From what he could tell from these photos, however unfair a basis that might be to judge, Rathe was sure Kirsty Villiers had known how stunning people would say she was. Alice, he knew, would never be so sure of her own beauty to be able to take it for granted.

The articles he found on Kirsty told him very little about the circumstances of her disappearance beyond what he could remember Alice telling him all those years ago. Kirsty had been on a Christmas night out with friends. Cocktail bars, music, dancing, taxi home with or without a takeaway, depending on her mood and her body's requirements. She had got separated from the group of friends by a need for more money, so she had gone to a cash machine further down the road from the Devil's Gate club. One friend had said she would come with her, but Kirsty had said there was no need. In hindsight, the friend knew she should have insisted, but at the time she had taken Kirsty at her word. The police had ascertained that Kirsty had withdrawn £100 from the cash machine and the CCTV in the area showed her doing it. The grainy image on the footage and the entry on her online banking statement were the last pieces of physical evidence of Kirsty Villiers's existence in the world because she had not been seen since.

Rathe took a moment to consider the friend. Not surprisingly, she had been interviewed more times than anybody else in the group who were out that night and Rathe wondered how she felt now about her decision to let Kirsty go off alone. He thought about how often she might lie awake, wondering if things might have been different if she had told Kirsty she was coming with her for money, no matter what anyone else said about it. He could not be sure but he suspected she had let that unanswerable question loiter in her mind for some considerable time. It might linger there still, of course, and Rathe could not help but think how quickly a bad decision could crumble into a sense of guilt.

The conclusion of his researches was predictably vague. He could not hope to solve a disappearance with a couple of Google searches and some introspective thoughts when a dedicated police team had failed to turn up any clue after a major enquiry. Nevertheless, that evening, as he sat with a glass of Merlot in the company of Mahler, he reminded himself that some new information must have come to light. Roger Gilchrist was proof enough of that. But it was useless to speculate and, for the rest of the evening and much of the following day, Anthony Rathe gave no more thought to

Kirsty Villiers, although he was unable to prevent his mind from detaching itself entirely, or at all, from the past memories and restored contact which he had made with her sister.

* * *

By quarter past seven the following evening, Rathe had made up his mind. He had been outside the bar at quarter to the hour, as arranged, but when the time for Alice to arrive had come and gone, Rathe had found himself with a dilemma. It did not take him long to determine that going into the bar alone was not a viable option. For one thing, he had no idea what Roger Gilchrist looked like and he had no way of being able to guess which one out of the many patrons of the place would be him. For another, it was not Anthony Rathe whom Gilchrist was expecting to meet, so there was no reason why he would speak to Rathe alone in any event. It was Alice alone to whom Gilchrist wanted to speak. But she had not shown up for the meeting.

Without any more thought being given to abandoning Gilchrist, Rathe hailed a taxi and gave Alice's address as his destination. Let Gilchrist sit alone and draw his own conclusions, thought Rathe; when it was obvious she was not going to show, the detective surely would have enough presence of mind to contact her the following morning and demand an explanation. Gilchrist could be left to his own devices. For now, Rathe's mind was more concerned with the reason for Alice's failure to keep her appointment. With a possible lead in her sister's disappearance in sight, Alice would surely be eager to find out all she could from Gilchrist. And yet she had not shown up. That conflict of her own interests was the reason Rathe spent the entire taxi journey with an ominous sense of dread knotting up in his stomach.

Alice's house was in darkness. It was the last property in a small cul-de-sac, sheltered from the main road by a fringe of trees which lined the street. It was a modest but respectable area, a haven of secluded peace in the heart of London, and Rathe felt that the increasing darkness of his purpose ought to have no place in the calm, suburban tranquillity of the estate. He waited for the taxi to disappear before he approached the house. He knocked once on the front door, but got no reply. He did not bother looking through the front window because he had already noted that the Venetian blinds were drawn. Instead, he walked down the narrow alleyway which Alice shared with her neighbour, making his way past the variously coloured wheelie-bins which lined the passageway, towards the back of the house.

It too was in darkness, but Rathe could look into the kitchen window as he passed, although he saw nothing untoward inside. He reached out to try the back door, but he was stopped at once in his tracks by the soft crunch of broken glass under his feet. His gaze drifted to the glass panel of the door and, with a quickening of his breath, his eyes took in the small hole above the handle. His sense of dread intensified and, for a moment, he wished he was anywhere else but standing at Alice Villiers's backdoor. He wanted to be doing almost anything other than finding that door unlocked and stepping into the kitchen into the silence of the house.

He resisted the temptation to call out her name. Something deep within him told him that it was probably a futile response to his situation. Refusing to speculate about what he might find the further into the house he went, Rathe walked softly across Alice's kitchen tiles. His fists were clenched and his jaw locked in a concentrated effort to make as little noise as possible. In the blackness, his sense of smell became more acute and he could detect Alice's scent lingering in the air, the faint traces of perfume and female domesticity seeming so vivid to his heightened senses as to be almost overpowering. His eyes had grown accustomed to the dark and he could tell now that there seemed to be no trace of any disturbance. The kitchen through which he moved, and the long hallway which he passed as he walked through the house, were as neat and organised as he would have expected from Alice's personal habits. Any suggestion that the glass panel had been broken for the purpose of burglary seemed to dissipate with each step he took.

From the kitchen, he walked through a communicating door into the living room. She had had it knocked through, he could see that, so that the lounge and dining room were one large space. It was modern, decorated in a contemporarily fashionable style, and in a brief moment of misplaced pride, he found himself thinking of how happy Alice must have been living here. It was cosy, comfortable, and hers; an area which she had been able to make her own. On one wall, he noticed large wooden letters which spelt the word HOME; on another wall, he would see later when the darkness had been illuminated, there were framed pencil sketches of tasteful studies of naked couples, celebrations of the human form rather than any sordid depiction of lust. The black and white of the furnishings were complimented by the occasional and well-chosen splash of colour of cushions, throw-overs, and the hearth rug on the laminated floors.

All those details, Rathe noticed afterwards. Almost at once, as he walked into the living room, his attention was seized by the grim horror of the figure which lay sprawled out in front of him. She lay on her side, her legs outstretched and crossed over one another, one arm splayed out to the side and the other buried under the weight of her body. Even in the absence of light, he could see the blood pooling around her, horribly black in the darkness, and he knew that she would never again reach up and kiss his cheek, or smile at him when he promised to help her, or show him the gap in her teeth with a coy smile. How long he stood staring at the lifeless body of Alice Villiers, of the girl he had loved once and might have loved still, Anthony Rathe could not say. But he was aware that it was long enough for the tears to well in his eyes and for him to become aware of the urge to drop to his knees and scream at the sky.

Suddenly, he was aware of light. A shaft of silver which broke through the darkness of the room, illuminating the horror which was spread across the living room floor, sending a cruel blend of fear, shock, and pain through Rathe's senses. He spun around in this abrupt spotlight, particles of dust dancing in the beam, but all he succeeded in doing was blinding himself. Behind the torch's light, he could make out the figure of a man, but it was no more than a silhouetted outline which was masked by the glare which assaulted Rathe's vision. There was a sharp curse in the confusion, followed by a small click, which preceded the living room lights bursting into life. Rathe's eyes took a moment to come to terms with the change in focus from profound darkness, to the glaring brightness of the torch, to the softer illumination of the ceiling lights. When his vision had settled, he found himself staring into the face of Detective Inspector Terry Cook.

"What the bloody hell are you doing here?" hissed the detective.

Rathe dumbly pointed to what had once been Alice Villiers. "I knew her. Alice. I knew her."

Cook moved past Rathe and approached the body. Forcing himself to look, Rathe saw the dark contusions around her throat and the darker, more terrible stains of death on her back.

"Stabbed to the back," said Cook, as much to himself than to Rathe. "Three... four times. Marks to the throat. He must have grabbed her from behind, half choking her so that she couldn't fight back, then used the knife. Four quick stabs."

He got up from his knees and turned round. Rathe was no longer there. For a second, Cook wondered where he could have gone, but almost immediately he heard from the kitchen the sound of gentle sobbing and Cook found that all he could do for the present was lower his head and allow a few private moments to pass unhindered.

* * *

An hour later, Rathe and Cook stood in the night air, leaning against the bonnet of Cook's car. They were watching the initial process of a murder enquiry unfold before them, illuminated by the flickering blue lights of the emergency vehicles. Alice's house had lost its peaceful contentment. It was now a crime scene, a place of official scrutiny and scientific sterility, a home no longer. The cold calculation of forensic analysis had usurped the domestic harmony which Rathe felt sure Alice had enjoyed in that small semi-detached house she had called home, a physical manifestation of the invasion of personal privacy which murder demanded.

"Did you know her well?" Cook asked now.

"We were a couple," Rathe replied. "Together. Once. Before… But we split up."

"Recently?"

"Six months." Rathe paused. "When the whole thing with Kevin Marsden started. It broke us apart."

"I'm sorry," said Cook, without any sense of obligation.

Rathe did not acknowledge the sentiment. "I loved her."

Cook looked at him, seeing the lean profile flashing blue in the lights of the police car beside them. There were no more tears in Rathe's eyes, but the sadness which seemed always to be in them was deeper now. Cook said nothing, unable to think of anything to say which did not sound crass.

At last, Rathe turned to face him. "Why were you there,

tonight, Cook? There was none of this official activity when I arrived, so you hadn't been called here because of her death. Which means you came here fully expecting to be able to speak to her. About what?"

Cook shook his head. "You show me yours first. I'm a serving police officer and I've just discovered a civilian standing over the body of a murdered woman. And that civilian has just said, pretty much, that the dead girl broke his heart at the lowest point in his life. So, you tell me why you were there first."

Rathe's expression was carved in ice. "Are you saying you think I killed her?"

"No." Cook shook his head. "I'm just saying that you need to explain to me as a matter of priority why you were at the scene of a murder, before I choose to confide in you why I was there."

"To eliminate me from the enquiry?" scoffed Rathe.

"If you like."

Rathe demonstrated his annoyance at Cook's approach by falling into silence for a moment. It was a petty display of petulance and Cook recognised it as such, but he supposed it was only fair to allow Rathe to have this sullen moment of anger. He waited for Rathe to speak once more, refusing to betray any impatience at the situation.

"Six years ago, Alice's younger sister vanished," explained Rathe. "You might remember the case, you might not. Kirsty Villiers was her name, and she disappeared on a night out with friends, last seen on CCTV drawing some money from a cash machine. Alone. She was never seen again."

"Rings a faint bell," said Cook without any particular confidence.

"A few days ago, Alice had a call from a private detective, asking to meet her in person, because he had something personal and private which he had to speak to her about."

"And she thought it was about this missing sister of hers?"

Rathe nodded. "She wanted me to go with her. Moral support, she said."

"So you agreed?"

"I didn't want her to go to meet a stranger on her own." Rathe paused for a moment. "And I didn't want to say no to her."

"And when she didn't show up, you came here to find her?"

"I couldn't believe she'd back out of the meeting if she thought it was about Kirsty. Nor could I believe she'd do it without telling me." Rathe looked over to Cook and lowered his voice. "I feared the worst the minute she didn't show, I suppose."

"This private detective who contacted her... he got a name?" Cook began to bite a fingernail.

Rathe replied with caution in his voice, his instincts on edge once more. "Roger Gilchrist, from RPG investigations."

"Shocker," said Cook.

Rathe leaned towards the police detective, lowering his voice. "You knew Gilchrist wanted to meet Alice tonight, didn't you? That's why you came here. To speak to her about it, ask what it was about."

"Your Alice's details were in Gilchrist's appointment book." Cook still refused to look at Rathe. "I know that because I've gone through it tonight. Personally."

Rathe buried his face in his hands, hiding the truth from his sight. "He's dead. Gilchrist... he's dead, isn't he?"

"Stabbed in the back in his office," Cook replied. "Four times."

"Oh, God... " was all Rathe could say.

Cook pushed himself off the bonnet of the car and slapped a hand on Rathe's shoulder. "Come on. Let's go and get a drink, for Christ's sake."

They found a small, traditional pub after a short walk. It was quiet. There were only four old men drinking in the particular comfortable silence only pub regulars have: happy with their own company, and willing to observe the unspoken etiquette of minding their own business. Only one of them looked at Rathe and Cook as they entered. The others hardly seemed to notice any disturbance. Cook ordered a pint of bitter, as though he thought it was the drink he would be expected to have in a place like this. Rathe ordered a scotch whisky. He doubted the wine would be much more than a few notches above vinegar. They walked to a small table in the corner and none of the regulars seemed to have anything to say in protest.

"Gilchrist was found by his wife this afternoon," Cook began to explain. "She'd expected to meet him for lunch but she'd got delayed at an appointment with the bank. They're having money troubles, apparently. Turns out Gilchrist is too fond of vodka and poker and neither of them are his friends. He didn't answer his mobile, so she went round to the office. Found him slumped over his desk."

Rathe was staring into the amber fire in his glass, his mind only half registering what Cook was saying. The rest of his thoughts were those few streets away where love had died once and for all. "Same killer," he volunteered at last.

"Looks like it from the wounds to the back." Cook drank some of the beer. It was warmer than it should have been. "Gilchrist's last client was a woman by the name of Eliza Graham. He'd been retained by her a week ago from what we can gather. As part of his investigation, it looks as though he came across Miss Villiers's name, which is why he wanted to speak to her."

"But what's his investigation got to do with Alice?"

Cook leaned forward, placing his elbows on the table. "Eliza Graham had hired Gilchrist to find out what happened to her daughter, Lyndsey Crane."

"Mother and daughter have different surnames?" queried Rathe.

"The girl's natural father died," said Cook. "Mother re-married a man called Elliott Graham, but Lyndsey wanted to keep her father's name. Mrs Graham let it happen," he added with a shrug.

But Rathe barely seemed to be listening. "What's all this got to do with Alice?"

Cook's voice lowered. "Lyndsey Crane disappeared... "

Rathe had that same sensation of history repeating itself. It felt like snakes crawling over his skin. "When?"

"A year ago. Police enquiry went nowhere."

Rathe slumped back in his chair, burying his head in his hands, the connections forming in his brain and the idea of coincidence dissipating with each link he forged. Kirsty Villiers vanished six years ago; Lyndsey Crane disappeared five years later. The private detective investigating what happened to the Crane girl contacted Alice saying he had something important to discuss. Within twenty four hours, Gilchrist and Alice had been murdered in the same manner, probably by the same man. The whole sequence of events made Rathe's throat constrict and, for a moment, he felt he would either cry or vomit.

Cook spread his hands, palm upwards, on the table. "So, we have to look at the possibility that Gilchrist found out something about Kirsty Villiers's disappearance."

"Or the other way round," muttered Rathe. "He might have hoped that something in the Villiers case would help him with his own enquiry into the Crane girl."

"Fair point," conceded Cook. "But there's a connection somewhere and we need to find it. I don't suppose, by any chance, Alice Villiers ever mentioned Lyndsey Crane?"

Rathe shook his head. "Not to me."

"Right." Cook had hardly expected the answer to be any different. It would have made things too easy, but he was too seasoned to such setbacks to be discouraged by it.

As though aware of the inspector's thoughts, Rathe spoke once more. "It doesn't mean anything though, does it? Kirsty could have met Lyndsey Crane at some point but not told her family."

"Why wouldn't she?"

Rathe shrugged. "All sorts of reasons. Did you tell your parents the names of everyone you met? There doesn't have to be a sinister cause for it. And another point: if the Villiers family heard about Lyndsey Crane's disappearance, there's no reason to assume they would have made a connection with Kirsty. Just because two girls go missing in London doesn't mean there's automatically a connection. Especially with five years between them."

Cook waved his finger between the two of them. "We're assuming one, though."

Rathe nodded. "But we've got the two murders to suggest a link. Too much of a coincidence otherwise. Alice and her parents didn't have that connection, did they? If they heard about Lyndsey Crane's disappearance, and we don't know they did, all it would have done to the Villiers family is open up old wounds. Assuming they had healed at all."

"Again, fair point." Cook had a sip of his beer. "So where does that get us?"

Rathe shook his head. He was suddenly aware that he had just been speaking to avoid a silence, an effort to keep his mind occupied so that it would not recall the tragic events of the last hour or so.

"I've no idea," he said, with something like a sigh but which might have been a repressed sob.

Cook leaned back in his chair, cradling his glass in his lap. "No sign of any break in at Gilchrist's office. Theory is that the killer pretended to be a prospective client. One of the filing cabinets was open, the one where he kept his client documentation and contracts. We reckon he went over to the cabinet to get the necessary paperwork and while his back was turned… "

"I get it," muttered Rathe.

"Right," said Cook again, accepting his dismissal for the second time. "I'm going to interview Eliza Graham tomorrow morning. If there is a connection between her daughter and Kirsty Villiers, I want to know what it is."

Rathe fixed his eyes on Cook, his lips pursed in anticipation. "Cook… ?"

The policeman was already shaking his head. "I can't. You know I can't."

"I don't want to have to beg you, Cook." Rathe had turned his gaze away.

Cook shifted in his seat. "I know you and Alice Villiers were close, Rathe, I get that. And I know you've got a vested interest in the case this time, not just idle curiosity. But I can't have you come with me. It's not right."

"I'll only look into what happened anyway, no matter what you say," Rathe pressed. "You know that."

"Then you'd be a bloody idiot," hissed Cook. "I know you're that too."

"I just want to know what happened to her," Rathe insisted, although he knew explanation was not necessary. "And why it happened. I want the truth, Cook."

"For your own peace of mind, like every other time?"

Rathe shrugged his shoulders and then, after a moment's thought, he shook his head. "No, for Alice's parents' sake."

Cook dropped his head once more and gave a crooked smile of resignation. As though to drown out his doubts, he finished the beer in one, long draught. He slammed the glass down on the table. Two of the four regulars were startled by the noise into a disdainful response, but Rathe remained seated, not looking up from his glass, waiting for an answer.

"I'll pick you up at eight, so be ready," snapped Cook, turning on his heel and heading to the door. "And don't outstay your welcome here."

Rathe watched the doors to the pub be pulled open and allowed to swing shut on their own accord. He looked back down at the whisky and finished it without hesitation. It would warm his insides for the long walk home he was compelled to make.

* * *

The first thing to strike Rathe about Eliza Graham was her sense of resolve. He had no doubt that in her private moments she had shed more tears than she had thought possible. Similarly, he felt certain that she had experienced her emotional state fluctuate between grief and despair at the loss of her child, before eventually turning into rage and fury at the injustice of it all, and finally into a determined resolution to do something about the situation herself. As she stood in front of them with her arms folded and her eyes glaring at them with defiance, Rathe could imagine the moment when she decided that it was time she took matters into her own hands. She retained the fierce expression of a capable and practical woman, someone who was not prepared to take life's cruelty any longer without at least some effort being made to retaliate against it.

She was older than he had expected, suggesting that Lyndsey was a late arrival. Her hair had once been blonde, according to the photographs which he saw on the hall table, but now it was so streaked with grey that it seemed to appear naturally platinum. Her cheeks were drawn but shaded with a pink glow which suggested warmth of character which was belied by the cold, piercing blue of her stare. Her lips were tinged with red but they had the pressed expression of sourness about them, as though the presence of Rathe and Cook in her house was offensive to her. Her face was not that of a grieving woman who floundered in her own misfortune; it was the face of a woman who had a definite course of action mapped out in her head but their arrival had interrupted somehow the smooth progress of that plan.

"The police being in my house can only mean either that you have something to tell me about my daughter or, yet again, that there is nothing to tell me," she said. "I suspect I know which it is. I don't see any reason to assume that the police have suddenly developed either an interest in my daughter's case or the capability to make any headway in it."

Cook wasn't about to allow her to walk away from that. "The police have always had an interest in your daughter's disappearance, Mrs Graham. You shouldn't think otherwise."

"They didn't manage to find her," she replied.

"That doesn't mean we weren't trying to," returned Cook, leaving her in no doubt how he felt about her implications.

Rathe had declined the invitation to sit down as readily as Cook had accepted it. Instead, he had chosen to stand by the entrance to the conservatory and look out onto the impressive lawns which stretched out at the back of the house. Flowers and shrubs whose names he would never know, but which his late father would have identified with ease, gave splashes of colour to the expanse of green and so beautiful was the display that the comparatively ugly gravel path which led down to a flagged raised patio at the end of the garden seemed less intrusive than it might have done otherwise. On that patio there was a small table and a couple of wicker chairs. Seated in one of them was a man reading a broadsheet, one leg crossed arrogantly over the other, his head tilted back as he looked down his nose at the pages of the newspaper. Occasionally, he would reach out to a coffee cup which was placed on the table beside him and take a sip, checking the cafetière occasionally to make sure it had not lost its heat. It was not a cold day but, in Rathe's view, nor was it warm enough to justify having breakfast or morning coffee outdoors. It somehow struck him as a pretentious gesture and, as if to show it the disdain he felt it deserved, Rathe turned his back on the man and looked back to Mrs Graham.

"Was it your frustration with the police which prompted you to approach a detective agency, Mrs Graham?" he asked softly.

"Sometimes one feels one must do something," was her reply. "There is only so much sitting about and waiting for news one can manage. I have done my share of lying awake wondering, worrying, and speculating. If one acts, one feels one is doing something proactive. That brings its own support, especially when there is no comfort elsewhere."

"I can understand that," said Rathe.

Cook cleared his throat, as though to remind them that he was present in the room. "I appreciate this may be difficult, Mrs Graham, but could you tell me what happened on the day Lyndsey disappeared? As briefly as you like."

She rolled her eyes as though the request was a party trick she was tired of performing. "The number of times I've had to tell this story to the police, it's a miracle to find an officer who doesn't know them."

"Just a brief recap will be fine," said Cook, his voice barely polite.

"It was a Saturday afternoon," Eliza explained. "Lyndsey was going to the West End to buy a dress for a party she was attending the following weekend. I had been with her to pick an outfit, see her try them on, and what have you. We'd narrowed down the choice to three and Lyndsey was going to go and have a last look at them and decide."

"You didn't plan on going with her that time?"

She shook her head, as though a different decision might have made all the difference. Rathe thought again about the friend of Kirsty Villiers who had not gone with her to that cash machine. History rolling back over itself.

"She told me that she didn't need me there to make the final decision," Eliza was saying. "God forgive me, I was relieved. I had some things to do myself that day and couldn't really spare the time to go with her. I realise how that sounds in retrospect."

"What time did she leave the house?" asked Rathe.

"Half past ten. She was going to get the tube, buy the dress, have lunch, and come home. My husband said he would pick her up and drive her home."

Rathe's eyes narrowed. "Lyndsey's stepfather, am I right?"

The woman nodded slowly. "Elliott and I have been married for ten years, but he took Lyndsey on as his own right from the beginning."

"Lyndsey's natural father died, I understand," said Rathe.

Her eyes were glaring at his impertinence in asking a private question, but something about his expression prevented her from expressing her disgust. It was something in those melancholy, dark eyes which suggested to her that he might not be probing after all, but seeking some way to help. Her offence remained, but her outrage at it was somehow diluted under that calm, yet tragic stare.

"Yes, when Lyndsey was a little girl. There are days when I still miss him," she added, placing her fingers to one of her eyes, ensuring that no tears were betraying her.

Rathe was fascinated by the woman's apparent desire to show as little emotion as possible. It seemed to him that she was almost pathological in her desire to demonstrate emotional austerity, even in circumstances when it would be entirely appropriate to give in to those most basic emotions, and he began to feel captivated by her reason for it. He felt certain that it was not simply her desire to be proactive in the wake of the police's failure to trace her daughter, understandable though that was, and he started to wonder what more powerful cause was behind the woman's sensual reticence.

Cook was oblivious to these nuances of behaviour. "Was it usual for your daughter to go into town on her own?"

"Not so usual for it to be the norm, inspector," replied Eliza, daring Cook to question her suitability as a parent.

"How old was she?"

"Sixteen when… it happened."

"Isn't that a little young to be letting a girl go to town alone?" stated Cook.

"I didn't think so," replied Eliza, her voice carrying a knife with it.

Rathe's voice was like velvet by comparison, covering the blade of her tone with a mellow softness. "When your husband went to pick her up, she wasn't there?"

"They'd arranged to meet at Waterloo. He waited, waited, waited. She was never late. She… "

Her eyes hardened at the memory and Rathe wondered again at her self-control. He would have expected tears at this point, but Eliza's command of her self-control was so impressive that she betrayed no sign of impending tears. Rathe wondered whether it would be a different version of Eliza Graham who appeared once they had left her home. He half-imagined furious sobs once the door had been closed on their backs, but he could not feel certain that they would fall.

"My husband insisted that we wait a few more hours before contacting the police, in case she turned up," Eliza said. "Teenage girls can be waylaid by meeting friends and getting carried away, he said. They can lose track of time. No doubt that's true. But, even then, I knew it was a false hope. I think I lasted an hour, a little longer, before I called the police."

Cook had been writing furiously in his notebook. Now, with the mother's summary of the events complete, he forced the conversation back into the present. "Was there any particular reason you approached RPG Investigations, Mrs Graham?"

"Not especially. They seemed capable and efficient."

"Did you speak to many agencies, or was RPG the first one you tried?"

"I did a brief internet search and made a choice," she replied, growing impatient. "Look, what is this about? Is there some news about Lyndsey or not?"

Cook stood up and placed his hands behind his back. "I'm afraid we have no news about your daughter, Mrs Graham, but we do have something to say which you need to hear. Yesterday afternoon, Roger Gilchrist of RPG Investigations was found dead in his office."

Rathe watched her reaction. Her cold eyes grew harder, widening in outrage, but her composure remained in place. She heaved her shoulders in an effort to retain her control of her emotions. The news had come as a shock, Rathe was sure about that, but he was impressed by the woman's refusal to display anything which they might take as a weakness or a lack of control.

"An accident?" she managed to say.

"He was murdered," said Cook. He saw no reason to decorate the truth with tact.

Eliza Graham put a hand to her mouth, as though she might be able to protect herself from the embarrassment of screaming if she forced the shock back down her throat. She walked out of the room, past Rathe, and into the conservatory. She banged on the glass and gestured for the man in the garden to come inside. By the time she was back with them, the urge to give a voice to her shock had subsided and her hand was back by her side.

"I want Elliott to hear all this," she explained.

Rathe was watching the man march down the gravel pathway of the garden. Elliott Graham walked into the living room from the conservatory, slapping his newspaper against his thigh with an impatient rhythm, irritated that his morning solitude had been disturbed. He went to stand beside his wife, but his eyes had narrowed in suspicion as they fixed themselves on Rathe and Cook. He was a tall man, lean without appearing emaciated, his thin lips drawn down in a perpetual sneer of arrogance. Those suspicious eyes peered down the long nose which protruded from the thin face and the entire expression cast by those features was one of scornful superiority. His hair was grey, swept back from the intelligent forehead, but there were still traces of the soft golden colour which it must once have been. Rathe supposed he must have once been a handsome man, but he doubted Elliott Graham had ever been a truly likeable one.

"Who's this?" he asked, the words clipped and precise.

Eliza Graham pointed to them in turn. "Inspector Cook and Mr Rathe."

Graham took a step towards Cook, leaning over him. "Police? About Lyndsey?"

Cook was the shorter man by some margin but he retained eye contact with Graham and Rathe felt that there could be no doubt amongst any of them that Cook was neither impressed nor intimidated by the man's posture.

"No, sir." Cook remained motionless, offering no more than a direct response to the question. "And, if you don't mind, I came to speak to your wife."

Graham sniffed and turned on his heel. "You'll speak to me too. Anything you want to say to her, you can say to me."

"Thank you, sir," smiled Cook. "But I'll decide that, if it's all the same."

He walked towards the couple and stood between them, purposefully, his hands in his pockets. Rathe resisted the temptation to smile at Cook's dismissal of Elliott Graham. Standing with his back to the arrogance, showing his easy control of the situation by keeping his hands in his pockets, Cook made it clear that Graham's presence in the room was of no concern to him or his enquiry.

"Did Gilchrist give you any idea of what he'd found out about Lyndsey?" he asked.

"Gilchrist?" interrupted Elliott Graham. "The private detective? What's happened to him?"

"He's dead, Elliott," said Eliza. "They say he's been murdered."

This time, Rathe watched Elliott Graham's reaction to the news. He showed no sadness because of it, but Rathe hardly expected him to. He suspected that Graham would have seen Roger Gilchrist less as a man and more as a business concern. The man's murder would seem to Graham to be a failed commodity rather than a loss of life. It did not surprise Rathe, therefore, to see him simply lower his eyes to the floor and give a minor, almost imperceptible shrug of his shoulders.

"Tragedy," he declared, without any suggestion of genuine empathy.

Unlike Rathe, Cook had given Elliott Graham no consideration at all and he had reserved his attention for the man's wife. "Did Gilchrist tell you whether he'd found anything out?"

She shook her head. "Nothing specific. He just said he had a number of lines of enquiry to follow."

Rathe stepped forward. "Did Gilchrist ever mention the name Kirsty Villiers to you at all, Mrs Graham?"

Elliott Graham held out a hand. "Excuse me, but who exactly are you? Are you a policeman too?"

Rathe held the man's eyes with his own. "No, Mr Graham. I'm not a policeman."

"Then I think you had better leave, don't you?"

Cook moved between them. "Even if you think that, Mr Graham, I don't. So he stays."

Graham's lips pursed in irritation. "Hardly an appropriate arrangement. Give me one good reason why I should answer his questions."

"Firstly, he didn't ask you the question, he asked your wife," growled Cook. "Secondly, if you only want to answer questions put by an official detective, I'll just get Mr Rathe to tell me what he wants to know and then I'll ask it. But that means we'll be here twice as long as necessary, so I suggest you let us do what we need to and get on with it. How does that sound to you, Mr Graham?"

Eliza raised her hands to her temples. "For pity's sake, let's just get on with this and get them out of here, Elliott. Please."

Graham waved a hand in Rathe's direction. It might have been a disgusted dismissal of the situation or a consent to Rathe's continued involvement in the proceedings. Graham walked into the conservatory and sat down, far enough away to express his dislike of matters, but close enough that he was able to listen to their developments.

Rathe looked back to Eliza. "Do the names Kirsty or Alice Villiers mean anything to you?"

"I've never heard either name before."

Rathe walked into the conservatory. "Have you ever heard those names, Mr Graham?"

The older man shook his head. "Never."

Rathe frowned, scratching his chin in thought. "Gilchrist didn't mention either of those names to you?"

The woman shook her head, but it was her husband who spoke. "We've just said so, haven't we?"

Rathe did not dignify the outburst with a reply. He walked slowly around the room, pulling his bottom lip as his dark eyes narrowed in thought. Cook watched him move, knowing that something had sparked a train of thought inside Rathe's brain. Rathe walked towards framed prints of coastal landscapes, eyeing them carefully as though they were the works of one of the master painters, but Cook knew that Rathe's attention was far away from the room and its adornments. Rathe moved across to a small table upon which stood a chess set, set ready for a game, the figures carved representations of the court of Henry VIII. Rathe picked up the King and studied it intently.

"Who is the chess player?" he asked.

"My husband," Eliza replied. "I've never been able to play the game."

"Could Lyndsey?"

Graham had walked back into the living room. "I tried to teach her many times. She showed promise, but she wouldn't persevere with it. Lost interest too rapidly."

"It was the same with the piano," confessed Eliza, unable to keep the regret out of her voice.

"Gave up on things too easily," declared Elliott Graham.

"You pushed her too hard." Eliza intended it to be taken as an accusation, and it was, but she had said it so calmly that for Elliott to make a scene as a result would have made him look foolish.

Rathe replaced the King and placed his hands in his pockets. "I've always enjoyed a good game of chess."

Eliza Graham was not listening, her interest in chess being so negligible as to be non-existent. Instead, she was looking at Cook, who became aware of her scrutiny and straightened his spine to confront it.

"Is Mr Gilchrist's death something to do with my daughter's disappearance?" she asked.

Cook shook his head. "I can't say, Mrs Graham. Not at this point."

"But it seems likely, doesn't it?"

"I'm not prepared to speculate about anything until I have more facts." Cook made it sound like a rehearsed line, delivered with ease but authority.

Eliza considered him for a moment, before clasping her hands together and raising her head in an assumed exhibition of proud dignity. "Well, will you tell me whether you think Lyndsey is alive or not?"

Cook had not been prepared for it to be asked so soon, or so directly, and it was clear that the question had embarrassed him. There had been no official curtain of rhetoric to hide behind.

"I can't say," was the vague reply he gave.

"I'm only asking for an opinion."

It was Rathe who came to the rescue. "Inspector Cook is investigating murder, Mrs Graham. It would be inappropriate for him to have a personal opinion without evidence to support it. And I think it is unfair to ask it."

Elliott Graham gave a sneering laugh. "In other words, if nothing useful can be said, it's pointless saying anything else at all."

It had sounded to Rathe like a dismissal and he, for one, was happy to take it as such. The room had suddenly become oppressive and he felt the need for air. He was not sure what it was which was stifling him the most: Eliza's rejection of her natural feelings, Elliott's supercilious contempt for Cook and him, or his own frustrating inability to grasp that single important fact which he was convinced had come to light.

* * *

"I don't think either of us expected to see you again, Anthony," said Sonia Villiers. "We were sorry about you and Alice."

"Yes, so was I," he said, lowering his head. "But I understand why she felt she had to… "

Sonia looked at him with those same eyes which had struck him so powerfully in her elder daughter. In the time which had passed since he had last seen Alice's parents, he had forgotten how similar she and Sonia had been. They shared those same feline features, the gap in the teeth, and the blonde hair, so that at times he felt sure he could know for certain what Alice would have matured into if she had been permitted to continue to live. Sonia was still an attractive woman and, in her younger years, she would have been especially beautiful. Rathe was sure that when Terence Villiers first saw Sonia, he would have had the same lurch of emotion and the same clutch of desire around his heart that Rathe had felt when he had met Alice for the first time. Now, Sonia laid a hand on Rathe's, but only for a moment, her gentle kindness towards him seeming to pass through him with her touch, her gaze, and her smile.

"We always felt that she should have stood by you when things went badly for you," she said. "I think you have a right to feel betrayed by her."

Rathe shook his head. "I don't think the way I was back then gave me any right to her support. I was selfish, vain, and proud. Not qualities which should be rewarded."

Sonia studied his face. "You look like a different man, Anthony."

"I think I am."

"A much sadder man."

He did not answer that. Instead, he lowered his head and studied his clasped fingers which lay in his lap.

Terence Villiers walked into the room with the tray of

coffee. Like his wife, he had changed little. He had retained his keen, blue stare and genial expression, but age had creased the skin around the amiable eyes and the gently smiling lips. His once dark hair had turned white but it had retained its luxuriance and it showed no signs of deserting him. A pair of gold rimmed spectacles now hung from his neck and there was a selection of pens in the pocket of the shirt sleeved shirt he wore. The collection of crosswords and puzzle books which Rathe had seen stacked on the coffee table in the centre of the living room had determined the purpose of the pens. Terence had always been a keen exponent of puzzles, believing as deeply as any faith that a sharp mind meant a healthy life. Judging by the man's appearance, Rathe found it hard to argue.

"A long time since we sat here having coffee together," he said. "I only brought milk for two, Anthony. I trust you still take yours black."

Rathe accepted the cup with a smile. "Yes, Terence, thank you."

Alice's father handed his wife her cup but he did not take one for himself. Instead, he placed his hands in his pockets and looked down at Rathe. "As I recall, you were never one to beat around the bush."

"Terence… " cautioned Sonia, detecting Rathe's abrupt embarrassment.

"He wasn't," insisted Terence. "I admired him for it. I hope I still can. You're here after all this time for a reason, Anthony, and I hope you're not going to wait an age to tell us what it is."

Rathe hadn't known of Terence Villiers's admiration for his plain speaking and he was surprised to find how much the admission of it meant to him. Realising that it deserved respect, he placed his cup down and rose from his chair, moving to stand alongside the man who in another life might have been his father-in-law.

"You're right, Terence, and I won't insult either of you by pretending otherwise," he said. "Nor can I say that I am here socially, although I wish I could say I was."

Terence looked across at his wife for an instant. "I think we can assume that you're here for a more serious reason than coffee."

Rathe bowed his head. "The truth is that I asked to come here in place of somebody else. I felt it might have been better for someone you know – at least, someone you once knew – to explain things."

Sonia had leaned forward on the settee, her instincts now arching their backs in readiness. "Anthony, what is it?"

"You're here in place of whom?" demanded Terence.

Rathe met his gaze. "The police. They will want to come here anyway but, for now, they've let me do it in their place."

"The police... ?" stammered Sonia. Then, once the idea had occurred to her, she placed her hands to her cheeks. "Not about Kirsty? After all these years… Terence?"

But her husband's mind was working quicker than hers, the crosswords and Sudoku proving their worth. "Not Kirsty. Anthony wouldn't be here for her. Oh, God… "

Sonia was on her feet now, attempting to keep her balance as her world shifted out of control beneath her. "Alice? This is about Alice?"

Rathe had clenched his fists unwittingly and his jaw had clamped shut against both the pain he felt and the crueller pain he was causing. He should not have come, he knew that now. He should have left it to Cook with his dispassionate and official sense of detachment, instead of coming here, carrying with him those reminders of broken engagements and troubled times, to shatter their world completely with his news of death.

"I'm afraid it is about Alice," he whispered, struggling to

retain control of his voice. "I'm so sorry. She... she's... "

"Dead," declared Terence Villiers. "Alice is dead."

What followed was confusion. Rathe would later recall Sonia rushing into her husband's arms, her voice making a noise which was barely human and which seemed to come from some place so deep her body seemed incapable of producing it. Terence remained firm, his grip on his wife as tight as he could manage, as though he was refusing to allow another of his family to be torn away from him by circumstance. How long the wailing lasted, Rathe could not say, but he knew that his presence there now was an intrusion. He mumbled a further apology, unable to prevent his own tears from falling, and in the days to come he would remember muttering something about being in the garden. As he attempted to walk away to give them privacy, he was surprised to find his movement blocked by a firm grip on his forearm. Terence Villiers had hold of him with one hand whilst the other arm remained wrapped around his wife. He grasped Rathe's arm with the same firmness of grip with which he held his wife, and when he shook his head at Rathe, his eyes pleaded with the younger man to stay, as though his presence were vital to keeping some stability in the chaos.

They remained like that for some minutes. In the end, it was Terence who moved, releasing his grip on Rathe and gently edging his wife back to the settee. Rathe moved to the drinks cabinet and poured a brandy for Sonia and two malts for Terence and him. Sonia's weeping subsided under the stern influence of the spirit and the fire in her throat brought her breathing under some form of control. Terence threw back the whisky and poured a second for himself. He looked at Rathe's glass, expecting the same, and Rathe complied. The second glass would be treated with more respect and, in honesty with himself, Rathe was glad of the sharp but soothing effect of the drink.

He gave them a summary of how matters stood, delivered succinctly but with difficulty. Sonia listened with intermittent sobs, closing her eyes against the effects of the more terrible details. Terence took in the information with a grim defiance, refusing to take his gaze from Rathe's face, forcing himself to confront every detail of the misery with courage and resilience. Rathe had spoken whilst still on his feet but, now he had finished, the strain of the past few moments hit him and he felt his knees begin to tremble. With an apology, he moved back to his chair and sat down.

"I want to say this, and I expect no dispute about it," declared Terence after a brief silence. "On behalf of Sonia and myself, Anthony, thank you for having the decency and the respect to come here and tell us in person."

Rathe responded with a shake of his head. Terence Villiers accepted the gesture for what it was: an acknowledgement of his own sentiment of gratitude and a declaration that nothing further on that particular topic need be said.

"You say the police are assuming a connection between Alice's death and that of this private detective," Terence clarified instead.

"It seems likely," said Rathe. "And it seems to me that if that's right, it's impossible not to assume a similar link between the disappearances of Lindsey Crane and Kirsty."

Sonia shook her head. "I can't believe there might be some news about her after so long."

"We have to take things one step at a time," cautioned Rathe. "It's only a theory until a fact proves it correct. You have to remember that, Sonia, however easy it is to forget it."

Terence was nodding. "But it does seem more than possible, doesn't it?"

"To me it does," confessed Rathe. "But I have to prove a link before we can act on it. Do you ever remember hearing the name Lyndsey Crane before?"

"Never," said Terence, giving voice to Sonia's shaking of the head.

"Given the age difference between them, I'm not surprised at that," replied Rathe. "It was a point which struck me almost immediately. Kirsty was quite a few years older than Lyndsey Crane, so it's unlikely they'd have anything to do with each other."

"What's your point?" asked Terence.

Rathe shrugged. "If there is a connection between the two disappearances then it can't be the girls themselves, because the difference in age makes it unlikely they knew each other."

Sonia looked up at him. "You mean the link between them is… what? A coincidence?"

"Something like that. There was a link which they didn't know they had. Same school, different years, for example. Same gym, but years apart in membership. Same dentist, same doctor, same… "

"Yes, point taken," snapped Terence. "A transient connection, that's what you're saying."

"Exactly," murmured Rathe.

"Which will make it harder to find, correct?" Terence stared at Rathe not with hostility or fury, but with a clear plea for honesty.

Rathe stood up, his legs feeling more secure now that the initial storm of grief had passed. There was something stabilising about these intellectual discussions which fortified his energy. "Not necessarily. We just have to look at things a little differently, that's all."

"Why are you getting involved in this, Anthony?" asked Sonia.

He could not look at her and tell her an untruth, so he turned away with a shrug and looked out over the garden.

He could remember sitting around the wooden table with Alice and her parents, sipping white wine and gins and tonic in the fading summer sun with the remnants of tapas or pasta on the plates in front of them. He could remember fireworks in the cold, dark skies of November evenings or New Year twilights, with Alice's head on his shoulder and her face illuminated by the multi-coloured explosions in the sky. So many memories in that expanse of green which stretched out beyond the glass of the patio doors. So many memories which he had allowed to slip through his fingers because of who he had been and the misery he had caused.

"I never knew Kirsty," he said now, turning back to face them. "I only know what Alice told me, which wasn't very much. She didn't like talking about what had happened."

"She never really came to terms with it," said Terence. "It was the pain of not knowing. You tell yourself that you can handle anything as long as you know the truth; that not knowing is worse than knowing. I think Alice saw it in those terms."

"Do you?" asked Rathe.

"It's not something I've been able to test as yet," replied Terence.

Sonia had moved from the settee and she had taken a photograph from the mantelpiece. She held it out to Rathe, who recognised Kirsty from his own online researches, but this photograph was professionally taken. It was black and white, elegantly lit, showing Kirsty looking to one side with her head dipped slightly, gazing up at the lens from under her long lashes. He was no expert, but Rathe suspected that her hair and make-up had been applied expertly.

"She was very beautiful," he said, almost without thinking. "Both of them were."

Sonia enjoyed the compliment and she smiled at him, although her eyes were still ravaged with grief. She took the photo from him and gazed at it herself. "Kirsty wanted to be an actress, Anthony. She had this taken for portfolios, auditions, publicity, what have you. From the age of ten, it was all she had wanted to be. *The Wizard of Oz* on television was all it took. Do you remember, Terence?"

"Of course," he replied, as the memory formed a film over his eyes.

"Did you encourage her?" asked Rathe, gently.

Sonia inclined her head, evasively. "To an extent, we did, yes. It wasn't something we felt was secure enough for her to have as a sole profession."

"Which is why her degree at university was going to be English as well as Drama," offered Terence.

Rathe looked across at the older man. "Going to be?"

"She only managed two years of the course," explained Sonia. Her tone of voice showed that their mutual disappointment had not quite faded over the years.

"Do you mind me asking why?" ventured Rathe.

Terence got to his feet. "Because she couldn't see beyond the present, Anthony. It was one of her failures. It's not easy to talk about your daughter's shortcomings, especially not in these circumstances, but I'm afraid it's true."

"She was just so ambitious," Sonia said, in defence. "She had a dream and she wanted to follow it."

Rathe became aware that the ground upon which he was walking now was infirm and unstable, as though each word might bring the conversation to an end. Rathe knew that he could not allow that to happen, because he had that tremor of instinctive anticipation across his spine which told him that something important was about to come out. When he spoke, his voice was gentle, almost soothing, his lips curled in a soft, disarming smile.

"Something had changed though, surely?" he said. "If she had done two years of the course, something in her circumstances must have altered for her to abandon those two years of hard work like that."

Terence turned his back on the conversation, as though the memories it was dragging back to life were too much for him to recall. For a moment, Sonia looked at her husband and debated whether silence was the right option. When she turned her gaze back to Rathe, however, she saw something so comforting and yet so determined in his dark eyes that she felt certain she could give him the trust which she seemed to beg from her and that silence would be nothing less than a betrayal of that trust.

"It was a letter," she said. "Kirsty received a letter and, once she had read it, everything changed."

"Who from?"

Sonia Villiers looked over again at her husband but, in truth, her mind was made up even without Terence's nod of the head. She put her hand on Rathe's arm and inclined her head towards the door. "Come with me, Anthony."

He followed her out into the hallway and up the stairs, passing the framed oil paintings of the various landscapes of Britain. Even to Rathe's untrained eye, they were obviously the work of a trained amateur and the small, neat "TV" in the right hand corner of each showed that Terence kept his mind active with art as well as lateral thinking. Rathe had a sudden image of a man trying anything to fill the void left by the loss of a child and, with a twist of his stomach, Rathe wondered what hobby Terence would take up now that the void had doubled in size.

Sonia opened a door on the landing and turned on the light. She led him into a large sized bedroom, tastefully decorated, with a single bed set beneath a large window in the far wall. A collection of small teddy bears and a heart shaped pillow were neatly gathered at the foot of the pillows, an oddly immature bundle of items but one which Rathe found it hard to dislike in the circumstances. Posters of productions of Shakespeare and Ibsen, amongst others, were framed on the wall to Rathe's right as he entered the room. Fitted wardrobes spread the length of the adjourning wall, with a mirror and dressing table set in the centre of them. Facing them, a desk and computer were set out, with a small bookcase fixed to the wall above it. Copies of plays and literary criticism books, as well as various biographies of notable actors and some modern movie stars. Next to the shelves there was a cork noticeboard, filled with various slips of paper and assorted photographs. Rathe saw Kirsty and Alice messing around on a beach; Kirsty wearing a hideous Christmas jumper with barely concealed embarrassment; Alice in her teenage years drinking wine from a bottle; Kirsty with a group of friends, as glamorous as any celebrities, drinking champagne and blowing kisses to the camera. Rathe wondered which of those friends, if any, was the one who chose not to go to the cash machine with Kirsty on that night six years previously.

Sonia walked to the noticeboard and flicked through the papers which were pinned to it. At last, she pulled one free from its place and read over its contents. She handed it to Rathe.

"Read it for yourself, Anthony."

It was an invitation to an audition and interview, following Kirsty's own approach which the letter had acknowledged. It was dated June 2012, six months before she disappeared. The header of the letter was written in Gothic script, Trebuchet Talent Agency Ltd, with an address somewhere in Soho. Kirsty's portfolio and publicity photographs had been impressive, it said, and a representative of the company would very much like to meet her in person. A date, a time, and a venue were given, with an offer of thanks and kind regards above an indecipherable

210

signature. Rathe read the letter several times, but he could see nothing of importance in it. He handed it back to Sonia.

"And that was the letter which caused Kirsty to give up university?" he asked.

Sonia was replacing the letter on the cork board as she replied. "She'd sent dozens of letters to similar agencies all over London, but the reply had always been to tell her she needed a qualification before she could be considered. Kirsty was an impatient girl, Anthony. One of my traits, I'm afraid."

"Did she attend the interview?"

"Yes. And a second the following month."

"Did you go with her?"

Sonia nodded. "Terence and I drove her there and picked her up afterwards. She was the happiest we'd seen her in ages."

Rathe took out his mobile. A quick Google search found the agency without any difficulty, with the correct address, and a phone number which matched the number on the letter head. He dialled it, was connected, claimed he had dialled a wrong number, and disconnected the call.

Sonia was looking at him. "Everything all right, Anthony?"

"Just an idea," he replied, putting his phone away with a shy smile. "And not much of one."

Sonia smiled back at him, as though sympathetic to the idea that an idea formed could be destroyed within seconds. She walked back towards the door and Rathe moved out onto the landing to make room for her. They walked back down the stairs, finding Terence in the hallway. He had his hands in his pockets, his head slumped on his breast, but as they approached he looked up at them with livid, raw eyes which showed that he had spent some private and painful time with his grief in their absence.

"I was just coming up," he said.

"We're done now," said Sonia, placing her hands in his.

Rathe moved past them and put his hand on the handle of the front door. "I think I should be going now. Leave you in peace."

Terence reached out to him, instinctively, then pointed to the lounge. "Stay for one more malt. Keep an old man company."

Rathe smiled. "Thank you, but no. I think I ought to go."

Terence contemplated him for a moment, as though his gaze alone would be sufficient to change Rathe's mind, before bowing his head in defeat. Sonia moved towards Rathe and kissed him lightly on his cheek.

"Thank you, Anthony."

Rathe lowered his eyes. "I'm going to find who did this, Sonia. I'll find you the truth."

She took his face in her hands, forcing him to look in her eyes. "I asked you this before, Anthony, and now I am asking it again. Why are you getting involved in this?"

"Because I let that kid die, Sonia. I put him in prison and he died, but he shouldn't ever have been there."

Terence was shaking his head. "It wasn't your fault. We told you that then and I'm saying it now. God, it was this that drove Alice away from you."

Rathe stared back at him. "Which is why I've got to do something about it now. Make amends. Find some way of putting it right."

"You can't do that by interfering with the police," Sonia insisted.

"I can't get Kevin Marsden out of my head," confessed Rathe, suddenly surprised at how the words sounded when he said them out loud. "I dream about him, I relive his trial, I go to his graveside. I see his mum, ask for her forgiveness."

"You don't need it," said Sonia.

"That's just what she tells me."

"And she's right," said Terence. "You don't need absolution about what happened from anybody but yourself, Anthony."

Rathe shook his head. "I can't forgive myself. Not yet… "

Terence Villiers put his hand on Rathe's shoulder and squeezed. "You'll have to. Otherwise, you'll never move on."

"Doing this helps," Rathe muttered, but his explanation for his actions sounded weak even to his own ears. "Trying to help the police seems to help me."

Sonia shook her head. "No, Anthony. All it does is shift the sadness and the guilt somewhere else."

She kissed his cheek once more. "Come back to see us. Please."

"I will, I promise."

Terence released Rathe's shoulder and opened the door, shaking Rathe's hand as he stepped out into the gentle afternoon breeze. "Take care of yourself, son."

Rathe did not reply. Instead, he smiled back at the two of them and slowly walked away. Once he had reached their garden gate, he looked back, but they had closed the door. Rathe began to walk again, Sonia's words echoing in his mind. He could not seem to stop them from reverberating in his memory and, with each step he took, they seemed to get louder so that by the time he reached the main road, they were screaming in his head. He tried to block them with thoughts of other things but they were too resilient against his efforts. So loud were they that he did not hear the mental click of the connection of several facts which his brain had made and which, once he could see it, would be the clue to the mystery.

* * *

Cook had not been idle. He did not need Anthony Rathe to tell him that the probability was that a link existed somewhere between Kirsty Villiers and Lyndsey Crane. The murders of Alice Villiers and Roger Gilchrist made that idea too vivid to be a coincidence. Similarly, Cook had formed the notion without Rathe's help that the age difference between the two girls made it unlikely that any such connection was between them personally. Cook had formed his own conclusions on that point and, like Rathe, he had determined that what linked the girls' disappearances would be transitory as opposed to direct.

As a result, Cook had undertaken a search of the databases of the files of all missing-person cases for the last six years involving girls of similar respective ages to Kirsty Villiers and Lyndsey Crane. After an hour, his stomach had rebelled and his eyes had begun to gloss over the words on the screen in front of him. Cook found reading from computers increasingly difficult, the glare from the backlight now causing more pain to his eyes than ever before. Andrea had told him more than once to get his eyes tested, but he had brushed off the command.

"I don't need specs," he had growled. "I can see fine."

"You're squinting at the TV," Andrea had argued.

"No, I'm scowling," he retorted, "because I can't believe what I'm bloody seeing."

But none of that bravado altered the fact that his eyes were becoming irritated by reading these computer files. He threw himself out of his chair with a curse and pulled open his office door. He called in a young detective constable, newly promoted and eager to please, and given her the basic facts of the Villiers and Crane disappearances. Pointing to the screen, he had told the young detective what he wanted.

"Any connections, however small, between what's in these files and on that screen," he had barked. "Got it?"

"Absolutely, sir."

"Right. Don't skim-read either. Put your glasses on if you need them."

214

The station canteen offered him nothing better than a corned beef and onion roll and stewed tea, but it would do. He checked his phone as he ate: two texts from Andrea, yet another email offer from Sky, and a notification that the phone wanted to update four apps which Cook never used, largely because he couldn't access them and didn't know what they did.

Nothing from Rathe.

Cook had wondered several times whether he had made an error of judgement in allowing Rathe to break the news of Alice Villiers's murder to her parents alone. It was a gross abuse of duty and procedure but Cook wasn't concerned about that so much. What went into his reports was down to him and what those above him didn't know they could much worry about. What concerned Cook was that Rathe was so close to the tragedy this time that his judgement might be impaired. Cook could imagine Rathe's interview with the Villiers descending into sentiment, shared memories, and mutual condolence. Although he would never admit it to anyone but his own spasmodic reflection in the shaving mirror, Cook could not deny that Rathe's ideas and perspective had been of use to him recently, which was largely the reason he allowed Rathe so much latitude. But now, on this case, Cook feared that the same perspective he had come to value might be disorientated by personal grief and the lack of any communication from Rathe was doing little to assuage Cook's anxieties.

Reaching for an apple as he left the canteen, then substituting a Bakewell tart for it, Cook made his way back to his office. The young DC was still in his chair as he walked in, kicking the door shut with his foot. He noticed she hadn't put on any glasses and he could not help but sneer in envy.

"Found anything?" he asked, spitting pastry casing into the air.

She was still frowning at the screen as she replied. "Nothing much, sir. I've found a link but it's pretty tenuous."

"I can handle tenuous," declared Cook, walking round his desk and leaning over her shoulder.

The Detective Constable pointed to two printed screenshots of the relevant files. "Holly Darwin, 23, vanished September 2014. Lisa Pemberton, 18, disappeared February 2016."

Cook looked at the printed images of both girls. Both attractive, smiling, filled with hope. Holly Darwin had been described as vibrant, slim, intelligent; dark haired, olive skinned, almost Mediterranean in appearance. Lisa Pemberton had been classified by her peers and family as shy, generous, thoughtful, athletic. Red-haired, freckled, younger looking than her years.

"Tell me more than this," murmured Cook.

"Holly Darwin was a bit of a party girl. Liked the high-life. Ambitions to marry a footballer, have her own fashion house, you know the sort of thing."

"Right up my street," snapped Cook.

"She'd go partying every weekend. From what I can gather hardly a barman or bouncer wasn't used to seeing her at some point from Friday to Sunday."

"Is there a point coming my way any time before this Friday or Sunday, or what?"

The girl smiled. "One of the places Holly Darwin liked to go more than most, sir, was the Devil's Gate nightclub."

The scowl on Cook's face dissolved into eager anticipation and his fingers gripped the papers in his hands with increased intensity. "What about Lisa Pemberton?"

The DC shook her head. "Nothing to suggest she ever went there and, to be honest, the statements from her family suggest it wouldn't have been her sort of place anyway."

"But… ?" Cook was leaning further forward now, his

elbows on the desk, so close to the detective that she could smell the onion from his sandwich when he spoke.

"Lisa Pemberton was a health freak, a talented athlete by all accounts," she said, somehow not minding the smell of his breath. "She ran for a local club, had visions of being a professional."

"Get to the point."

The girl smiled. "As you might expect, she was a member of a gym. Went there every day, right up to the day she disappeared. Sometimes in the morning, sometimes in the evening, but every day, without fail."

"You're losing me," cautioned Cook.

"The gym Lisa was a member of is owned by a company called Castle Leisure Facilities Ltd." She switched screens on the computer and brought up a website. "Gyms all over London. But they take the term leisure in its broadest sense."

"Meaning?"

"The company owns all sorts of places where you might spend your free time, sir. Gyms, casinos, bars… "

Cook was smiling, but it was not a pretty sight. "Nightclubs?"

The detective smiled back at him. "Including Devil's Gate."

Cook pushed himself off the desk and stood upright. He was staring at the website for Castle Leisure Facilities Ltd. His shirt suddenly felt very close to his skin and he wondered whether the temperature of the room had increased or whether his instincts had just ignited within him. He looked at the young detective sitting in his chair, but he saw no sign of her finding the room suddenly too hot to accommodate them both. He nodded to her, the grim smile still lingering over his lips, and he motioned for her to get out of his chair.

"I was just about to try to find out who owns the

company," volunteered the DC. "If you want me to, I mean."

Cook shook his head. "No, thanks. Can't have you taking all the glory and getting yourself promoted above me just yet. Go back to your desk and do whatever it is you do all day."

She stared at him in disbelieving anger, her cheeks flushed with sudden fury at his arrogant, belittling attitude. She let out an involuntary snort of air and threw open the door. Before she could slam it behind her, he whistled to her. She turned back, the crimson anger in her cheeks intensifying.

"Quality work," he said, nodding, his eyes suddenly saying more than any of his words had done.

When the door closed, it was not with a slam but with an efficient snap, and Cook did not need to see the smile of pride on the face of the officer whose name he had noted not only in his head but also on his notepad for future reference.

* * *

Late evening.

Rathe sat in silence in his living room, the lights turned low, his only company the bottle of Shiraz which he had opened. He had considered some music but he knew that he would not hear any of the notes or melodies, so the idea seemed worthless. The wine had seemed like a much better idea but, even so, he had yet to touch any of it despite his lust for the drink as he had poured out that first glass. He had no idea how long he had been sitting there before the knock on the door. When a man is sitting alone in almost silent darkness, it seemed to Rathe, time loses its meaning; or, more accurately perhaps, the man loses his perception of it.

He was not surprised to find that his visitor was Cook. The inspector looked tired, more so than usual, and Rathe found himself wondering how much Cook had eaten in the last few hours. He said nothing about it, knowing that any

218

recrimination he uttered would be hypocritical. Rathe himself had dismissed the idea of food several times that day. He invited Cook in, told him to help himself to a drink, and sat down in his armchair. Cook went into the kitchen and opened one of the bottled Italian lagers which he had expected to find in the fridge. With a shrug, he opened a second. Something told Cook that the first wouldn't last too long.

"I think I know what happened," said Rathe, once Cook had slumped on the settee. "To Kirsty, to Lyndsey. To Alice, to Gilchrist. I think I know."

"So do I." Cook half-drained the first bottle of beer. "At least, I think I know who made it happen."

"Any proof?"

Cook held the cold bottle to his forehead. "Piss in the wind."

Rathe picked up the wine and stared into its deep, red darkness. "What made you suspect him?"

"The companies. Gyms, nightclubs, casinos. We've found connections between several missing girls and leisure facilities owned or controlled by him in one way or another. Girls going to bars, to clubs, working in casinos, joining gyms, waitressing in restaurants."

"Auditioning for talent agencies," added Rathe.

Cook peered over at him. "New one on me."

"It's how he got Kirsty Villiers."

"Right," nodded Cook. Then, after a moment, he added, "Tell me in your own time. What put you on to him?"

"Chess." Rathe sipped the wine. "Other stuff too, but mainly chess."

Cook did not ask for further clarification. It did not seem to be the appropriate time and Rathe did not seem as though he wanted to demonstrate any clever twists of his ingenuity. He looked as though he wanted to get drunk but, from what

Cook could see, he was doing nothing about it.

"We need proof, Rathe," he said.

Rathe drank more. "I don't. I know it was him."

"That's not enough."

"We can make him confess."

Cook snorted. "You don't believe that any more than I do. You don't think a man like that gets his hands dirty, do you? He won't have stabbed Alice and he won't have killed Gilchrist. Whoever did that will be far away now. If he's still alive."

Rathe was shaking his head. "It can't be left like that, Cook. It can't go unresolved, or… "

Cook leaned forward, his voice hardened with danger. "Or what?"

"Unpunished."

An unpleasant silence settled over them, a blanket of sin which gave neither of them any comfort from the horror of their thoughts. Cook stood up, finishing one beer and starting the next, suddenly wishing he had opted for something harder, something more controlling.

"Don't talk to me like that, Rathe. Never."

"We must do something," hissed Rathe, banging his hand down on the table beside him. "We can't let him walk away from it and if we can't prove it then we have to… "

Cook held out his arms. "What? Do what, Rathe? You tell me what you want to do to punish him."

But the words would not come.

Rathe's mouth moved but they breathed only futile silence. He raised his glass to his lips and by the dim light reflecting off it, Cook could see that Rathe's cheeks were glistening. There were no tears now, but there had been, and not long before Cook had knocked on the door. Cook looked around for evidence of more alcohol consumption than the single bottle which stood on the table beside Rathe, but he found none. The man was sober. Cook tried not to think about what thoughts Rathe might have been having, or what tears he might have been shedding, if he had drunk more than he could hold.

Cook took a step towards Rathe and then paused. For a moment, neither of them moved. Then, Cook bent down onto one knee and rested his arm on his raised thigh, the bottle hanging loosely from his fingers. His eyes looked up to Rathe.

"I know this hurts, right, and I know why it does. But we've got to let it go until we find some proof. Got it?"

"It's not all about Alice," said Rathe, his teeth clamped together.

"Fair enough. But most of it's about her."

Rathe was shaking his head. "It's as much to do with the ones we don't know about, the ones we've never heard of but who have gone the same way as Kirsty and Lyndsey. It's about all of them, Cook. How much has he got away with and for how long?"

"Too much and too long," replied the inspector. "But without proof, we've got nothing, Rathe. You know that, as well as I do. And you know better than anyone that neither of us is going to manufacture any proof."

Rathe scowled at the vague reference to the Marsden case, but he said nothing about it. He found that he was trembling, the tears forming in his eyes, but he knew that they were not the product of grief or guilt this time. It was frustration and anger which consumed him now, sitting there in his armchair, resisting the urge to tear his home to pieces in a useless rebellion against the injustice of it all.

"I made a promise," he whispered. "To Alice's parents. I promised I'd find out what had happened."

Cook placed his hand on Rathe's arm. It felt nothing near unnatural or misguided to either of them. Later, they might have reflected that at one time it would have been an unthinkable move for either of them to make or receive; but at that point in existence, no other gesture seemed appropriate.

"And you have," said Cook, "but you can't do anything else about it, not right now. He's been allowed to walk away from his crimes for too long, no doubt about that. But before... right up until this moment in time, Rathe, that bastard could get away with it. Why? Because he didn't have you and me chasing him. But now he has – and God help him if he can't run fast enough to get away from us. Yeah?"

Rathe held Cook's glare for several seconds before he nodded his agreement. Cook held up his bottle of beer, inviting a toast to their agreement to continue to seek the evidence they needed, and Rathe accepted the gesture by gently knocking the rim of his glass against the neck of the bottle. To Cook, it sealed a pact between them and he drank in honour of the promise they had made.

Anthony Rathe drank too. But as he did so, in the back of that raging sea of a mind, a plan had formed which he hoped would bring justice for them all whilst still honouring that covenant he had made over beer and wine with a man whom he had come to consider a genuine friend.

* * *

Elliot Graham listened with patience, but Rathe knew that beneath the cold arrogance of his stare, an emotion far beyond mere contempt was at work. It had been a simple ruse to secure an interview with him alone. A telephone call to the house and the request to speak to Graham away from his wife; the minor lie that it was concerning his arrangements about picking up Lyndsey from the tube station on the day she disappeared; the further trivial untruth about Cook being indisposed on another line of enquiry; and Rathe's suggestion that it be a private interview, to spare Eliza

Graham any further and unnecessary upset. This last part at least, Rathe reflected, had been true.

And so they sat in the garden, on that raised patio where Rathe had first seen the man he now knew to be guilty of kidnapping and murder, drinking coffee in a warm, autumn breeze, like two old friends catching up after a period of absence from each other's company. The juxtaposition, to Rathe's mind, was almost perverse.

"What is it, precisely, which you are accusing me of, Mr Rathe?" Graham asked.

"I think you know." Rathe was staring into his coffee, itself as black as his mood.

Graham shook his head. "No, no. I think you will have to make it clearer."

Rathe fixed his eyes on Graham's forcing himself not to let his eyes drift from the man's own unctuous yet guilty stare. "You own a number of businesses, Mr Graham."

"Indeed, I do."

"Castle Leisure Facilities, for one?" Rathe raised an eyebrow. Graham nodded in reply. "And the Devil's Gate nightclub for another?"

"Yes, but I don't see the relevance of any of this."

"And Trebuchet Talent Agency. That's one of yours too?"

"You're trying my patience, Mr Rathe," cautioned Graham. "What have any of my business arrangements got to do with Lyndsey's disappearance?"

"Everything." Rathe sipped some of the coffee, its bitterness complimenting the tone of his voice. "I had a suspicion that you were the owner of all those business concerns even before the police confirmed it. You're a chess player, you said as much yourself. The use of the term 'castle' might not be enough to suggest a link between a leisure group and a chess player, but the name 'Trebuchet' would only occur to an aficionado of the game. You know

223

what 'Trebuchet' is, don't you, Mr Graham?"

"It's a type of reciprocal zugzwang occurring in pawn endgames," explained Graham with a sneer.

Rathe had the feeling his adversary might think Rathe was incapable of understanding the terminology. Rathe smiled at the petty tactic. "Exactly. Where whoever is next to move must lose the game."

"And is the next move yours or mine, Mr Rathe?"

It was an unexpected question and it caught Rathe off guard because, in truth, he knew that it had to be his turn to play and that the endgame for him was not what he had wished or hoped for. But, he decided, it was not obligatory to lose the game without a fight. Similarly, he knew that there was more than one way of winning any type of game. It was all a question of perspective.

"From the outset, I had been convinced that there had to be a connection between Lyndsey's disappearance and that of Kirsty Villiers," Rathe said. "The murders of Alice Villiers and Roger Gilchrist showed there had to be a link. But the difference in ages between the two girls suggested that the connection had to be transient. The police have determined that Kirsty had been approached by your talent agency and had been going to the Devil's Gate nightclub on the night she disappeared. They have found records of unsolved missing persons cases involving young girls, where the girls concerned have used your businesses for recreation or leisure purposes. And your step-daughter has vanished too. You see? You keep turning up in this investigation, first under one stone and then under another."

"Coincidence." Graham spat the word as though it were a hair in his mouth.

"At least four girls, all missing, all connected to you."

Graham held up a finger. "Vicariously connected to me. Hundreds of girls go to my clubs and gyms, to my restaurants and bars, but they don't all disappear."

Rathe leaned forward across the table, his eyes never moving from Graham's face. "Perhaps not all of them fit your requirements."

Graham's jaw clenched in anger and his lips curled in disdain. "Meaning what? Are you saying I'm some sort of paedophile? Because if you are, Mr Rathe, you'd better make sure one of your old colleagues is readily available on the end of a phone."

Rathe shook his head. "The ages of the missing girls don't suggest anything like that."

"So what are you implying?"

"All these girls disappearing, all of them linked to you, and all of them also connected by the fact that they are young, healthy, and beautiful."

Graham's eyes flashed towards the house, ensuring that Eliza was nowhere in sight. "Just what is it you're suggesting?"

"I'll leave that to your intelligence."

Graham's fingers had balled into fists on the table. "I'd rather you say it out loud."

Rathe leaned back in his chair, a smile flickering across his lips. "This talent agency of yours… Does it often approach girls for interview for possible representation when they've not been formally trained?"

"I don't… "

"Kirsty Villiers had applied to a whole collection of agencies as well as yours. They had all said the same thing: she needed a formal qualification from stage school or university before she could be considered. But not Trebuchet." He pointed a finger at Graham. "Not you. You were prepared to see her when she had had no formal training at all. Why is that?"

"I couldn't say."

"Perhaps it was as simple as ensuring that you could meet her alone and on your own terms. Coaxing her to you with the promises of fulfilled ambitions."

"Or perhaps we just saw something in her." Graham regretted the choice of words immediately, but Rathe was unable to prevent the snort of contempt from exploding out of him.

"I'm sure you did," he said. "A viable commodity, no doubt."

Graham shook his head. "I find these insinuations not only offensive but tiresome."

Rathe sprang forward in his chair, slapping a hand on the table. Coffee spilled from both cups into their respective saucers. "Why would attractive young women keep disappearing from nightclubs, bars, gyms, and so on which you own? Why? What might you think is the likeliest explanation?"

The outburst had been sufficient to shake Graham out of his arrogant apathy. Now, he saw Rathe's eyes darken with anger and the sensitive mouth snarl back in fierce disgust. Graham contemplated Rathe's change in demeanour, his throat constricting with sudden discomfort, and he released his fingers from themselves, spreading his palms on the table in an effort to steady his nerves.

"If – if – there were any criminal activity going on in my club involving anything of the nature you're suggesting, it does not mean I knew anything about it."

"And what is it I am suggesting, Mr Graham?"

"You know."

"I want you to say it."

Graham had regained some of his previous disgust. "You will have seen the newspapers and TV reports over the last few weeks, Mr Rathe. Modern slavery is becoming an increasingly problematic concern for our society."

"Selling women to sexual predators, here or abroad," Rathe nodded.

"And if anything like that was going on in my enterprise, I would make sure something was done about it."

"I don't believe you. I think you're in the thick of it."

Graham shook his head. "And Lyndsey? Do you think, in this wild fantasy of yours, that I would sell my own step-daughter? In fact, she seems to be something of a fly in your ointment, Mr Rathe. If these disappearances are somehow all linked, how do you account for Lyndsey?"

"I think she had to disappear," Rathe said. "You wanted the others because they would be good business. But Lyndsey? I think she vanished because she had to, not because you wanted her to."

"And why?"

Rathe shrugged. "Had she found something out? Overheard you setting up one of your… transactions? Read an email she shouldn't have seen? I can't say, but it was something like that, I've no doubt."

Graham remained impassive. "You've not explained why you think I had anything to do with my step-daughter's disappearance at all. I told you that I went to pick her up and she wasn't there."

Rathe nodded. "True, you did. And when I met you that first day, something occurred to me and I knew I had heard something important. But it wasn't until later that I realised what it was. We only had your word for what happened. You say you went to the tube station to pick her up, that you waited, but she didn't turn up."

"Which is true."

"But we only have your word for it," pressed Rathe.

Graham pursed his lips. "Is that all?"

"Not quite," replied Rathe. "Something else was said which I couldn't account for. The police… Why did you ask

Eliza to wait until she called the police?"

"I didn't want to cause panic if there was no need," answered Graham, with a dismissive shrug of his shoulders.

"Or were you delaying things on purpose? You see, I can't imagine a concerned parent being that lucid. In fact, I would expect a concerned parent to start to think about calling the police within a few minutes. Just like Eliza did. Because she was a genuinely concerned parent." Rathe pointed a finger at Graham once more. "Not like you."

Graham grinned, allowing a small laugh to escape from his mouth. "So, you think I use my various businesses – all of which are extremely successful, I should add – in order to procure young women who I can then sell on some abominable black market of human beings, but that my step-daughter discovered it somehow and so I had to dispose of her in the same way?"

"Yes," admitted Rathe.

"And you expect me to accept all of that?"

"No," confessed Rathe.

Graham laughed once more at his candour. "And these murders? Did I commit them?"

Rathe sighed gently. "I don't know for sure. The same man did, certainly. The method of murder was the same. But I can imagine you having one of your many employees, expendable or otherwise, doing it for you. Part of me feels sure you are unlikely to get your hands dirty." He paused, shaking his head. "And yet… "

"And yet, what?"

"Cook's theory is that the murderer approached Gilchrist as a potential new client. When the private detective's back was turned, the killer struck. Alice… " Rathe's attention wavered for a moment, as his memories came back to squeeze his heart with their fingers of ice. "She was killed because the murderer feared Gilchrist had made the connection between Lyndsey and Kirsty Villiers – the connection being you. The killer had discovered Gilchrist and Alice were going to meet, because Gilchrist had put it in his diary, which was open on his desk. The killer couldn't allow that meeting to take place, but he also couldn't be sure what Gilchrist had already told Alice, so she... had to die."

Graham had listened to Rathe's summary of the official theory of the killings with barely feigned interest. "But you don't believe this theory?"

Rathe raised his eyebrows briefly. "Most of it. Up to a point, I think it must be accurate but, for me, something about it isn't quite right. You see, Mr Graham, I find it much easier to believe that Gilchrist would open his office and put himself off guard if the person who had gone to meet him that day was the husband of an existing client. After all, in discovering the disappearance of Kirsty Villiers, Gilchrist felt he had made something of a breakthrough in finding out what had happened to Lyndsey Crane. He would want to give an update of his success as soon as possible. If, by coincidence, he received a call from his client's husband, he might forget his promise of confidentiality for just a moment. In the wake of his excitement with his news, you understand. See my point?"

Graham contemplated Rathe for a moment and then allowed his eyes to roam around the garden. Rathe continued to watch him, wondering what thoughts were going through the man's head. Despite his assurances that he was right, Rathe knew that nothing he had said could or should cause Elliott Graham any disquiet. What Cook had said was true: there was no proof, nothing which Graham couldn't explain away by one lie or another.

"You've said a great deal to me, Mr Rathe," Graham said, at last, "so I think it only fair that I have a right of reply. But my only response to what you have said will make me sound like a broken record, I fear, because I can only repeat what I have told you previously. I deny every allegation you have made and, without proof to support what you say, the only guilt I can see here is yours of slander."

It was not an unexpected answer and Rathe felt no threat from it. He had known it would be the response Graham gave; if truth be told, Rathe knew that there was no other reply the man could give. But all that meant was that Rathe had come prepared for it.

"Inspector Cook is as convinced of your guilt as I am," he said. "He'll find some proof eventually. He'll crawl over your accounts like insects over a carcass until he finds some evidence of a transaction. And it will take only one transaction to prove what you do behind the closed doors of your companies, Mr Graham. After that, it will be forensic examinations of Alice Villiers's home, Roger Gilchrist's offices, your home, your offices. Search after search until they find that one fibre or that one trace which places you at the scene of one or both of the murders. When that happens, you'll be closed down and put away. I only hope I'm here to see it."

Graham drained his coffee. It was cold, but he barely noticed. "All that takes time, Rathe. If I am what you say I am, the process of Inspector Cook's investigation will give me enough time either to cover my tracks or to shut down my businesses and move away. Either way, it looks as though it is you and not me who is in in Trebuchet."

Rathe did not share the smile which Graham gave to his remark. Instead, his eyes had hardened once more and his lips had curled over his teeth in a feral snarl. "You're going too fast, Graham. The law may be required to take its time but the tabloid press isn't. A court may demand evidence to support allegations, but a headline needs only a whiff of truth and scandal to make itself heard."

It was Graham's turn to scowl. "What the fuck do you

230

mean by that?"

"You close down right now and vanish yourself or the papers get a phone call."

"That's blackmail, you sanctimonious bastard!" Graham spat. "I'll have you prosecuted."

Rathe's smile had more than a trace of wickedness in it. "Never heard of anonymous tips? The press don't betray sources and you'd never be able to prove anything against me, just as I can't against you. But mud sticks and the damage to you would be done."

"You bloody hypocrite!"

"You deserve a life sentence, one way or another," hissed Rathe, rising from the table.

"I thought you believed in justice, Rathe," goaded Elliott Graham. "The rule of law."

Rathe looked down at the man for whom he felt neither pity nor remorse. "Sometimes justice and the law have nothing to do with each other. If I could prove your complicity, I wouldn't hesitate to see you stand trial, but I can't. But that doesn't mean you should get away with it."

Graham remained seated, his eyes flickering around in confusion and distress. It had not been a move he had anticipated. Rathe had felt cheap making it, but the thought of Graham going about his business without any form of opposition made Rathe feel worse than cheap. Graham stuttered some words, pleas to reconsider or formulate some sort of deal, but Rathe shook his head, closing his doors to them. Graham's mouth continued to move as rapidly as his eyes, but no more words came out. Turning on his heel, and without any sense of regret in his heart, Anthony Rathe walked away from Elliott Graham with the most acute feeling in his heart that the two of them would never meet again.

* * *

"I'm just sorry I can't give you anything definite."

Sonia Villiers took his hand in hers. "You've done more than we could ever have hoped or expected from you."

Terence was staring out over the lawn, not yet able to meet Rathe's eye. "Now that this man, Elliott Graham, has done what he has, I don't suppose we'll ever know the whole story."

Rathe lowered his head. "Not necessarily. Graham's suicide means that he isn't around to hinder any police enquiry into his affairs. Inspector Cook is confident that something will turn up soon."

"You trust this man – Cook?" asked Terence. "He's a friend of yours, am I right?"

Rathe took a moment to answer. "I think so, yes. And I certainly trust him."

Sonia was not listening to their conversation. "It's Graham's wife I feel sorry for. As well as learning what he might have been, what he might have done to her daughter, she has to live with the memory of walking in on him in the bathroom. All that blood she must have seen. It's horrible."

Terence Villiers turned to face them both. "I don't give that a second thought."

It was an admission which threw them into silence for a long period. Rathe was wondering precisely how he felt about Elliott Graham's death. It had not been unexpected that the news of it had brought back memories of Kevin Marsden and, for a long time after Cook had given him the facts of Graham's suicide, Rathe had known that his actions towards Graham and his threats of scandal had contributed to the man's decision to end his life. And now, Graham had cursed Eliza to the same sense of loss and shame with which Kathy Marsden lived. Rathe could not help but incline to Sonia Villiers's point of view about the effect of Graham's death on his wife but, in equal part, he felt he could understand Terence's reaction to the situation.

Rathe thought back to that telephone call with Cook. It had been characteristically brief, but the exchange between them had not been lacking in its mixture of truth and lies.

"I can't say I'm sorry," Rathe had confessed.

"Nor can I," Cook had admitted. "He was a shit and he deserved everything he got."

"You'll still try to find evidence that he was at the centre of it, won't you? I still want to know what happened to Lyndsey and Kirsty."

Cook had been adamant. "Investigation's on-going and it won't stop any time soon. Seems a bit sudden, though, doesn't it? Graham cutting himself open like that."

"Perhaps."

"Something I should know about it?" Cook had asked, his voice betraying that he knew the answer only too well.

"No," Rathe had lied. "What do you mean?"

"Just a thought I had. Came to me in a flash when I heard what Graham had done."

And then the call had been terminated, seemingly as quickly as the thought of Rathe's involvement in the death had entered Cook's head.

Now, Rathe thought once more about Kevin Marsden. He had been an innocent young man, betrayed by a system of justice which saw him as expendable. His death had been entirely unjustified and Rathe now seemed to understand more clearly that it was this quality of it, which weighed heavily on his shoulders. He had played his part in condemning Marsden to his own death, but he had been entirely innocent. Could the same be said of Elliott Graham? Rathe doubted it very much and, for a reason he could not clearly define, he did not feel as though Graham's death would stay with him alongside the memory of Kevin Marsden for any length of time.

He stayed with the Villiers for a while longer before making his excuses to leave. At the front door, he received a small kiss on the cheek from Sonia and a firm handshake from her husband.

"Keep in touch, Anthony," demanded Terence. "We must hold on to what family we have." ·

Rathe had permitted himself a smile. "I will. And I'm sorry for everything which has happened."

Sonia shook her head. "You have no reason to apologise. We know what you've done and we're grateful for it."

"I'll let you know as soon as Cook has any news about things," he promised. "Anything to connect Elliott Graham to Alice's death. And any news about Kirsty. I'll tell you at once."

"We know," said Terence.

That day, Rathe walked home slowly, allowing his mind to drift over a collection of different thoughts. He gave none of them any special attention. He was tired of imagining horrors, deciphering facts, and analysing questions. His mind felt drained, cramped, and a small hum of pain began to form at the back of his head. He wanted to permit himself to wonder only about banalities, to listen to some conversation which had no meaning for him and no expectation of any response from him. He wanted to watch an escapist film, read a comic novel, listen to music which would stir his soul into wonder. For the remainder of that day, and many more to come, Anthony Rathe did exactly that and the past few weeks seemed to distance themselves from him, losing themselves in time.

It was three weeks later when Cook found Rathe standing at Kevin Marsden's grave. The inspector's face was blanched, his cheeks sallow, and the growth of beard on his chin spoke of several late nights and early mornings. He stood next to Rathe, his hands in the pockets of his crumpled suit, his eyes staring down at the ground.

"How did you know I'd be here?" asked Rathe.

Cook sniffed. "Lucky guess. You weren't at home and you weren't in my office. Where else would you be?"

"You're a cynic."

Cook looked around him. It seemed they had the churchyard to themselves. "I don't know why you come here, Rathe."

"I wouldn't expect you to understand it even if I told you."

"Can't do you any good."

"That doesn't mean it isn't necessary."

Cook offered no reply other than to shake his shoulders. "How long do you normally stay here?"

"It depends."

"On what?"

Rathe turned to face him. "What are you doing here, Cook?"

Cook sighed heavily. "There've been some developments. We've traced some of Elliott Graham's business financials. Most of his restaurants and bars launder money for some of the bigger names in our sights. Some of the shits he does business with are known for drugs and prostitution. At least one is being investigated for trafficking."

Rathe smiled. "Then we were right."

"Looks that way. There's something else." Cook paused, shifting his position, as though the pressure of the words he had to say was too much for his body to manage. "We've found Lyndsey Crane."

Rathe's heart seemed to slump in his breast and he felt a surge of nausea pass through him. "Where?"

Cook was shaking his head. "She's alive, just. There was a raid on a place near Kings Cross. She was in there as a worker. That much junk in her she doesn't know who she is."

Rathe ran a hand down his face. "Dear God. But the doctors think... ?"

Cook nodded. "In time, she'll recover. In a long time."

Rathe ran his hand through his hair. "Eliza Graham will be relieved, no matter what."

"Of course." Cook closed his eyes against the thought.

"When will Lyndsey be able to talk?" asked Rathe.

"Once she's clean," said Cook. Then, with a sigh, he added, "What she remembers and what use it'll be, I can't say."

"At least she's alive."

The silence which followed was so intense that Rathe's instincts were aroused at once. He threw a glance at Cook and saw that the inspector's pale cheeks had turned a sickening shade of alabaster.

"Cook?"

"There's more news. A body was found in Leeds, a young woman. Known to be a prostitute under the control of one of the main criminal families up there. This gang keep their girls under control, know what I mean?"

"With drugs?"

"Just enough to keep them addicted and compliant. These girls are reserved for the high flyers: businessmen, visiting diplomats, politicians. She died after a nasty beating. Some pretty horrible wounds to her back and arse, probably from the buckle end of a belt. Signs she was tied at the ankles and wrists. That's just the start of what he did to her."

"Rape?"

"Everywhere you can imagine." Cook cleared his throat, as though to dislodge some of the unpleasantness of the world from his throat. "It got out of hand, so whoever her punter was phoned the gang and they cleared it up."

Rathe was looking down at his feet. "Who was the girl?"

"Leeds police have got the man who did it, but he's

naming no names," said Cook, as though he hadn't heard the question.

"Who's the girl, Cook?" pressed Rathe.

"We'd sent photos of all our missing girls to forces up and down the country," Cook explained at last. "You never know what another force might come up with. We got the call this morning. This girl in Leeds… "

Rathe looked at him. "Kirsty Villiers?"

Cook's silence answered the question better than any words. For a moment, it seemed to take Rathe by surprise. His eyes flickered and his lips twitched, as though he could not bring himself to accept that he was standing by the grave of a dead man whilst hearing the news of a dead girl. He looked around at the stone markers of people who had lived and died and it began to seem to him that he was surrounded by death, as though death was part of his own being, a morbid thread of the fabric of his own life, and nothing he could do would ever allow him to escape death, because nobody could ever run away from themselves. He was barely aware of Cook's hand on his shoulder but that touch of friendly support was enough to bring Rathe's consciousness back out of itself and return him to the reality of what his mind had been forced to process.

"There's no doubt?" he asked.

"None. I'm sorry."

"What about evidence against Graham?" asked Rathe, his voice suddenly brusque and professional. "Any progress there?"

Cook nodded. "We've got his car on CCTV in the vicinity of both Gilchrist's office and Alice's house."

Rathe was shaking his head. "But no physical evidence to get him for either murder?"

"Not yet."

Rathe looked down at Kevin Marsden's grave once more,

his eyes narrowing and then closing. Cook knew better than to interrupt, so he kept quiet and let his eyes wander aimlessly around the churchyard. At last, Rathe took a step back from the grave and began to walk.

"Come on," he said. "Let's go."

"We'll keep looking, Rathe," said Cook. "I promise."

Rathe nodded, although he wondered now whether it mattered any more. It was impossible for him not to accept that Elliott Graham had sold his step-daughter into prostitution to keep her quiet about his illegal activities, just as it was an absolute in his mind that Graham had murdered both Gilchrist and Alice. All that was unknown as far as Rathe was concerned was how many of the girls still classed as missing in London and beyond had been targeted and sold by Graham and how many of them were dead, like Kirsty, or still barely alive like Lyndsey. The thought was almost too much for him to contemplate and, for a brief second, he felt as though he would vomit.

He forced himself to think of something better, something which proved there was still goodness somewhere in the world. Almost at once, Alice's face appeared in his mind's eye and he felt his heart drag itself towards the light once more. The world was dark, Rathe knew that, and any chance of redemption had to be seized and kept close for as long as possible. If he could do nothing to stop the violence or the death, he must try other things to balance the scales. Sonia and Terence Villiers had spent years not knowing what had happened to their youngest child. Despite the tragedy of the truth, they could now at least know what that truth was. If he could do nothing else, Rathe could give them that certainty, however painful. And Alice could be reunited with her sister. He was not religious, nor was he given to sentiment, but Rathe could believe that amid the darkness and the horror, even those small glimpses of hope and honesty had to count for something.

They were at the gates to the churchyard when Cook spoke. "I don't suppose you fancy a beer, do you?"

"I may well do. But not right now – later perhaps. I'll ring you. There's just something I have to do first."

"Such as?" asked Cook.

"I want to go and see Sonia and Terence Villiers."

Cook shook his head. "Not a chance. If it was my case, no problem, but it's not. It's a Leeds case and the boys from up there will want to tell the parents. I can't let you do it."

"Make a phone call."

"I can't."

"I'll buy the first two, no, three drinks later. I promise."

Cook growled angrily, but he took out his mobile in any case, his grubby fingers struggling to handle the device before he made the call. For himself, Rathe looked back towards the cemetery and wondered whether or not he would ever come back. It did not take him long to give himself an answer and the knowledge forced his lips into an uneven, humourless smile. Cook was engaged on his call for no more than five minutes and he was compelled to end it with an assurance that he would return the favour as soon as it was possible.

"Right, got your own way again, Rathe," barked the inspector. "So you owe me three drinks. I don't suppose you want to tell me why I've just put myself out for you yet again, do you? No, course you don't."

"I will do actually," said Anthony Rathe. "It's just that I made a promise to Terence and Sonia Villiers and for once I want to be able to say I kept it."

Sparkling Books

We publish:

Crime, mystery, thriller, suspense, horror and women's fiction

All titles are available as e-books from your e-book retailer.

For current list of titles visit:

www.sparklingbooks.com

@SparklingBooks